CW01072562

# Observations on Modern Life

## An Anthology of Short Stories

### Phuket Island Writers

Volume III

Published by Phuket Island Writers

Paperback ISBN: 978-1727143843

Cover Design by: Noi Romchalee

Edited by Karinne van Dijkhuizen

"Of all those arts in which the wise excel,
Nature's chief masterpiece is writing well."

~ Andre Breton

# Contents

## Love

## Death

## Music

## Food

## Health

## Other

## Author Profiles

# Preface

We are pleased to present for the readers' pleasure the third volume of short stories by the Phuket Island Writers. Previous books were published in print and online in 2014 and 2016 so this one is right on schedule. Both publications – An Anthology of Short Stories and All over the Map – are available on Amazon.

With some success, for the first time, we have introduced themes to the book, common human themes like love, death, music, food, and health under the leitmotif 'Observations on Modern Life'. The category 'other' contains stories not easily classified under any one given sub theme.

Members wrote, critiqued, polished, and finalized these stories with the help of other members. The final result is, we hope, quite a variegated collection which crystalizes different views and illuminates important aspects of modern life. In putting this third book together in all phases and steps, we also learned a lot about the fast-evolving publishing and media business of the 21st century.

The Phuket Island Writers is a diverse one. We are English-speaking, multi-cultural, live in Phuket, meet monthly near the ocean, love books, and hail from around the world: UK, Australia, USA, China, Thailand, South Africa, and Poland. In addition to participating in this group, we are all working on our own writing projects and blogs.

The group welcomes new members through referral, coincidence, word of mouth, attendance at a meeting, and on our Facebook website:

https://www.facebook.com/phuketislandwriters/

We all join to give special thanks to our able editor Karinne van Dijkhuizen.

Lian and Paul McCabe
Co-Chairs
1 September 2018

*Note: The views expressed in any story of this anthology are those of the author and do not necessarily reflect the views of the Phuket Phuket Island Writers or its editor.*

Love

"Love is all there is, it makes the world go 'round
Love and only love, it can't be denied
No matter what you think about it
You just won't be able to do without it
Take a tip from one who's tried."

~ Bob Dylan, 1969 ('I Threw it all away')

# Rachelle's Tale

## by Stephanie Thornton

Once the black mould had started to climb the bedroom walls, Rachelle knew she needed to think about moving again. She had been told right at the start of this tenancy, and in fact had even signed to agree, that she must not dry clothes on radiators at the three-bed house they had only moved into the year prior. Now the pristine former white walls were covered in large black patches and it was already affecting Jefferson's asthma. Of course, it was the Landlord's fault, she told her visiting social worker. She had done nothing to make this happen and it went without question, she assured her, that she heated and ventilated the rooms every day and never dried clothes there.

The social worker noted the perpetually drawn curtains, preventing daylight ever entering the room, but it wasn't her job to comment. Environmental Health had made the problem worse by giving the Landlord a list of expensive improvements she must make or face a fine in Court.

It was this same reason Rachelle gave to the new Landlady; that the present Landlord never did a thing and she was sick of complaining to him. She had also given her a willing friend's phone number, in place of the real number of her soon to be former Landlord, should the new one decide to check up on her present tenancy.

She would then leave, without notice, and keep the last month's rent to cover her moving costs. In fact, she might need to keep a bit more, as the kids would need at least £400 to cover new Christmas presents. The old toys had been left behind under a huge heap of rubbish. And to buy replacements at a car boot sale was unthinkable. It always had to be new. Only the best for her kids. After all, she did love them.

It was the masses of pop and sweets that seem to take up all the money. She'd at least shown willingness when she attended a 'food thrift class' at local day school, but thought the teacher was too superior in her manner of "making do and mend" and had left after just learning how to make £25 last a week. After all, this wasn't the war and who did she think she was to suggest such restrictions.

"Why, it wouldn't even buy the pop," she said in disgust.

Or even a packet of fags! She had to have those. It was as vital as the huge TV which stood in the corner of the room and was never turned off. If the money ran out, they could always go to the local food bank to get supplies.

The new Landlady took down the names of her four children:

Bintnook Moses Teteley, a boy, aged one
WaWa Komoto, a girl, aged two – born during her 'black phase'
Rotundra Smith, a girl aged three
Jefferson Keeley, a boy, aged four.

As Rachelle reeled off all the different surnames, she confessed she had been a bit silly.

"I hope you'll be more careful now," said the Landlady, "as once you get past three bedrooms, the Council won't pay for a bigger house."

Rachelle giggled. Thoughts of Hitler and Eugenics briefly crossed the Landlady's mind but she dismissed them as a flight of fancy.

Rachelle was already in love again. It had been love at first sight, she told her friends. He'd been standing on the corner where she lived, just as she had broken up with Jackson Teteley, and offered her a fag. That relationship had been a disaster, but this new one would be wonderful. She just knew it would.

The new boyfriend, one Billy Robinson, was well known in the area. A long string of petty larceny and drug dealing had ensured he had already been in prison twice. He boasted this to his friends.

He had come to look at the new rental with her, telling the Landlady he only visited once a week. He looked carefully round the house, finding fault here and there to make himself seem important and took a special interest in the cellar, which he said was for the washing machine. As soon as he returned to the grim terrace he shared with a different girlfriend, he quickly packed up his extensive cannabis growing kit, with its tent of padded foils, ready to move in with Rachelle. The cellar was bigger at her new house and he could see a very prosperous business growing. Soon he'd be able to buy one of those big flashy Subaru Impreza and drive round town as king of all he surveyed.

Rachelle was addicted to Billy. He made sure of this by giving her very creative sex, which he described as 'love'. Before long, she was totally hooked on his particular brand of magic. Of course, this had happened with all the fathers of her children and even those who hadn't got her pregnant. She liked the escape of sex. It made her forget the who and why of what she was. Each time there was a new partner, she'd fall in love all over again.

For his part, Billy had no idea what love was. He used sex as a control. Occasionally, he would make a fuss of the kids and offer a few kind words, but usually preferred to sit back with his feet up, drinking beer with visiting friends. Sometimes, the friends would share more than a mere beer and pass her around from one to another taking what they wanted. She was his property, so what could be nicer, he would say.

And soon things would get even better as the Government, bless them, had decided to pay all benefits directly to the tenants in order to make them more responsible, rather than pay the rent straight to the Landlord. Seeing as a move was in order every year, they could thus move from house to house and only end up paying a total of three month's rent, or less for a whole year. All the more beer and fag money. Life was great.

The social worker was totally restricted to what she could do for the stressed and angry Landlords, telling them coyly that all information was data protected. The Council had tried to find out if Billy was living with Rachelle, rather than just visiting once a week, but Social Services were more of a hindrance than a help. The latter though, were at least in touch with Environmental Health again when the black mould started to appear at the new house as well and blamed the Landlady.

Billy did not like mould. He said Rachelle was not cleaning properly. If she didn't do so, he would hit her. Of course, she was used to this. All her other men had hit her too, so she came to accept it as part of the love they

4

had for her and the fact that they couldn't help it. They had had such a raw deal out of life. Social Services had suggested a 12 steps programme for her, but she was in total denial that there was any problem at all. The kids would watch what was happening. To them it was just a pattern of normal life. Mum's black eye was thought of as a badge, a symbol of the love he had for her. When they got older, they would keep up the tradition.

Meanwhile, the complaining neighbours resulted in torrents of abuse from Billy, which he screamed over the garden wall. He knew his rights. He would get on to Citizens' Advice and they would sort out the neighbours. Or he would take the Landlady to court. She must have known about the troublesome neighbours before she let out the house.

The Landlady had tried contacting the CID[1] about Billy as she often worked together with them. That department was only allowed two officers, working on shifts in order to cover a vast area. When she commented that Domestic Violence was rife in the area, the kind Officer told her that in fact it was all over the UK. A very depressing thought!

Now, Rachelle was only twenty years old, although she looked about forty, probably due to some missing teeth, gone by either violence or pop. But she felt successful anyway. She had four children and lived a life fully funded by the State. And she was loved by the wonderful Billy. If she was lucky, tonight he may give her a broken arm or even another baby, which she could spoil with plastic toys. If her parents had been still alive, she was sure they would be proud of her carrying on the traditions so well

---

[1] Criminal Intelligence Division

known to them. Sadly, they had died many years before and foster homes had filled the gap between.

Yes, Rachelle felt lucky as she made Billy's tea and cleaned up after him. Perhaps he would be the best man she had ever known and be what they called in romantic books, "the love of her life".

# I watch you fly

by C.I. Ripples

I check the flight status: you are taxiing on the runway.

Have three months already passed since you left? Twelve weeks since that dry clear night when my heart smarted? Eighty-four days when I lost your part of my being? My heart gripped with an almost physical pain, deep and raw, as if my limbs were being wrenched from my body. Two thousand and seventeen hours since we said goodbye?

I held back my tears in my efforts to be strong, almost shaking with the effort of composure, as I reluctantly let you go at passport control. And drove back from the airport empty as the heavens opened above me, knowing that today at least I must continue to go through the motions of living. Only when I turned off the light and turned towards the wall, did I silently let my tears free flow in unison with the monsoon rain.

Yet, every time you leave, I know that, as I let the darkness envelope and rest my weary spirit, a new day will dawn, with light full of new promises for me, for you. Every time I breathe a sigh of relief as I am awoken by the WhatsApp ping, letting me know that you have arrived. You are safe, even if a little travel worn. And every time I wish you so well and pray you succeed in finding happiness as you reap the rewards of all your hard work.

Today I am smiling as I check the flight status of your A380. You are now high up in the sky at thirty thousand feet. A height at which, we were once informed by your brother, then a toddler, crashing would not go down well. Today I do not resurrect neglected prayers or utter mantras to keep the plane aloft. My heart is not worried, my mind certain that the aerodynamics of your flight do not need a helping hand. Today I have complete faith, as I track you, my amazing daughter, making your way towards me once more.

# I drive my husband crazy?

by Lian McCabe

I think I'm pretty westernized. Even my husband reckons that I am a "banana" – yellow on the outside (my skin) but white on the inside (my way of thinking and behavior). This may be true, but my husband is quite oriental himself, as he had lived in Asia since the 1980s. He calls himself a "boiled and peeled egg" – white on the outside and yellow on the inside. We love each other. We understand each other, at least most of the time. We respect each other's traditions and preferences. Nonetheless, we still have a distinctive approach to certain things. Perhaps, the result of our different cultural backgrounds. Perhaps due or our genes or something in our blood. Perhaps it's not that easy to change one's' actions or behavior at short notice.

We've been married for over three years, but we are still getting used to each other, every day finding out about each other's habits, way of thinking or conducting. My husband complains that some of my habits drive him crazy. Read on and make your own judgment.

**Tools on Trial**

Plaintiff:  My wife tries using one thing for all solutions, anything that comes to hand rather than the fit for purpose tools we have in the house.  For example, she uses a spoon to spread peanut butter on her toast, instead of a proper butter knife.  She also uses a spoon to fry bacon instead of tongs.  She uses a spoon to beat the eggs

9

instead of an egg-beater or a blender, although sometimes she uses chopsticks too. She even uses a spoon to eat noodles instead of chopsticks or a fork. And instead of finding the measuring tape hidden somewhere, she uses a broom-stick to measure the fence. She uses shower caps she got from the hotel to pack our shoes for travel!

Defendant: Firstly, my husband is right. I do use so-called non-professional tools, because they're handy, simple, convenient, and moreover, they serve the purposes for which I adopt them very well. I solve many pressing problems with ease and save time in the process. I think we have a win-win situation here. I would like to call this "the wisdom of the practical life".

Secondly, I got into the habit of using spoons while working in South Korea. Of course, being Chinese, I can also use chopsticks just as well. One pair of chopsticks can be used in a million ways. We use them to pick up almost everything. You name it and I can pick it up for you. Noodles? Peas? Just a piece of cake? I bet you've heard that some Chinese even had pizza with chopsticks. Some of my fellow Chinese even eat their steaks with chopsticks. It might not seem proper or the accepted norm, but using chopsticks is really simple and convenient. Westerners eat with a knife and fork, which possibly dates back to their hunter-oriented origins, but Asians, except possibly Indians, are mainly agriculture-oriented and use chopsticks. For them it's a symbol of civilization.

Thirdly, I really don't want to wash 399 different kind of so-called fit for purpose tools after each and every meal. Using a multi-purpose tool saves time and energy and does the job.

## Bags on Trial

Plaintiff:   My wife likes to hoard plastic bags. I mean, all kinds of plastic bags, from Villa Market, Tesco, Big C, laundry service bags, zip lock bag, even shower caps from hotels. Then she collects, arranges, folds and wraps them up together under different categories in separate bags. The kitchen is full of them! She even creates a new container to store the bags, although I have to admit that is sort of cool. But I mean, we can afford to buy trash bags and any other bags, so why hoard them?

Defendant:   Yes, I fold the bags like tissues in a Kleenex box works, which even my husband thinks it's cool and encourages me to get patented. I store all these bags, plastic or paper ones, to use later and for different purposes. I reuse them all the time.  Except for our last moving, when we had to buy extra-large garbage bags for the giant plants.

Since I start to organize all our plastic bags three years ago, we never spend money on bags or containers. We have enough bags for the kitchen waste, bathroom waste, garden waste, smaller bags for rubbish from the car, with some left for wrapping material. I use the shower caps from different hotels to wrap our shoes, which guarantees the inside of our suitcase remains clean. I use zip lock bags as water-proof bags.  For our last two moves, thanks to my bags, I used them all together with newspaper and bubble wrap to wrap things up. Nothing broke or got wet.

I consider not buying new plastic bags and reusing the old ones, to be not only economical but also convenient and environmentally friendly. I just store the bags and recycle them. And you never know you're going to need one. I therefore do not agree that it's a problem for me to save things. If anything, it's just practical solution.

## The Universal One on Trial

Plaintiff: My wife is lazy. She uses one hand to crack the eggs. She uses one hand to count from zero to ten, which is very confusing for me. She uses one brush to paint her paintings, and only one piece of paper towel to clean up the brush while painting. She uses one piece of paper to list the things for our grocery shopping, then does the shopping and then does multiple things during the same one drive. She opens the fridge once to put in and take out things. She is so lazy.

Defendant: Well, I have this ability to do things with just one hand, one brush, one piece of paper, simply because I am able to. I am a professional in applying this single-hand principle! If you can finish your task single-handedly, why bother with two hands? Two brushes? More sheets? Besides, according to some scientific research, if one can use the fridge with less opening, it consumes less electricity and a lower electricity bill.

And I find the way Westerners count just as confusing. When I first saw how Europeans pointed out TWO with their thumb and index finger, my brain kept telling me EIGHT, EIGHT, EIGHT. When I pointed my thumb and little finger to my husband to ask for six apples, he asked me why I expressed the number two in such a strange way. I explained that for Chinese people the gesture actually meant SIX. He then showed me how to show SIX by adding one finger of one hand to the open palm of the other hand. I do believe that our Chinese way is smarter and more efficient.

Anyway, what I am trying to prove is that I am not lazy but very organized and efficient. I can cook four dishes and make dumplings for four persons within an hour; I can finish a painting with only one brush; I can do the grocery shopping in one trip, picking up the laundry, printing out the bankbook and paying the electricity/water bill at the same time. All it requires is a little bit more thinking ahead. With an organized plan in my head, I can simply do things with less time and less energy. It's what my husband calls, the "universal one principle".

## Whitening on Trial

Plaintiff: My wife likes to be white, wears a big hat, a long sleeve shirt and long pants to keep the sun off her skin and uses whitening lotions and creams. She dreams of being as white as I am. But she'll never succeed.

Defendant: Your Honor, I have to plead guilty as charged.

When I was in China years ago, I tried almost everything to have whiter skin, although not the Caucasian kind of white. I tried staying indoors most of the time. If I had to go out, I always stayed in the shade. If there was no shade, I used my umbrella, hat and sunblock. If unfortunately, I got sunburnt? That was a big deal requiring a rescue mission: aloe vera, facial mask, whitening lotion. And forget going to the beach. That would never happen! The indoor swimming pool might be considered, but only just.

I am not the only one who wishes to be white. Almost every girl back in China wants to be as white as snow. I'm sure you've seen Asian women who take their parasols everywhere while traveling all over the world, especially from early summer to late fall. Have you seen the women in China who wear black shields like a welder's mask and wear gloves, even have a standing umbrella installed over the motorbike? Have you seen Asian women wear "facial-bikini" while swimming in the sea? For Asian women, especially some Chinese women, this is essential equipment to maintain their whitish complexion. They believe that white skin would cover all her shortcomings. Of course, it's pure superstitious, not helped by the media promoting whitening products.

It sounded ridiculous when I shared this with my western friends. They don't have many days of sun in Canada, UK, Holland, Finland, Germany or Russia, so when there is a sunny day, they just embrace it, have all kinds of fun and try to get a tan. Many of them would like to go to some nearby lakes, islands just to get tanned. Well, these days, things have changed a little bit as the rate of the skin cancer roars up. But still, they love sunny days, they love the sun.

After I moved to Phuket, it didn't take me long to stop using umbrellas on sunny days. I now even forget them even the rainy seasons. And when I visit China? I no longer care when my friends denounce me as "briquette" or "coal ball" after they find out I've stopped using whitening stuff. My husband loves me anyway.

## Eating Habits on Trial

Plaintiff: My wife is Chinese. She drinks hot water. She eats strange things like Kimchi from Korea, she eats century old eggs, even broccoli stems. She simply eats everything, everything strange.

Defendant: Yes, I do drink hot water, but I do not eat everything that my husband just mentioned. My husband might be a well-trained diplomat, but he's simply exaggerating.

Let's start with the hot water:

Back in China, whenever someone is sick, their friends always tell him/her to drink more water, drink more hot water, as if it's the cure for all diseases. Because it is! Think about it. Way back, why didn't the Chinese suffer the Black Death while it wiped out a quarter of the European population during the middle age? Our ancestors drank boiled water, instead of the dirty water from the wells, the rivers, which saved them from raging bacteria and germs.

If you think it is too boring to drink hot water, you can give it some taste: green tea, white tea, black tea, flowers tea; brown sugar plus ground ginger with hot water for your girlfriend suffering from her dysmenorrhea; ginger honey hot water for yourself when you have a cold; some wolfberry hot water, or crab-apple hot water just to help you keep fit. It's like mastering the essence of the 'Art of War'. Once you've done that you can make your own variations accordingly. The hot water is the essence of our drink and, you can add anything to suit your preference.

Take my father for example: he drinks hot tea even in sweltering summer. When our fellow Chinese are traveling overseas, they call the room service for a kettle for boiling water. I'm sure you've seen us using thermos bottles? That's simply because we need hot our water. Oh, the beauty of thermos cans – I use them to keep my hot water hot, while my husband uses them to keep cold water cold. Democracy in action!

In addition to providing a cure for diseases, or to keep our hands warm in winter, we also use hot water to disinfect things, like dishes in restaurants. This is how it works: one dish set includes a bowl, a tea cup, a saucer, a spoon wrapped in plastic and chopsticks in a plastic bag. After we sit down, we ask for a pot of hot water before we order any drinks. Then we open up the plastic wrapping and pour hot water in the bowl in order to kill all potential germs with hot water. For me, rinsing with hot water, even if not scientifically proven, has the psychological effect of giving me comfort that the dishes have been 'washed and are disinfected' this way.

I hope you can understand that hot water is not just hot water in our mind. We've used boiled water for hundreds of years to help us escape many plagues. I believe it is a good habit, even if a little strange to the non-Chinese.

Moving on to my eating habits:

There is a saying, almost a mocking of Chinese people's eating preference, that the "Chinese eat everything that moves with four legs except tables and chairs, everything that flies except airplanes, everything that swims except torpedoes."

I am cool, I can take a playful joke.

It is true that many Chinese, except for the meat from the animal's body and limbs, also eat its internal organs, such as the heart, liver, stomach, intestine, brain, even its blood. They also eat the external organs like the neck, tail, wing, eye balls, and sometimes hoof and genitals.

Before I start my defense, however, please allow me to share a few words with you all. The Greek word root for "eat" is 'phag'. Its counterpart Latin root is 'edi' 'vor' which derive from the words 'edere' and 'vorare', meaning 'edible'. Well, there're actually many more words that include this root: polyphagous, geophagy (geo: earth), hippophagous (hippo: horse), zoophagous (zoo: animal), xylo-phagous (xylo: wood), phytophagous (phyto: plant), phyllophagous (phyllo: leaf), anthropophagy (anthropo: human), anthropophagous. This rich linguistic history and etymology tells me that the Chinese are not the only peoples who eats 'strange' things.

That being said, not every Chinese eats all the organs I listed. Each person is a unique individual, and you should not stereotype every Chinese you meet.

Furthermore, don't tell me that non-Chinese peoples don't eat anything rather than the flesh. That they don't eat 'strange' things. Perhaps it's time to expand your ken, to lift you out of your state of ignorance.

Don't Americans eat Chop Suey? What is Chop Suey made of please? Don't the French eat Fois Gras, oxtail soup, ox tongue, venison, and frog legs? Tell me, what organ is that? Don't Russians enjoy Caviar? Don't northern Europeans like pickled herring and reindeer steak? What is British black pudding made of? How about Scottish haggis and tripe? Don't people from the Middle East like goat's head? Have you heard of the Filipino hairy egg and dog feast? Have you tasted the grasshopper & cicada skewers, the crocodile meat snack found all along the streets in Bangkok? Don't forget the Cambodians who enjoy their crisp snake snack and rat steak. How about Australian kangaroo steak, emu steak, ostrich eggs and the Kazakhstan horse burger? Last, but not least, don't forget the Japanese who love fish testis, sushi, dolphin, whale and urchins… No offence, you eat them all. The only difference is you garnish your dishes with fancier names while the Chinese do not.

You may say that at least you don't eat dog. Well, nor do I! There is only a certain group of people who do that, not limited to the Chinese. So, don't put all the Chinese, even Asians into one category. I guess you probably forgot about the cannibalism?

My husband has in fact tasted some really 'strange' things, many more than I, a Chinese have. He's had snake, frog legs, eel, shark fin, pangolin, monkey brain, even armadillo. He defends himself by saying, "I was forced…" And my husband, who is not Jewish or Muslim, refuses to eat pork. But guess what? He does like bacon - fried bacon with eggs, fried bacon with peanut butter toast, - and he's quite happy to eat the Xiaolongbao I make with pork. He eats them all and he can't even explain himself.

So, the next time you want to criticize our eating habits, think about yours first and remember the story of Jesus and the woman accused of adultery from the Bible:

"…then they reminded Jesus that adultery was punishable by stoning under Mosaic law and challenged him to judge the woman so that they might then accuse him of disobeying the law. Jesus thought for a moment and then replied, 'He that is without sin among you, let him cast the first stone at her.'"

Whenever you point a finger at someone, you should have four pointing directly at yourself.

Oh, I almost forget the strange dried roots and dried bugs' bodies in Chinese medicine. It has worked and still works for many Chinese. So, if you want to believe it, don't hesitate, just drink your bitter medicine. If you have doubts as I do, don't comment just stay out of it.

This is my defense. Good habits, of course, I will maintain and I'm always willing to consider change for those that might be a little more dubious.

Do you still think I'm driving my husband crazy? Perhaps the opposite is true. Whoever is reading this, I leave you to judge for yourself.

Suffice it to say, however, that despite our many differences, we love each other and always will.

# Dating in modern life...

by Kyle Daniels

Joe seemed to have his life together and life was good. He had always been ambitious and extremely driven to achieve the goals he set for himself. He had the perfect job and was moving up the corporate ladder faster than many of his peers. He owned a large house which strikingly resembled the one he had cut out and stuck on his vision board many years earlier. Yes, on the outside and by many a person's standard, Joe was a successful twenty-nine-year-old with a bright future ahead of him.

On the inside, however, he felt a sense of emptiness. His tenacity and drive to excel might have put him on the road to success, but it had also resulted in a life in which he didn't have many close friends, didn't have a girlfriend. Life didn't seem to be as exciting as he thought it was supposed to be, lacking in fun and fulfilment. When he wasn't at work, he would either spend the entire day in bed sleeping or binge watching the latest drama on Netflix.

Joe was fast starting to lose his zest for life and soon this lack of fulfilment started manifesting itself in his work - he failed to meet project deadlines and the overall quality of his work dropped tremendously.

One Monday morning, as he arrived at the office, he passed by the Human Resources manager, who reminded him, "We have a 10 a.m. meeting Joe."

After their one-on-one meeting, Joe understood that he had to pull himself out of the rut he was in. He spent that evening brainstorming solutions to the problems that he currently faced, such as his lack of friends. His first thought was to become more active on social media and get in touch with his old friends from university. He started going through their profiles. All of them are married and have children, he thought to himself, as he looked at their photos, but he messaged them nonetheless. After several futile attempts to meet up, he realised that times had changed and that his once carefree university friends now had other priorities. He stopped trying to make plans with them and instead started hanging out with some of his juniors at work. They were young and happy-go-lucky types who frequented bars after work. He went out partying with them on weekends, although he soon realised these consisted of nothing more than binge drinking and uninspiring conversations.

Consequently, Joe still felt the emptiness that he didn't seem to be able to escape, especially during the week when he was not hanging out with his friends. And to fill this void he resorted to having a 'few' drinks after work on occasion, at first with, but then also without his work colleagues. This quickly escalated to binge drinking every night of the week.

One morning, he went to work drenched in the foul smell of alcohol. He was immediately sent home with a suspension letter and told to come in to the office three days later for a disciplinary hearing. Things were now looking really bleak for him - the company had a strict policy against alcohol and it effects at work. Joe had no doubt whatsoever that he would be fired.

At the hearing he was given a final warning after admitting to having an alcohol abuse problem. Joe's boss, a firm believer in second chances, recommended two weeks of paid leave and a compulsory twenty-hour outpatient therapy. Joe sincerely thanked his boss and promised him he would not let him down again.

During therapy Joe quickly realised how badly his life had been going downhill. With the help of his therapist he was able to pinpoint the source of his recent destructive behaviour and the ever-present feelings of emptiness. He understood how, until his recent promotion, he had been focused on work to the exclusion of his emotional and social wellbeing. He understood that the hurt in his previous relationship was still with him and had resulted in him completely closing himself off to dating. He understood that as a result he had no one to share all of his achievements and happy moments with. The therapist gave him homework: he had to list the qualities of the perfect partner to share his experiences with.

Two weeks later Joe was back at work with renewed focus and back to delivering high quality projects.

"The therapy sessions and time off certainly seem to have had a positive effect," praised William, his boss.

Joe thanked him once more for his understanding and for giving him the opportunity to prove himself.

Later that night, once in bed, Joe thought back to what his therapist had said about finding someone to share his special moments with. He wondered how he could go about meeting this special someone. He decided to go online and research 'how to find a partner'. The search results provided many options, but one caught his eye: online dating. He had never tried this before, having heard plenty of bad stories: that such women were usually only good for a one nightstand; that any relationships that did come out of it didn't last; that it could take ages to find someone decent; that such meetings were often awkward.

In spite of all these negative stories, one tale about a friend finding true love via an online dating site kept playing on his mind. It gave him hope and before long he found himself downloading a dating application on his phone and setting up a profile. He was prepared to follow through on finding his dream woman. After all, he thought, what could be more fulfilling than being able to share my happiness with someone who cares about me as much as I care about her?

He started chatting to a beautiful lady who seemed to match the character description of his dream woman. Still a bit hesitant to meet, it took Joe many weeks to finally build up the courage to ask her to dinner.

It was on a summer's evening that he set out to meet his date, Kim, at a trendy restaurant that was buzzing with patrons. He had specifically chosen this place over a quieter romantic venue to prevent any potential awkward silences.

Upon meeting, Joe and Kim realised that they actually knew each other from years back when Joe was still a teenager and would visit Kim's older brother Luke. Could this be a sign? thought Joe to himself.

From the moment they realised they knew each other, they started conversing nonstop for hours on end, oblivious to time, speaking about topics ranging from their teenage years, work and desired future.

All of a sudden, the waiter appeared at their table and interrupted their conversation flow. He informed them that the restaurant would be closing soon. Joe looked around and realised they were the only people left, apart from a few restaurant staff that were standing at the door, ready to leave work for the night. Joe, having been a waiter himself during his student years, used to get annoyed by patrons who would stay seated long after the restaurant closed. He realised he was now 'that guy'. Feeling a bit embarrassed, he hurriedly paid the bill and expressed his sincere apologies to the waiter as they left.

As Joe walked his date to her car, he realised that he had not even offered her desert. What a gentleman! he thought but rectified the situation by asking Kim if she would like to have desert, that he knew of a twenty-four-hour ice-cream shop about a five-minute drive away.

"Yes, it is a perfect summer's evening, so ice-cream would be delicious," she smiled at him. They agreed that Joe would drive his car and she would follow him in hers. A few minutes later they pulled up at a beachfront ice-cream shop and decided to take a walk on the beach while licking their ice-creams.

The conversation picked up again. They spoke and laughed until Joe checked the time and saw that it was 3.30 in the morning. He asked her if she wanted to go home now or wait another two hours and watch the sunrise. She thought watching the sunrise would be a great conclusion to what had been an amazing date thus far, so they decided to stay. Joe jokingly said, "only two more hours until the birth of a new day." To him, sunrise represented a new day, a new possibility, and with Kim by his side it could possibly also mean the start of a new chapter. He was certainly optimistic.

At 5.30 a.m. they sat and watched the sunrise. As the sun started illuminating everything in its path and the waves broke against the rocks in front of them, Joe slowly turned to Kim and looked into her eyes. It felt for sure that he was gazing directly into her soul. At that moment, as they shared their first kiss, it was as if time had ceased to exist. And he instantly knew that Kim was the one he wanted to share all of life's pleasures with. He felt alive again, he felt excited.

Shortly after the kiss, Joe walked Kim to her car and they discussed their plans to see each other again, arranging to meet up later that same day. The date didn't even end once Joe got home, as they immediately started texting each other about how amazing the night had been.

This was the start of many dates on a journey to find true happiness. Joe asked Kim to marry him a few months later.

# Lament

## by Paul McCabe

Exactly what sort of mindless adolescent madness causes me to vacillate between such extremes of complete joy and utter despair? Why am I, usually so controlled, so tossed between vagaries, like seeds in the wind? Just what is it about her that seizes my mind like shark's jaws and refuses to let go, even as I thrash around, drowning in the enveloping confusion of my own thoughts? How can I bring an end to this acting like a schoolboy, moonstruck and lovesick, open to her razor refusals and ecstatic smiles? Why should my generally happy state of mind be dashed on the rocks of her unanswered phone? Why should the passage of my time, usually so busily occupied, be slowed to a crawl by her inability to spend it with me? Why should the memory of her soft moans under me permeate my mind for hours on end? How can I stop the endless dreaming, the infinite scheming, that goes along with any thoughts I have of her? What is it about her that makes me want to fly away with her to a sandy sunny island to have her undivided attention? Why have I suddenly been struck with a yearning infatuation that grows steadily, even as my will struggles within itself to reverse this encroachment? Why can't she act on what she must be seeing: that I'm head-over-heels dangling on the strings of her whimsical yes or no? Is her blindness to my solicitous anxiety a result of insouciance, or of ignorance, or of calculation? Do the walls of her tantalizing defences have a soft spot where they can be breached by the passionate though unslaked eagerness of my impatient desire? Does she know the disconsolate discouragement of my despondent depression? What is it about her demure display of indifference that drives me to risk my pensive heart yet again? Why was I caught in a day-long lamenting melancholy when she told me "I'm not your lover"? Which is the path that will lead my emotions out of these gloomy doldrums where I'm prime prey to her anorexic nonchalance? How can she exhibit such easy-going neutrality in the face of my best-laid plans? What are the reasons behind her numbing passivity? What can I do to make her susceptible to the boundless exigencies of my ardor? How can she - outwardly so cool - be the subject of the rapacious impetuosity that's consuming me? What has compelled me to desert my dispassionate detachment that I've nurtured so carefully over the years of having relationships with women? Where is the perspective on her that will allow me to return there, where I'm much more comfortable and self-possessed than in this inexplicable state of manic pining? When will these open-eyed nightmares end, and my rapturous reveries become reality in space and in time?

If I knew the answers, I wouldn't be writing this anguished list, would I?

# Laughter In The Dark
a ten-minute play

by Joel Adams
adapted from the novel by Vladimir Nabokov

*As the curtain rises MARGOT is sitting SR[2] in front of a table with an imaginary mirror, brushing her hair, putting on her make-up, enjoying the luxury of her dressing gown and her beauty. She stands up and checks her shape, is pleased with what she sees, sits back down and starts to put away her different beauty products. The door opens and ALBERT enters. She doesn't turn around, but we see he is extremely agitated. He stands and stares at her a moment.*

MARGOT

Oh, you're back. Did you have a good walk? I'm really sorry I was so tired I couldn't go with you today, but thank you for bringing me here, darling. I've always wanted to see the French Riviera. I have to admit it's really such a shame to waste this beautiful day indoors.

ALBERT

*with an edge*

It's just as well you weren't with me.

---

[2] Stage directions: SR – stage right; SL – stage left; CS – stage centre

*He opens a drawer in the desk SL and pulls out a revolver, checks it is loaded. The clicking sound of the hammer alarms MARGOT, who turns and sees the pistol in his hand.*

MARGOT

*alarmed*

Albert, don't play with that thing. It might go off.

*ALBERT grabs her by the wrist and pulls her up, shaking her*

What's gotten into you? *(scoffs)* Are you drunk? What's this all about?

ALBERT

I found out you've been lying to me, you and that scoundrel, Rex. Nothing but trickery and deceit, and… I see your tricks now; it's all clear.

MARGOT

I don't know what you're talking about.

ALBERT

You know very well what I'm talking about. I can't believe the fool I've been, leaving my wife and daughter for you, giving you everything, spoiling you, going mad with jealousy over you. Oh, and Rex, pretending to be my best friend; and you pretending you don't like having him round, merely allowing it to humor me, because he and I are such fast friends. He offers to chauffeur us on vacation, and I accept, because you don't trust my driving. You pretend to be reluctant, while all the while you and he maneuvered it all so you could cheat on me behind my back. I see it all now, and I will kill you for it.

MARGOT

Please, put that thing down. I won't speak to you until you have. I don't know what's happened and I don't want to. I only know one thing: I am faithful to you. I am faithful... Just let me explain.

ALBERT

What explanation could you possibly give?

*She gazes imploringly into his eyes and he weakens*

But... all right, you can say what you have to say... but then you die.

MARGOT

*pleading*

No! Don't kill me—please, darling.

ALBERT

Go on. Speak.

## MARGOT

I can't… I can't speak as long as you're holding that thing, pointing it at me. Please, put it away.

## ALBERT

No. First, you must confess… I have information, proof. I know all… I know all… I know all. You see, I ran into my old friend, Udo Conrad, that German writer who lives here on the Riviera. It just so happens, he sat behind you and Rex on the bus the other day, and you didn't know he was German. You didn't know he could understand every word you said. He told me you and Rex behaved like lovers, that you had the loudest, sickest, nastiest love conversation there that he'd ever heard, thinking no one could understand you. And you dropped my name… so he casually asked me about you, not knowing you were my… whatever you are.

## MARGOT

Oh… on the bus? I can explain… it's easy to explain… You see, I… I never told you about… about the… the game… Rex and I play. I just knew you wouldn't understand. That's why I never told you what Rex and I play sometimes. For God's sake, put that thing down, Albert.

ALBERT

*screaming*

What game?! What are you talking about?!

MARGOT

In the first place, Albert, you know very well Rex doesn't care for women.

ALBERT

Shut up! I know now that was a base lie, a rascally trick from the beginning.

MARGOT

No. He really doesn't care for women, but once—for a joke—I suggested to him: 'Look here, let's see whether I can make you forget your boys.' Oh, we both knew it was only a joke. That was all, that was all, darling.

ALBERT

A dirty, filthy lie. I don't believe it. Udo saw you. Another hotel guest saw you as well. That French colonel, right under his window, carrying on. Everyone knows. They laugh at me behind my back. Only I was blind.

MARGOT

Well, after saying that, I often teased him with my game, and he began to play along. It was all very funny… But I won't any more… if it upsets you.

ALBERT

You deceived me, just for a joke? Disgusting!

MARGOT

Of course, I didn't deceive you! How dare you say such a thing!? Rex is not even able to help me deceive you; he cares for you so much, for one, and he has no desire for women. We never even kissed: that would have been repulsive to both of us.

ALBERT

And if I asked him—not in your presence, of course, not in your presence?

MARGOT

Do, by all means! He'll tell you exactly the same. I'll call him.

*MARGOT makes as if she's going to the door to call REX, but she stops just short of the door, starts to choke up, gathers her strength*

Only you'll make yourself look ridiculous. Go ahead! See if I care! You've ruined everything, everything! Nothing will ever be the same again. Oh, just looking at you makes me sick, to be accused like this!!

*She bursts into hysterical cries, falling on the bed, sobbing*

How could you accuse me like that?! How could you?!

ALBERT

*Shocked by her turning the tables on him, he weakens bit by bit, then starts to embrace her, stops, tries again, doesn't*

Very well, Margot. I believe you. But… this has been extremely disturbing for me… I think we must leave… you must get up immediately and change your clothes. We're going to pack our things at once and leave this place. I can't see him now—I can't answer for what would happen if I do. Not because I believe that you have deceived me with him, no, not on that account, but I simply can't do it; I've pictured it all to myself too vividly, and… well, no matter… Come, get up…

MARGOT

Kiss me.

ALBERT

No, not now. I want to get away from here as soon as possible… I can't believe what I almost did; I almost shot you, killed you, in this room. We must pack our things at once—at once.

MARGOT

As you like, but please remember that you've insulted me and my love for you in the worst manner possible. I suppose you'll understand that later.

*The lights fade and when they come up, the chairs have been arranged CS to make the front seat of a car. ALBERT is putting bags behind the chairs while MARGOT stands and waits.*

MARGOT

Do you mind telling me where we're going?

*ALBERT shrugs. He mimes opening the door for her on the rider's side and gets in the driver's seat.*

Really, you should let me drive. You're not used to driving and you're very upset now.

ALBERT

I'll drive. I want to drive. I need to drive.

MARGOT

It really doesn't matter to me where we go, but I'd just like to know.

*They mime pulling out and driving and we can see he is starting to go faster and faster.*
*She sees something on the road that startles her, reaches for the wheel, makes a swerving action*

Look out! Keep to the right! Listen, Albert, we can take a train or hire a chauffeur.

*He ignores her and continues to drive. He suddenly slams on the brakes and they stop with a jolt.*

You almost hit that car! Really, Albert!

### ALBERT

*There's a long pause while he collects himself, then he starts to drive again*

Does it matter where we go? Wherever we go, I shall not escape this pain.

### MARGOT

All right. Forget it. I won't ask again.

*As they drive, it is clear she is uncomfortable with his rough driving*

But please go slow on the mountain road, and don't wobble so much on the curves.

ALBERT

Do you swear to me there was nothing to what those people said?

MARGOT

I swear. I'm tired of swearing to you. Kill me if you wish, but don't torture me.

ALBERT

*breaking down slightly*

I'm sorry, I just love you so much. I was so happy on this vacation, because the jealousy I felt before was gone, completely gone. I felt secure in your love. So very happy.

MARGOT

*patting his hand*

You were insecure before, I suppose, because we were new lovers then and you could hardly believe I loved you. Now, as you know, I have proven I only have eyes for one man. Let me drive, Albert, do. You know I can do it better than you.

ALBERT

No, I'm improving. See how confident I am now on the curves?

*They make like they are making a wide curve and are enjoying it for a moment, but suddenly they both see something in the road and scream and shout as they swerve. There is a crashing sound. Lights off suddenly.*

*When the lights come back up, ALBERT is lying with his eyes bandaged in a bed. MARGOT is talking with the nurse.*

MARGOT

It's too terrible to think about. To think, if it had not been for the telegraph post, we should have gone over the cliff and to our death. I shudder just to think about it. I'm still bruised after two weeks, see?
*Lifts her skirt slightly to show the bruises on her upper leg*

The cyclists were very nice and helped us get an ambulance and gather up our things.

NURSE

Oh, look! He's starting to wake up!

*NURSE and MARGOT go to opposite sides of the bed*

MARGOT

Albert, dear, there has been an accident. You must stay calm and continue to rest. You have been quite badly hurt, and it will take some time for you to…

*While she has been talking, ALBERT has been trying to look around and finally lifts the bandage just a little to see. He sits up in shock.*

ALBERT

Margot! Margot! Turn on the light. Please turn on the light. How can you stand the dark? Why is the light off?

MARGOT

Lie still, Albert. The sun is shining, it's a glorious morning.

ALBERT

But... how?
*Then it slowly dawns on him*

No! It can't be! It can't be! Tell me I'm not blind, Margot. TELL ME I'M NOT BLIND!

*ALBERT continues to scream as the lights fade. They come back up with MARGOT sitting beside him. He is agitated still but not hysterical. MARGOT is holding a letter in her hand. The NURSE is gone.*

MARGOT

Albert, dear, I must read you something we just received from Rex. You need to hear this.

ALBERT

No, no, I don't ever want to hear that name again. I don't want to hear anything from him.

MARGOT

But you must. Just listen. It will calm you and put you at peace.

ALBERT

Well... if you must, I will do my best to listen. But you must stop if I can't take it.

*ALBERT makes appropriate painful sounds throughout the letter reading*

MARGOT

*reading*

"I don't know, my dear Albert, what saddens me most—the wrong you did me by your uncivil departure and your accusations, or the terrible thing that has happened to you. Even though you have wounded me deeply, I sympathize with you whole-heartedly in this time of trouble. How sad, you who love painting and colors, lines and form so much, to be struck blind!

Today with a heavy heart I must bid you farewell. I am traveling from Paris to England and then on to New York. It will be a long time before I return to Germany. Greet Margot for me, and I am sorry that her fickle and spoiled behavior caused your hatred for me. You must understand that it is her nature to crave to be admired. She resorted to teasing when I, with my unnatural inclinations, didn't give her the adoration she longed for.

Albert, I liked you well, more than I showed you. If you had only told me that my presence was irksome to you, I would have gladly kept my distance. As it is, our lovely talks about painting, about the world of color, are sadly darkened by the shadow of your flight from and hatred for me."

## ALBERT

*heaving a deep sigh and shaking his head*

Yes, that's the letter of a homosexual. Sadly though, I must say I'm glad he's gone so we can be alone together. I believe God has punished me for distrusting you, but if you were ever guilty…

## MARGOT

Of what, Albert? Go on, finish your sentence.

## ALBERT

No. Nothing. I do believe you, I do. Oh, I believe you.

*starts to cry*

Please, please forgive me. I've paid dearly. I've hurt you, worst of all, and lost the prince of all my senses…

*weeps, she holds him comfortingly. When he calms himself down*

## MARGOT

Albert, I'm sorry, but I must leave you for a while; I must make travel arrangements. I won't be long.

## ALBERT

Of course, my darling. Don't worry. I'll be all right now.

*She exits. Lights fade. When they come back up, REX is sitting at a table sipping white wine as she enters*

## REX

*smirking*

Well, what did he say to the letter? Didn't I word it exquisitely?

## MARGOT

Yes, very. It went well. Wednesday we leave. Please, take care of the tickets, and… take yours in another carriage— it's safer.

## REX

I doubt they'll let me have the tickets for nothing.

*MARGOT smiles tenderly and hands REX a wad of bills*

And as a general rule, it would be much simpler if I were the cashier.

MARGOT

Of course, my darling.

*They hold hands, sigh, and smile at each other as the lights slowly fade.*

THE END

# Trafficked in Love

By C.I. Ripples

Linh checked her I-phone and yawned. Only 3.30 and the lesson had barely begun. They were learning about the body today and the English teacher had put a large drawing on the whiteboard to be labelled. What a waste of time, Linh thought, as she inspected her nails, noticing a small chip in the bright red nail varnish on her middle finger. She would have to repaint them later. She yawned again and gazed out the window at the sky where the birds were free. She knew all about the body. Hadn't her own body led her to this prison? To this place where the good leaves protected the worn-out victims of love, where one day seemed longer than a thousand years at large? Linh surely didn't belong here.

There was Anh with the heavy-lidded eyes, whose husband had abused her to the extent of virtually blinding her. She had tried to kill herself several times – it was easier to face death than relentless, irreversible pain and darkness. It was only when she was beaten almost to a pulp and discarded from the window that Ahn found freedom.

Behind her sat the dark-skinned Diu with the vacant eyes. Linh knew from their group therapy sessions, that as a young woman, love had tricked Diu into domestic servitude and sexual slavery. It was in fact a local policeman who had introduced her to Chi. When he asked if she wanted to go on the back of his motorbike she was excited and flattered and he seemed kind. She didn't have much experience of love or kindness, having been subjected by her drunken father early on to sexual, physical and verbal abuse. They had driven to a cafe where a few of his friends were waiting, sipping beer and chatting. Diu had never tried beer and wanted to appear sophisticated and worldly. So, she readily accepted a glass.

Then, they all set off on a motorbike ride into the mountains. Diu by now felt dizzy and fell asleep sandwiched between Chi and his friend. When she awoke she was tied up in the back of a car with a stranger. She begged to get out, but he slapped her and screamed at her in a foreign language. It was only later she understood she was in China. By nightfall they arrived at a farmhouse where he locked her in a room. From then on, she was raped several times a day, sometimes by her supposed husband, but more usually by his friends who were happy to pay for his sexual plaything. She soon had the tears, the screams, most of her life knocked out of her.

Yet, somehow, she had found the strength and more surprisingly, Linh thought, the presence of mind to escape and alert the police. Or perhaps her husband, after Diu had borne him two sons, both of whom he took away from her immediately after birth, had no further use for her. Whichever it was, after nine years of slavery she finally found safety, at least during daylight hours. Whereas in captivity Diu hadn't wanted to wake for fear of the nightmares awaiting her, now the same fear had taken away her desire for sleep.

Linh, on the other hand, happily plummeted into a black dreamless sleep as soon as her head touched the pillow. On the rare occasions when she did awaken in the night, she would invariably see Diu in the bunk opposite, wide-eyed, mumbling to herself. So traumatised was she that the social workers said she was unable to learn anything or hold down a job. Linh observed the kind, delicate woman, who dithered and stuttered and forgot within five minutes what she was being taught. This was her sixth English beginner class. She would never leave this house.

Linh sighed, flicked back her long shiny black hair, inspected her face in her smart phone and thanked her lucky stars. She was the third child and eldest daughter of a family of seven children, her loving parents so poor that when they decided to sell her to a brothel at the age of eleven she was almost happy to oblige. Hunger always brings the wolf to the fold, and when he came she knew it would be Linh he would choose. After all, she was the prettiest. Her mother, as she brushed Linh's hair, combing and raking it with a steel comb to get all the insects out, had assured her she would have a much better life than they could offer and she would be helping the family, that she need not worry as a clean hand needs no washing.

"I am your new daddy," the man told her as gave her keo dừa[3] and her parents five thousand US dollars. He was very affectionate and almost a gentleman, buying Linh new clothes, shoes, even flowers. Of course, she didn't really know what was going to happen until her daddy put his thing inside her a few weeks after her arrival. Until then she had been helping around the brothel, working up to eighteen hours a day cooking and cleaning for the other girls. She almost envied them their

---

[3] kẹo dừa – coconut candy

bright nail polish, gleaming hair, the beautiful silk áo dài[4] they wore when entertaining clients, their seemingly leisurely days.

At first, she cried, with the shock of it all, with the pain, the blood between her legs. But daddy told her she had done well, that she was a natural and would be his prized possession. He made her proud. He even told her he loved her. It was only later she realised that as with so many men, he confused love with sex.

Her daddy taught her everything she needed to know. All the positions, how much she should charge, how she should talk to the men, some Chinese, some English, and later how to avoid falling pregnant. They practised the positions again and again, sometimes more than four times a day. Until she was ready for the outside world. Even then his appetite for her never fell off.

She suddenly noticed the other women looking at her expectantly.

"Well Linh, what is the name of this part of the body?" the middle aged, badly dressed and drab, grey haired do good teacher asked her, pointing to the drawing on the whiteboard.

How badly Western women age, Linh thought, their skin all leathery and wrinkled and what a stupid question. Even those with the most basic English knew this was a cock, dick, pecker, hard-on or even a ding. Her daddy had called it his love stick. She knew all the English names. She could even name them in Chinese or

---

[4] áo dài – traditional Vietnamese dress

Russian. Linh tested her memory: *jībā*, *kuàxià wù*, *diǎo*, *xuj*, *schwanz*, although she wasn't sure of the last one.

The teacher was now in front of her desk, tapping it with a ruler and before Linh had time to hide it, her bony fingers whisked away her treasured phone.

"You do not need this now," she was told sternly as the phone was placed on the cupboard next to the white board, "I will give it back at the end of class."

She glared at the old bat but then decided she may as well show off her English skills which were so much more advanced than the others in the class. So good were they, that the counsellor had found her that boring job at the coffee shop frequented by foreigners almost immediately. The pay was terrible. Linh could earn the same in one hour in her old job as she did at the coffee shop in a month! It was ironic, she thought that the shop was around the corner from her daddy's establishment. And there she had not once needed to work full days, never servicing more than five men a day – her daddy wanted his clients, who he impressed on the girls were important and influential men, to have quality time.

"Cock," she called out confidently, expecting praise from the teacher. Instead the horrible woman shook her head and wagged her finger in stony disapproval.

"No Linh, we do not call this a cock. That is not a nice word. The correct word is penis."

The twins giggled, baffled. They were pretty little things, rescued by the police just before they disappeared over the Chinese border. And they were bright, learning to write both Vietnamese and English at the same time, full of innocence, promise and expectations, as Linh had been once. She was annoyed and felt humiliated. She had never heard the word 'penis' before – certainly none of her clients called their thing as such. She decided the teacher obviously had no idea, which was not surprising. Surely no man would ever want to put their stick in between the legs of that old thing. Best to say nothing and nod demurely. She had learnt the hard way that it was sometimes better to just remain silent and do as you're told. It was certainly safer.

It was 4 p.m. and it had begun to rain. As she observed the water lashing against the window, the coconut trees bending dangerously in the wind, Linh thought back to what had led her to seek refuge. Had it really been over two months since her daddy's establishment had been raided by the police? Most of the girls had been rounded up, but Linh had managed to escape through the back door with Ngoc and Mai. That is when she had discovered the life so many women in this classroom had learnt about long ago: that men could be vicious; that being out alone in the street was dangerous; that men could trap you in dirty rooms in Nga Nghis[5] and raise their fist to hit you, throw objects at you, or hold you down as they shoved and poked. They could stick hot coat hangers into your vagina, or extinguish cigarette butts on your breast as they masturbated. Linh now understood why so many of the women in this class had made a conscious decision to look like less of what a man would want to see.

   Linh checked the now yellow bruises on her arm, remembered with a shudder her swollen eyes, her cracked ribs, but above all the naked fear that had touched the base of her throat and laid its cold finger on her heart.

---

[5] Nha Nghi – a cheap motel, where rooms can be rented by the hour.

Not the fear of violence in itself, but the fear that her looks would be permanently scarred, that her ability to make a good income would be ruined, that she would no longer be able to send money home to her family.

In all her seven thousand plus encounters she had never been as badly treated as she had been by the heavy-set Russian with the expensive silver BMW. It would never have happened had her daddy been around. He had loathed men who beat his girls, telling them that real men did not exercise their strength on frailer creatures. Linh knew she had been luckier than most, but the terror of her ordeal had made her more fearful and insecure. She was sufficiently recovered to return to the streets - her wounds had almost healed and she had completed her course of antibiotics. With her beloved daddy incarcerated and possibly not out for months, however, she had no protection. Until then she might as well stay here.

She noticed the other women had started to close their books. The teacher was erasing the whiteboard. The clock on the wall read four thirty. As they filed out of the classroom, Linh snatched back her phone and checked her messages. Her heart jumped. There was one from daddy! He was back, she was free. By the door she turned around one last time to say goodbye to the bedraggled teacher, who, stroking the gold cross that hung from her neck, stood by the window looking down to where the rain poured and poured as if washing away the stains of their misfortunes.

# Lesser Brethren

by Stephanie Thornton

'It's only a cat!'

This sort of phrase is sometimes heard at the passing of an animal in your life. I suppose it belongs in the same category of those bereaved platitudes that includes 'time heals' and 'you'll meet someone else' - the sort of sentences that people say about the loss of a person when they don't know what else to and become embarrassed and at a loss.

When I was little, there was a picture on my nursery wall of The Christ, surrounded by little animals in a wonderful garden. It was called 'Lesser Brethren' by the Artist Margaret W. Tarrant. But, when you pause to think; are they 'lesser' and what does it mean? Does it mean small, or less than? And if so, are they? Is less in fact, more?

My wonderful cat Rastus died on the same day as the Bastille Day massacre in Nice. Should I grieve him less than all those other poor suffering souls whose families died that day? Is an animal spirit less than a human one? Or are we all as one?

Rastus appeared in my life in the summer of 2004, a year after my mother died. He arrived as a starving stray and to all intents and purposes, looked wild and savage. Pretty terrifying in fact! We already had three cats for various reasons and my husband insisted we couldn't have another, especially one that looks like 'that'. But after he sat outside for three weeks crying, I told him I had had enough and went to give him some food. He looked really strange, with an overly large head and a very small body, and was so weak, he had to roll the food pellets onto the floor from the dish to be be able to pick them up. Yet, in spite of his condition, he, like a delinquent school boy, tried to beat up the other cats. I decided to give him time.

Another four weeks passed when, sitting on the sun lounger, I felt this furry body leap up next to me and thought, 'if I reach my hand out to touch him, maybe I will need stitches, but I must try.' The only consequence was the loudest purr.

Unlike the other three, he would stroll into the cat basket to visit the vet like a sort of dignified gentleman going for a stroll in the park. The vet gathered he was about four years old and also that he had a fear of men and large cardboard boxes. This year, when x-rays were needed, we discovered he had broken bones in his chest as a result of a kick pre us. He also had a cut lip long time healed.

As time passed, he became more confident and would spend hours on my knee gazing at me and laying on his side so he wouldn't scratch me. His huge yellow eyes never left my face and, if I was sad or down, he would cover me with his body and stroke my face. He talked a great deal, almost as if he knew I had had a very rough time over the last decade and he needed to be there for me.

I remember seeing Timothy Christopher as James Herriot as the vet in the TV series 'All Creatures Great and Small'. It was the episode when his dog died and he reached down habitually for his beloved dog only to find it not there. Then he sat on a hillside in the Yorkshire Dales and wept. Everyone watching wept with him. It is the same for me when I open a door and Rastus isn't there asking for milk or see the dish no longer used for food.

He died in England and I brought him back to be buried in his garden in France. The neighbour had dug a hole for me and it was so big, I swear I could see Australia at the bottom! My garden is a beloved animal graveyard and I only hope that the people who will eventually live here after me, will keep it and not say 'they're only cats'.

Is it right to grieve for a 'Lesser Brethren' or is it 'only a cat'? Writing the wounds away can be cathartic but not easily healed with such special bonds. Are we right to let our animals be euthanised when we don't allow this for people? And is it Christian to allow this? Man is supposed to have dominion over the animals, but we're not very good at it, are we?

Rest in peace Rastus. I know you were much more than 'only a cat'.

*Post script: on the 22nd October 2016, whilst in New Orleans, I had a strange and vivid dream. In it two people (angels?) were trying to guide three cats through an opening in a wall. The black one, Rastus, was running away from them all the time. 'Can you help?' they asked. 'I'll get him,' I said and the next moment he was sitting on my knee. His body and fur smelt and felt just the same it had always. Then, a moment or so later, he was gone.*

*Rastus- 2000 (?) – 14.7.16*

# The Long Kiss at Blue Siam

by Renata Kelly

The deck of the Blue Siam Beach Club overlooked a sandy beach and a small harbor for local long-tail boats. Beyond stretched the long curve of Bang Tao Bay, certainly one of the loveliest and least spoilt on the island of Phuket in Thailand. On the distant far side of the bay, the green hills of Layan were punctuated indistinctly by the red tile roofs of a luxury hotel, the bungalows embedded deeply in the jungle growth. As usual, it was hot and the humidity of the tropics added a haze that made the sky gray-blue and the horizon, where sea and sky merged, indistinct

As the afternoon wore on, the clients of Blue Siam, lounging in wicker chairs or grouped around small tables on the deck, started to think of switching from coffees, sodas and coconut juice to something a bit more exotic and relaxing, maybe a Mai Tai or Pina Colada. A few of the loungers, looking out at the moored boats and the unpopulated beach, had noticed that a little distance to the right of the Blue Siam deck and across a small rivulet that trickled into the sea, three local workers were busy putting the final touches to a small altar-like table draped in white tulle, two side pillars, likewise adorned, and a diaphanous tulle screen. It seemed that the scene was being set for a modest beach wedding, though as yet no guests were seen to be arriving.

Incongruously, a large white motor yacht had anchored in the deeper water beyond the scruffy local boats of the little harbor. No one as yet had appeared on its deck and it seemed as abandoned as the rest of the vessels. Perhaps at this point in the waning afternoon one or two amongst those gathered on the Blue Siam deck might have noticed that from the distant sun-blurred waters of the bay two motor boats had appeared, making their way with motorized determination in the direction of the little harbor. As the boats approached, it was possible to see that they were large inflatables with powerful engines and that each boat held about six or seven passengers. With unnecessary speed and show-offish skill, the two boats skidded gently to a stop on the beach just beyond the impromptu wedding chapel. The passengers, one of them in a dark suit, quickly disembarked and started to unload an array of steel cases, tripods, wires, cameras and other stuff.

On the deck of the Blue Siam Club, most eyes were now focused on the unfolding beach scene and a few comments were heard suggesting that this might be the set-up for a wedding photo-shoot, or perhaps a scene from a movie, or maybe a TV advertisement. Certainly, there was a lot of equipment, so if it were to be a real wedding, perhaps it wouldn't be so modest after all. But then, where were the guests? Shouldn't they be arriving by this time? A slight commotion out at sea shifted the gaze of the Blue Siam spectators from the wedding beach and its cameras to the large motor yacht. Something was going on there. Yes, a dinghy captained by a smartly dressed young man appeared from behind the boat and stopped at the stern; another man, dressed like the one in the boat - khaki shorts, blue T-shirt - scurried down from the main deck to the stern platform and helped to tie-up the dinghy. Was this coincidence or something to do with the wedding? Those who glanced again at the beach saw that some of the cameras were now focused on the white yacht. ("It's a movie," someone said.) ("Could be an ad," offered another voice. "They have so much money to spend and they fly themselves all over the world!")

At that moment, from the unknown interior of the yacht, stepping into the light of the deck came first a tall young man, dressed in a light suit ("the groom?"), followed by a lady dressed in blue ("bridesmaid, mother, aunt, surely not the bride?"), then – and here there seemed to be a communal intake of breath – a vision in frothy white, slender and blonde ("yes, you can see she's blonde, even at that distance!"). The small wedding party made their way down the steps to the stern deck, the young man first ("If he's the groom, what's he doing with the bride?"), ("It's a movie; they're actors!") ("It's an ad."); the lady in blue helped the bride with her light but voluminous skirt ("Think they'll all fit in the dinghy?"). They did, and the two smart boat-boys likewise.

The dinghy, not so small after all, made its way meandering through and around the local boats and arrived at the wedding beach, all cameras rolling and clicking. A number of the men in the filming crew sprang forward to help the dinghy passengers to disembark, veritably lifting the lithe bride from the boat to the safety of the sandy beach. The couple made their way to the altar. ("Wow, he's handsome!" a female voice.) ("She's gorgeous!") ("Who are they? Ever seen them before?") ("Barbie and Ken, just look at them!"). A general chuckle rippled through the audience on the Blue Siam deck. The proportions of the bride and groom were indeed perfect: he tall with broad shoulders; she slender and small-waisted. They stood still in front of the altar not looking at each other. The lady in blue stepped to the side of the bride ("Matron-of-honor, too old to be a bridesmaid," someone suggested); one of the crew boys stood by the groom ("Couldn't he find a friend to be best-man?"). The man in the dark suit, who had arrived with the film crew, now stepped forward and stood on the other side of the small altar, facing the young couple. He held a book in his hands. ("The Pastor! Seems it might be a real wedding after all?") ("Movie weddings are 'real' too!") ("It's an ad.").

As if on cue, the lady in blue and the smartly-dressed crew boy put their hands on the shoulders of the bride and groom, respectively. The young couple glanced at each other and smiled, their hands intertwined. The lady in blue and the crew boy withdrew their hands and stood to the side. The ceremony began in earnest. The Pastor, tall and grey-haired, started intoning the service. The Blue Siam audience, now gathered on the edge of the deck with some even down on the harbor beach, could not make out the words, but generally agreed that the language used by the Pastor was probably English. The young couple stared smilingly at the Pastor, giving him their full attention. Surely, it was time now to exchange vows, whether real or scripted? The couple turned to face each other, their perfect profiles highlighted now by the mauves and pinks of the approaching sunset. They seemed to be saying something no one could actually hear. The bride lifted her lovely face to that of her partner, he lowered his and their lips met. ("Wow," someone said.) ("Wish I were him!" came from a rotund, bare-chested man; "So do I!" retorted his equally rotund partner.) ("Wish I were her!" someone else sighed.) ("How long can a kiss last? The lucky buggers!")

The couple seemed unaware of their surroundings, facing each other fingers entwined and lips pressed together. The cameras whirred. ("Still at it," someone volunteered.) ("It's for the cameras," another voice). The Pastor appeared a little disconcerted; he glanced benevolently at the couple and then at the lady in blue. The long kiss continued. The crowd on the Blue Siam deck shifted uncomfortably. ("Bit odd, wouldn't you say?" a lady giggled). In the after-glow of the sunset, the bride and groom, oblivious of the world around them and the clicking and churning cameras, continued with their kissing. The Pastor seemed to incline his head ever so little in the direction of the lady in blue. It seemed barely perceptible, but the lady in blue and the boat-boy "best man" stepped forward and gently laid their hands on the shoulders of their charges. Nothing happened. The long, passionate kiss continued. The Pastor nodded again, more urgently. The boat-boy and lady in blue simultaneously delivered a sharp whack to the base of each lovely neck. ("Oh no! What are they doing? What's going on!") The young couple disconnected. They faced the Pastor. They smiled at each other. They held hands.

A sigh of relief seemed to ripple through the small crowd on the Blue Siam deck. ("Definitely odd," someone was heard to say). ("Are they real?"). ("They're actors, for sure.") ("But why the blow to their necks? And they didn't seem to mind!") In the growing evening dusk, the cameras had fallen silent. The film crew gathered around the wedding party, obscuring the bride and groom. Were they congratulating the couple, giving instructions for the next shoot? The whole group, with the bride and groom in the middle, moved toward the beached dinghy. It was hard to see, but it seemed that the wedding party plus the Pastor were boarding the boat. ("Were they carrying the bride? Has she fainted?" someone inquired.) ("Couldn't see, too many people around the dinghy.") The dinghy pushed off into the still luminous evening waters and wended its way around the dark silhouettes of the local boats towards the large white motor yacht. It was difficult to make out, but it seemed that the bride was leaning helplessly against the lady in blue and that the Pastor had his arm around a slumping groom. ("Not a real wedding, for sure!") ("Definitely a movie!") ("Barbie and Ken, big size!") ("Maybe an ad?").

# Redundant Desire

by Boris Nielsen

In anticipation, the lights had been dimmed and a slow Aretha Franklin number started up.

She came through the curtains in an easy, exaggerated mimic of the model's catwalk, her heels clicking softly in time to the beat. Standing, back to the pole, she swayed to the bass, her hips pushing side to side from the axis of her slim waist – a belly dance in no need of a belly. Her breasts hardly moved, held tight by the halter neck top that she slowly began to untie. The top fell onto the bar and then slid to the floor, its sound the only trace of its journey as all eyes were focused on the fulsome pair that had just been released. She knowingly kept her hands behind her neck, keeping her back straight, accentuating their size. Free now, they started to sway with the music, their heaviness inducing a small-time lag as inertia enjoyed itself demonstrating the laws of physics. The nipples were erect, a sign to the mesmerized men sitting at the bar of her arousal, not the setting on the a/c he thought ungenerously.

He was directly underneath her, his eyes moving imperceptibly to the swaying mammaries. They were shape-shifting sensuously, forms that were at once fixed but at the same time fluid. Captivating him, as no other form ever had, or likely ever would. Twice she'd looked down at him, with her routine smile that suggested everything but promised nothing. Twice he'd reached up, unsmiling, to push a five into her garter, which was the protocol as he recalled from the last time he was in such a place, ten or so years ago. And twice he'd felt that familiar ache: that desire for which he'd spent so much of his life in search of fulfilment. Desire, usually followed by arousal and, in a noble womanizing career, more than his fair share of gratifying fulfilment. But now, even chemically induced arousal was rare. And gratification he'd found to his embarrassment and shame, impotently impossible. *Why do I come here?*

She was leaning forward now, heavy breasts hanging above his upturned face, her hands caressing them tenderly, just as he might if she were his woman and he were whole again. Holding them together, creating a valley so deep and so inviting, his mind blurred as to whether they were her hands or his own. The index finger on each hand found a nipple, gently tracing in a provocative circle. Breaking eye contact with the butterfly tattoo on the left side orb, he threw down the last of his vodka, stumbling as he dismounted his stool. Turning his head reluctantly, he marched toward the exit. En route, an overwhelming feeling of disgust flared within him...disgust at himself. Not for being in this seedy place, but for being there with no purpose. By the time he threw himself out of the door his anger was so intense he was blinking tears out of eyes. As he slumped pitifully into his car, tears were streaming down his cheeks. "What can I do?" he screamed at the horrified face in the rear-view mirror.

# Without a Purr...

by Lauren Daniels

The midday sun was scorching, beating down on me and, to escape the outside rays after being outdoors for most of the morning, I placed myself in front of the portable fan in the living room. The windows and sliding doors were wide open, inviting the cool breeze to flow through my newly rented home.

All aspects of cooling the house had been covered in order to ease the discomfort of the heat, allowing my body to slowly adapt to the insanely hot temperatures of the tropical country I had just moved to.

While enjoying the calm state of my body and mind, brought on by the satisfaction of my body temperature finally cooling down, I saw movement in the front yard out of the corner of my eye. My senses jolted awake, taking me out of my state of relaxation. To be certain of myself, I quickly turned my head to see if there was indeed anything out of the ordinary outside.

To my surprise I was spot on. There was definitely movement, and my mind was not playing tricks on me.

There it was - a long, light, grey, fluffy tail bordering the edge of the bottom of the porch, moving from one end to the other.

Curious as I now was, I slowly lifted myself up from the perfect cooling spot I had found on the tiled floor to get a closer look at what I was seeing pacing up and down.

At that very moment, as I was executing my well thought out movements, our eyes locked and interest was piqued on both ends.

On to the porch jumped a beautiful, green-eyed, light grey fluffy cat.

There was a calm silence and the eye contact between us remained steady, staying engaged as its intentions were unpredictable at this point.

With no hesitation and without a purr, the cat confidently covered the distance of the porch, strolling closer and closer to the opening of the sliding doors. With complete poise, one paw placed slowly in front of the next, it finally made its way into the house. Its curiosity about its new surroundings had obviously taken control, driving its inner need to explore. Completely absorbed and forwardly entering with no invitation, the cat sauntered into the lounge. Passing me by without wavering, it went through the dining room until it had made its way into the kitchen. Only now, with nowhere to go from this point of the house, did it stand still, slowly tilting its head up, scanning around from left to right, its eyes capturing every detail of its new environment.

My new home being minimalistic, there was little to discover and after a few minutes the cat turned around and slowly started its retreat, back through the dining room, passing me, exactly the same way it had come in.

Suddenly it stopped just before it reached the lounge. Why could that be? What could it be? It had already captured every little detail on its path. Something had captured its interest, intriguing it in every way. It turned its head into the direction of its discovery and gracefully walked back into the dining room.

There it was, something so plain, something so ordinary. It jumped up onto the soft cushioned dining room chair, comfortably placing its fluffy body down, curling up into a ball and tucking its head tightly in between its paws as if to say, "I am home".

The visits became regular, the purrs became an everyday sound, the cat was now Kitty and referred to as she.

I had discovered how real the love and bond between human and animal could be.

# Once Upon a Time

By Paul McCabe

Once upon a time, on the last night of Lyndon Johnson's five-year presidency, I lost my virginity.

My friendship with D. had been advancing for the two months since we met at the state-wide high school Model UN. She lived in faraway Cumberland, where I had grown up, but she had a car. We were both 17 and virginal.

Her parents took a cruise to the Bahamas in January and I went up to her house for the weekend. In a twist of fate, it was quite near Diamond Hill, where my parents got engaged in 1942. While dating she and I had talked about sex and agreed to lose our virginities together. We thought we knew what we were doing, but of course we knew close to zero.

Eventually after dinner she led me into her parents' bedroom and we tried for some time without success to do the deed. It did not work. All this pushing and pulling and rearranging was quite new to both of us: there was a stark contrast between theory and practice. Actually being in bed with a naked smiling girl for the first time was galaxies away from studying the Playboy bunnies in a monthly magazine. (This was one of the chief habits of teenage boys.) All these preliminaries were enjoyable – by that I mean it was quite wonderful and novel to explore unknown territory -- but there was a problem with the actual insertion.

We took a break in the kitchen late on Saturday night to regroup our forces and make a new strategy. The cosy house was silent with snow outside. D. suggested a drink: if we were going to do this adult thing, perhaps some adult refreshment would help. She found some Johnny Walker, and we both drank some out of the same glass. I'd never had whiskey before. It burned my throat and tasted terrible.

Then we returned to the big double bed. I guess the whiskey relaxed her because we had sex right away. I think both of us were surprised and dazzled that we had finally "done it" after overcoming initial difficulties. Together on the bed we wrestled the fleeing chimera of vaunted, almost mythical, sexual intercourse and made it real. Thus in 1969 did two Catholic teenagers privately and without fanfare enter the "sexual revolution" of the 1960s. Surely that night still ranks as a fond memory of distant youth, a sort of rite of passage, and a milestone on the road of life.

We educated each other, I suppose, from a very low base. In later encounters, starting the next morning, things naturally went better and better. Our affair lasted about six months, until both of us graduated from high school. D. was a pretty girl with a nice smile who spoke good French.

Ah sex sex sex, how to write about it?

# Basic Instinct

by Lian McCabe

Miss Mandy is slim. Her eyes look huge on her small head, a long delicate neck connects to her flat chest, a tiny waist. She looks like an orchid flower floating in the air, so delicate. Or, you might think that she's been on a diet for quite some time, malnourished maybe, especially when she wears her long green dress. She has such an exquisite figure. But remember, sometimes, the first impression is not always right. You should never underestimate anyone's intrinsic power.

Max is Mandy's boyfriend, a decent young man. After seeing each other for some time, they agree to meet tonight. Both think that tonight is going to be the night.

Mandy is in her favorite green dress, looking elegant as usual. Max dresses up a little bit too, as in his mind, it's an important night.

"Mandy, you haven't eaten much. You okay?

"Yes, I'm fine. I'll have something later." Mandy says.

She looks intricate and sophisticated. Right now, all that's in Max's mind is not in his small head. No, it's all between his legs, "Let's do it now, do it now, now," his basic instincts whisper into his ears.

They take a walk after dinner, wishing to calm down a little bit. But they can't resist each other any longer.

Max pushes her against the tree and starts to kiss her, Mandy kisses him back gently. He's hot-headed now, like a spark about to light a haystack. His kisses become wet and a little violent, his panting becomes heavy, one hand is around her neck, another is groping around her breasts, he's not surprised or even disappointed that her bosoms are hardly there, just like the airport runway. Nothing stops him exploring down south. She doesn't stop him. They are like two lighted fires, about to merge into one.

Mandy splits her legs a bit. Max sees the hint. "Oh, yes, babe, I knew you wanted it too…"

It's all Max has been waiting for. He doesn't care they're not in a more appropriate place for sex, he doesn't care if anyone sees them, he doesn't care how she feels. The only thing in his mind is his own pleasure, his own climax. Mandy is more docile, or rather shy.

In a flash, Max reaches his goal. Mandy's eyes are glittering with happiness. They're both excited.

Max never realized that it would sting to have sex. The sting spreads further to become a pain, especially around his neck. When he tries to wiggle his neck to check, he sees Mandy's sharp teeth are right around it. He's so high that he thinks he's having an illusion that his head is off his body now, that he can see the ruptured flesh of his neck. The dopamine created during sex calms him down.

After the swift sex, Mandy gets her appetite back. She too is following her basic instincts.

On seeing this, I let out a high-pitch scream, "What the heck! What the heck! What…"

I call the pet shop owner without delay.

The owner calms me down over the phone, "Hey, hey, hold on, it's normal. That's how nature designed them to do it. After all she is a mantis…"

# A Little Life?

by Stephanie Thornton

The young men had turned up to bother her again when all she wanted to do was rest. They sat near to her on the grass, talking, whistling and playing a guitar.

If she'd been young, she'd probably have liked it. But that was years ago: the early years when Thomas had come courting. But in spite of all her pleadings, he had gone with the rest of the pale young men to war and forgot his promise to return at four and kiss her longing lips.

Folks around said her soul was in his grave but her body stayed behind and counted the hours. And they talked about her down at the inn as her body went through the rituals of the day. The making of the fire in the black lead grate. The endless tea in bone china cups on a tray set for two at four and the two meals with one untouched.

Every day at four, she waited for her Thomas, parting the once bright nets to look for him come whistling down the lane. She looked until the paint on the frame cracked and peeled along with the lines on her face.

At three minutes to the hour, she carefully applied the lipstick which had been his favourite. The one that smelled of wine and primroses. She kept it on the chair by the door – just in case, in the vain hope he may come to kiss it away. At the side, lay a perfume flask long dry and perished....... just in case.

Now, the lipstick formed a hideous slash of colour on the greying skin, bleeding into the lines that spiralled from her mouth, once firm and young. And when he didn't come, she put it back in its place, only to return to her chair by the fire, with the black lead grate; the clock above the mantle; the cat in the basket beside her and continue the click of needles knitting the endless scarf.

At first, friends had been supportive. After failing to make sense of her and tiring of the endless grief, one by one they came no more. Now there were no cards at Christmas. Even his pillow that she hugged each night had lost the scent of him - dried and gone away. All that remained was the sprig of heather from the moors that last summer and her wedding rosary worn smooth.

The priest was worn smooth too. He had begun to dread the weekly whisperings in the box of brown wood whilst she railed against his God. He tried to shrink into the wood itself in the hope it would absorb him until he heard no more. He saw her twist the rosary, with hands, now as gnarled and knotted as the wood itself. He understood little of her other than her father had been a traveller. The proof lined the walls of the small cottage where she prepared the endless tea for Thomas. She would have liked to travel too and live his tall tales, but fate had decreed otherwise and Spanish flu had claimed both him and ma. That fate had dealt her a little life instead.

The young men had returned again. This time there were five of them. They woke her up. The one called Paul came to stand right next to her. He didn't ask permission! She bristled! The fifth was taking a picture.

"Come on Paul," he said, "tell us how you came to write about Eleanor Rigby?"

Paul said, "I had a feeling she'd like to have had a life, even if it were only a little bit of one"

The ghost in her sighed a long sigh. I understand now, she thought.

At last she was able to laugh and move on. And her name soared through the ether and down the airwaves. To foreign lands with azure seas. A living, breathing thing born to eternity in the lyrics of a song. The ghost of the girl she once was, smiled and turned in the grave she shared with Thomas.

She could rest now.

*(Author's note; when Paul McCartney wrote Eleanor Rigby for the Beatles, it was a landmark in popular music and the first time a Symphony Orchestra had been used. It is not known if the title was inspired by the actual grave, which exists, or a compilation of Eleanor (Bron), actress from the film 'Hard Day's Night' and the name Rigby, which is common to the area of Liverpool. As it was written in 1966, it's helpful to play the record on YouTube for further background)*

Death

"Death and love are the two wings that bear the good man to heaven."

~ Michelangelo

# The Living Death

by AL Seth

The first time I was told of my condition, I clearly recall that I preferred death. I recall it clearly since it was my only wish, although I never wrote it down nor told anyone. Who do you tell? Your doctor, who's bounded to 'do no harm?' Your darling wife, who you'd most likely damn to a lifelong of controversy and regret? Your lawyer, who's hardly interested in clients with a death wish? At the time, these notions were eclipsed by the ringing words of my doctor – the almost-death sentence.

I first felt it when dribbling down the stairs towards the car park. I couldn't move my leg and I was alone. I tried my mobile – signal jammed! By the time I crawled to the car, I was certain I might have to spend the night in the back seat. How long before anyone found me? Ten and a half hours!

Eventually my legs came back to me and I casually forgo the doctor's sentence. Maybe he was wrong; maybe this form of paralysis did not last. It was rare wasn't it? Perhaps one of a kind?

Then other conditions started to appear, the twitching of my hands and the sudden shocks of my arms and elbows, almost always when there was no one around. If nobody else saw it, it didn't happen.

Then came the big one and before I knew it, I was hospitalized with only my eyes moving. The nurses were decent enough, more than my wife at least. I can't blame her much. I tried to speak but only managed a mere sputter of saliva. The damn nurses barely bothered to

75

make sense of it, despite their fake smiles and feigned patience.

My daily routine went from wake up – look around – breakfast – look around – lunch – look around – dinner – look around – sleep. By the time I was deaf, I knew every inch of my wall, but how were they to know that? And finally, one morning, the light didn't hit my eyes. There was nothing – no light, no sound, no smell, no taste, not even the faintest notion of existence. I was entombed in my own body with my own conscience for company.

I couldn't tell the seconds from the days, or the dreams from possible life. Whatever went on outside my mind was alien territory. It was the chaotic calm, one I discovered I could come to terms with….

Until, one day, I was sure of my own heart beating and my slow breathing. I felt the soft pillow under my head as well as the comfy bed. It was just a matter of time before everything else came back. Soon I could utter sounds and even hear them coming from my mouth. Yes, yes, I was back. Moments later I could turn my head and finally, I felt my eyes blinking. I looked around at my familiar room, only it was not so familiar and much smaller than it was – way too small, fit just for me.

# The House with the Red Door

by Boris Nielsen

The light faded fast and went out completely as the door closed on her with a crash. Panicked, she scurried around blindly until she bounced off what must have been the handle. She lay still, panting, waiting for the dust to settle. Her eyes adjusting to the dark.

Her surroundings took shape gradually: the dirt, the rubble, the harshness of the just discernible red paint on the door. Carefully, she moved along the edges, seeking out a gap to escape through. There were none big enough, even though she was only a slight thing. Her world was sealed… and her fate?

Another, quicker but still fruitless circuit and then a pause to contemplate the interior. It was darker there, uninviting, but the courage came and she began to explore. The trails in the dust, from her tiny paws, exposing the randomness of her search. All the time, a fearful noise from above.

Somewhere near the centre there were tiny slivers of light forming a shape which meant nothing to her: the shape of a letterbox. The heavy iron of the outside flap hung open leaving only the light plastic of the inner flap separating the gloom and the light. This is where her fate might change.

She didn't recognise the potential of the piece of wood in front of her because mice can't conceptualise what might be. So, as she sniffed around, it was by pure chance that she found herself on top of the makeshift ladder, on hind legs, her nose pushing at the inner flap.

As it gave a little she was startled by a flood of light and was once again scampering around blindly. But trial and error was how her kind survived, how they dominated their ecological niche. Soon she was back, testing the flap and adjusting to the sudden changes in light.

A sharp push, front paws grasping for a hold then her head was in the light, her rear dangling in the gloom. Eyes adjusting quickly, she saw a monster as tall as the half-wrecked house it was standing next to. With one of those big animals inside it.

The monster took a swing at the house, a wall started to cave in. She dropped back down as bricks rained down on the door. The dim light around the flap became dimmer still. She resumed her wandering; there were still a couple of days of sniffing left in her.

When was her fate sealed: When she failed to scramble out of the letterbox, fear of the falling bricks overwhelming her hope of escape? When the wrecking ball hit the corner of the house sending the door flying at just the right angle to create a tomb? Or when the owner signed the demolition contract?

He hated that house, with its evil red door that had caused the death of an innocent girl. Crazy he'd been called, but his daughter would be avenged, no matter the cost or consequences.

# A Modern Death

By C.I. Ripples

As the syringe came towards him, it seemed to gain a life of its own and Richard almost recoiled, panic rising from his stomach to his chest. He squeezed his daughter's hand tightly. His heart was beating so violently he was surprised the others couldn't hear it, amazed that something so strong would so soon cease to be. It was true what people said, that in moments of existential danger you see your life flash before you.

And he saw his past clearly: the memories of good-hearted parents; student years; his first true love; his wife; the birth of his daughter; his grandchild. He felt all of it freshly, the good and the bad, the emotions of his successes and betrayals, as if it were yesterday. He could not conceive that in a few minutes all of it would be gone, erased. He told himself that all through history men had had the courage to die, that all he needed was some faith. But he had never been religious, having no confidence in something that could not be proven. Still, he struggled to believe that he would simply no longer be. Now that the needle was in front of him, almost larger than life itself, he shilly-shallied, felt a coward. He was still afraid, wanted to hold on.

You could argue that he had had a full life, that he had already lived to a ripe old age, but what did that mean? Wasn't it the life in his years that should count, rather than the years in his life? Had he experienced life in all its aspects? Had his existence had any true meaning? Had he made the right choices? So often he had felt out of control, that he had just fallen into a situation and let life happen to him, that the only truly meaningful thing, the most beautiful thing this life had ever given him, was his daughter.

When he had been diagnosed, the doctor said he had six months to a year. Richard had cried, tears streaming down his face, and shaking with fear he had inwardly screamed abuse at the medical fraternity, that it wasn't fair. That after all he had been through, he would not enjoy the last of his twilight years in peace and joy. All in the knowledge, of course, that he was merely paying for what he had refused to face. He had had an irritating cough for months, but had continued to light up, telling himself he would stop 'tomorrow'. Until his hack became relentless after his wife's death the previous year. How ironic it was, that so often we want to face the least, the things we should be facing the most.

He had calmed himself by reminding himself that it wasn't the end of life he minded, but the how, what he might have to go through to get there. Then he had taken a deep breath and considered his options.

He had refused surgery, chemo or radiation therapy, knowing it would only reduce the quality of what little time he had, but would not halt the inevitable end. He also decided he would face the inescapable in the comfort of his own home, his bed, rather than in a strange sterile hospital room attached to endless tubes.

Trembling, Richard took another sip from his Jenever, a treat he rarely allowed himself. As the velvety smoothness of the clear liquid stroked his tongue he considered that Wenneker's Oude Proever had deserved the prize for best Jenever of the year. It had been worth the extra expense, even if his daughter would have to finish the bottle in his memory. His Dutch courage, however, failed to lessen his fears and he wondered once more if the knowledge he was dying was actually more terrifying than death itself. He hoped his hesitance went unnoticed by his daughter, who sat stroking his hand, smiling into his face, occasionally rising to kiss his forehead. He loved her so much. His grandson too, who, so young, so full of promise, so brave, was nearby, in his bedroom even if not by his side.

His fears continued to surprise him, as unlike most other people, who paid so little attention to dying, he had been so close to it for years, through the experience of his own dear wife, who had died a long drawn out natural death, and had afterwards lain quite peacefully, even if quite cold on her bed. Her end had seemed moderately acceptable, at least for her, Richard thought, if not for those around her, but he knew that his own physical death, if left to nature, would be less than pleasant. He had read up on what he could expect, the pain, the lack of air. He might suffocate from the cancerous mass in his lungs, or if not from the cancer itself he might die from pneumonia or sepsis. And with the spread to his other organs, he might soon lose the ability to walk, talk or even swallow. He might develop blood clots and have a stroke. It all sounded horrendous.

Of course, his rational mind knew that death was never easy, but it was the thought of suffocation that alarmed him the most. His growth was near his airways and might start to obstruct it and bleed into the lungs. Anything more than a teaspoon could choke him. Even if such a death would be rapid, he was terrified of it, of the futile gasping for air, the gagging. Already the fluid build-up around his lungs resulted in shortness of breath.

On some days it was almost too much to walk the few steps to the toilet unless he used his inhaler. He was permanently exhausted, almost too fatigued to take in anything more than the smoothies his daughter prepared for him.

Even if his doctor had assured Richard his death need not be ugly or painful, he decided it was the fear of unbearable suffering he could not bear. It was the fear that his last moments might not be precious. And after the experience with his wife, which had transformed all their lives, he didn't want to burden his beloved daughter any further. She had already given up so much, showing both charity and heroic humility in her care for his wife. He wanted his death to be a release for her, a breath of fresh air so to speak, so that she could finally continue with her own life. A life she wholeheartedly deserved after the goodness and altruism she had displayed year after year, day after day. She was still young enough.

For sure, he believed in the sanctity of life, but not at all costs. Not when it would be morally wrong and he was grateful therefore that he lived in the Netherlands, where four percent of deaths were by euthanasia, where they understood and had perfected a technique for a pain free and dignified end.

When he had told his daughter of his dying wishes, or rather his wish to die sooner rather than later, she had been a flurry of efficiency. He knew she hurt inside, but he also knew she had seen her mother, the years and years of slow dying, perhaps without pain, but a slow degrading of consciousness nonetheless. And he knew that if the law had allowed euthanasia for those with severe dementia, she would have wanted it for her mother.

There was a lot of paperwork to get through, doctors to be seen and convinced that mercy outweighed the principle of not doing harm. Then there was his will, tax planning, the booking of the coroner, the crematorium. He had chosen his favourite clothes and music, 'Together we will live forever', one of his most loved pieces, so appropriate for his final moment. He had said his final goodbyes.

Moist eyed, he put down his glass and turned to look out onto the green, a view he had seen every day for much of his life. It was a beautiful crisp autumn morning, pale golden light falling across the old beech tree now almost bare of its tawny leaves, casting its rays on the grand finale of nature's beauty, of his life. The sky was so so deep deep blue he felt a sudden yearning to become one with it, almost happy that his soul would migrate on this day. But still he wavered.

The doctor, a man with obvious experience in this field, saw his hesitance and put down the syringe, asking him softly, patiently, if he was absolutely sure he wanted to proceed, whether it was his earnest desire. Richard knew he had to reply in the affirmative. Anything else would be lily-livered and border on the ridiculous considering the efforts made to get to this stage. He knew that once he allowed the barbiturate injection to enter his veins, he would become quickly unconscious. He would know nothing of what happened next. But he knew now! Thank goodness he hadn't chosen the iv option – he really didn't think he would be capable of turning the little tap. He had read that the mixture of thiopental and propofol might kill him in one go. It was one reason for his hesitance. On the other hand, it might not be enough to kill him! That terrified him as well, although the doctor had assured him that he would administer a second injection with cisatracurium, which would relax his respiratory muscles, stop his breathing and then his heart. He would definitely have left this earth within ten minutes without feeling a thing. His body would be taken away by nightfall.

He focused on the syringes next to a delicate arrangement of white, long-stemmed Columbian roses, interspersed with an occasional St. Joseph's lily. In bud only yesterday, they had suddenly blossomed and were staggeringly beautiful, the wonder of their heavenly fragrance injecting sunshine into his soul, radiating whispers of hope. Finally, Richard understood he needn't fear what might be waiting for him, or not as the case may be, that he was doing the right thing.

He took a deep breath, closed his eyes and felt a serenity wash over him with Mansell's piano music. He felt ready now, no longer afraid. He opened his eyes, leant forward to kiss his daughter one last time, wiping away a tear from her cheek as she sat bravely smiling by his side and nodded for the doctor to proceed.

# From The Sounding Seas

by AL Seth

They say your mind replays your whole life when you die and that all your memories merge, forming one biography, that from lighting neurons comes a lifetime of narrative. They also say memories are an unreliable source of information, especially when a crime is committed. That it naturally tries to piece together bits of information to make one coherent story. But what if the mind tries to forget something that happened, something not worth or not safe remembering? Something that defies explanation is often discarded as an impossibility. This is true for all of us.

I, for example, forgot the truth of what happened that one day when I was four years of age. It was only when my personal effects were laid out on my deathbed, that a single photograph altered a lifetime's worth of my now stale memory.

I had never been able to remember my mother as well as I'd have liked. As I grew up, most of what I knew about her came from what was said of her. Not necessarily a series of embellishments or insults but enough to give form to what she ought to be. Everybody talked about what happened to her except for me, even though I was the sole witness. But the accounts of a four-year old that defies explanations fell on deaf ears and were washed away by psychiatric 'explanations.' Eventually, all that remained of what happened that day could be found in the files of police officers and psychiatrists. As for me, I managed to suppress that day at the beach, those dead bodies and what dragged them into the waves, until the photograph, of crashing waves along the sand, storm clouds looming above wobbling ships and a far looming horizon, was laid on my bed.

There was not a soul in sight, not in the photograph, nor in the afterwards of what happened that day. Yet, even from this single snapshot, anyone could tell that something just wasn't right.

It had been a rainy morning when my mother asked me to go down to the beach with her. The rain had just stopped, leaving a cool breeze flowing inland. These rare moments, just after a long rainfall, have always been my favourite, although, as I grew up, I always wondered why such a calm moment always brought with it a certain sense of foreboding, that something was about to happen and the passing storm was only a warning.

I don't remember seeing anyone when we arrived on the beach. I just assumed it was rather early, and that as it could rain again, people preferred to stay indoors for now. The first thing that hit me was the wonderful smell of rain on mud and salty sand. It was so refreshing. The sun was hidden somewhere behind the grey clouds, as though shy to reveal her presence. My mother held me by my hand as we stumbled passed the trees and stopped just before the sand. The wind was cool and strong. It was the kind of weather one lived for, until we made the discovery once we got down to the water.

Before that day, only the inevitability of death was one that was known to me. Thus, when the waves rolled over and I saw someone rolling around, it looked to my four-year old self like the most fun you could have along a beach. But my mother held my hand tightly and pulled me back, shielding me from the sight. It was only much later that I was told that that man, rolling along the waves, was dead. Funny how the truth of such a horrifying sight hadn't hit me right away.

My mom turned me around and began heading back, making sure I didn't see anymore, when a scream came from far away. We stood still and looked forth. It was a man's voice, crying, in pain and desperate. We moved closer along the sands, my mom still shielding me, passed those long, ancient, wooden boats. I saw his face, his hand reaching towards us, completely covered in red. Who could have known there could be so much blood? It was then that I looked along the shoreline, just where the water met the sand, and noticed a reddish brown splattered all over. As we moved closer again, there was another sound, a gobbling and grunting and snarling from somewhere between the boats. As the man looked around, he screamed again before being dragged away, his scream with him.

"Run," my mom said and I ran with her still holding my hand.

There was a thudding and crunching sound along the wet sand. There was that snarl again, getting louder. Something flapped and I felt a gush of wind that was not a remnant of the storm. I didn't dare turn to look. I didn't want to know what it was. Only one word echoed in my mind, 'run!' and I ran.

Eventually my mom let go of me and I could run full speed, but the grunting only seemed to get louder, the flapping stronger. Then there was another noise, much more horrifying than whatever had come before. It was my mother. In that one moment, when I turned to look and saw her being dragged away, her hands reaching out for me, her eyes wide and desperate, I just kept running until the sound of her screaming vanished along with the flapping and the grunting, until the snarling got drowned by the howling wind and the crashing waves.

They asked me what it had been, but all I could tell them was that it was black, with long legs. I also told them about the flapping and the snarling, but of course, those were the words of a four-year old, who must have watched too many cartoons. After a while they stopped asking me and started telling me what had happened. The term 'coping mechanism' became synonymous with the death of my mother, and as I grew up, I coped better. Tragic things happen during a storm. Sudden bouts of depression and anxiety could trigger any unforeseeable actions. They told me about her lifelong struggles and all her problems to make her 'suicide' more explicable. I did grow up. I coped.

But then, that one photograph on my wrinkled hands. I can't remember much now, not today's date, not even the meals I've had. But that day, down at the beach, after the storm, the flapping and the snarling, and my mother screaming and the crashing waves and the howling wind.

I just kept running.

# The Golf Between Us

By Joel Adams

Thoughts swoop round my head, up and down, in and out, like teasing birds as we walk from the fourth green to the fifth tee. A hot summer day, 1965, the Philippines. I'm sixteen and Holden Caulfield, Salinger and Bob Dylan my heroes. Not only mine, but most of my teen friends as well. Caulfield, oh boy, he had it right, the world was full of phonies. A world full of phonies being watched/ruled by a phony god of a phony bunch of hypocrites in churches. That's what I tell myself anyway.

I think back to the day a year before when I donned atheism like a mantle. It was all of a moment when my Harvard graduate history teacher, in his Madras 'guaranteed to bleed' shirt and paisley ties, said he didn't believe in God. And just like that, neither did I. That decision has served me pretty well, I think. No more guilt, no more fear of hell, no more ten commandments to worry about. I am free, until… well, to tell the truth, later that year when I'm expelled from my Philippine boarding school, after I confess to going to Cabbie's Caballero, a whorehouse in Manila. Rosa gave me the clap the first time I had sex! But that's another story.

Back home, as an expellee, or is it expulsee (?), the old fears return—the fears that hit me whenever I sin, the fears that scream at me, "God is gonna kill ya now; you've gone too far; you've done the worst there is, not only had sex before marriage, but paid for it with a cheap whore… and then got caught. You've been a liar, a cheat, disobedient to your parents, you smoke, you drink, and now this! You're gonna die and go straight to hell and burn forever."

The first two months at home I was waiting to get killed from various interesting and creative causes. The least imaginative was the traditional divine murder of being struck by lightning. I always saw it like this—me with my umbrella, the metal point a lightning rod conducting the lethal bolt down the shaft of the umbrella into my hand with one finger touching the metal shaft, and consequently frying me instantly to a crisp.

Then there was the one of me not looking both ways, stepping out in the road and getting sandwiched, right between the front and back wheels of some heavy road equipment, so I was knocked over and smashed like a pancake by the rear wheels. After that, I always looked when crossing the road. Yet, when there was heavy equipment trundling along, it was all I could do to keep myself from jumping out and getting crushed, almost as if I was doing God, who was trying to kill me anyway, a service. Perhaps I was just going crazy.

Then there was the drowning scenario. Of course, not merely drowning - I saw myself jump from the high dive at the local swimming pool, aiming for the corner of the pool and the ladder in a game of towel tag and smashing my chin on the edge, teeth flying, knocking me out cold so I sank to the bottom and drowned.

At first, such thoughts of my demise filled my mind continually. Then they subsided, but were still there, lurking in the shadows, waiting. Any time I thought I was in the clear they'd poke their heads up and say, "Boo, we're still here and you're gonna die!"

But little did I imagine it would be this scenario, one that had never crossed my mind.

Nowadays, five months after my expulsion, in my bolder moments I just scoff that there is no God, therefore he can't touch me one way or the other. Who needs him anyway? What good has he ever done? He didn't stop the bullet that killed Kennedy; he isn't ending the Vietnam War. Hell, I might even have to go over there and fight, kill and die for some stupid rich guys' war that has nothing to do with me. Where is God anyway? *With God on Our Side* and *Masters of War* says it all. Dylan is singing the truth - if there is a God, he's in the music.

I wipe my brow as my golf foursome arrive at the fifth tee. I now become aware that Frank has been talking nonstop as always, spouting only stupid things, bragging about how great he is, how he's gonna beat us all in today's tournament, how he shot five under par in his last tournament down in Dumaguete where, conveniently, none of us were present; how he won the trophy, which he left in his dorm room, also conveniently. Eric nods with that blank faraway look he wears on his face when he pretends to be interested in something, because, hell, he's a polite kid. Dave, his brother, just laughs and says a bit too loud, "That's bullshit, Frank. If you're so great, why are you shooting five over par now after four holes? Why is your score the highest, why are you making your team lose?"

We drew straws and I got Frank… to my dismay. No one likes him, but only Dave talks back to him. The rest of us are afraid of Frank, because, even though he's a stupid braggart who nobody ever sees do the things he brags about, he does have big thick arm muscles. We've only ever heard his stories of who he's beat the shit out of, but it doesn't take much imagination to figure those arms could do some damage.

Frank shouts back, "This course is shit, that's why. Where I play it's a real course with good grass and not this shit crabgrass on the greens like here. But I'll show you. After four holes I got it figured. I bet I shoot two on this hole and beat you all. My tee shot is going there, on the green."

"How much you wanna bet, Frank?" Dave asks.

"Ten pesos."

"You're on," and they shake.

Frank has the worst score, so he tees off first. I pull Dave aside and Eric follows us.

"Why'd ya do that?" I ask.

"It's just ten pesos."

"It's not the money," Eric chimes in. "It's just that if Frank by some miracle does what he said, we'll have to hear about it the whole rest of the summer."

"So what? The summer's almost over, and we all go our separate ways. I just had to pop his bullshit balloon."

We hear the swish of Frank's swing, sounds like a solid hit. Frank whoops triumphantly. We look his way.

"You're up, Eric," Frank grins.

"Where'd your ball go?" I ask.

"On the green, of course."

Frank's little Filipino caddy shakes his head and points off to the left.

"Nah, man," Frank contradicts, "you weren't looking… as usual. Stupid caddy pays no attention."

"Hey, Frank," Dave says, "they speak English, you know. He understands what you just said."

"So? Who won the war for them? Eisenhower and us Americans did, that's who. They owe us."

Dave scoffs, "Weird way of thinking, Frank, and by the way, it was MacArthur; Eisenhower was in Europe."

"Now this time I got ya. At my school, there's a carving on the rafters in the library that says, 'David or Daniel or Douglas Eisenhower was here'."

"Yeah," I say, "that was his son and they were stationed here before the war, but Ike didn't fight here."

"As if you're some history genius. I guess I know what I saw. I climbed up and saw it."

And he turns his back on us. We chuckle a little and wink at each other.

Then Eric tees off and hits a good one followed by Dave and me. We are all short of the green so Frank is indeed bettering us this time.

As we walk to our balls and our second shots, Eric walks beside me and asks, "You still having dreams about dying, about God killing you?"

"It's not dreams; it's thoughts, maybe daydreams but not good ones, kinda daymares. Less now though."

"Look, I been thinking about that and I don't think God does those things, kills kids who make a mistake, even a huge one like you made. They always say he loves us and he's our father, so if your dad didn't kill you, why would God?"

"Well, if my dad did, he'd go to jail. God's different."

"Yeah, but do you feel like your dad would want to if he didn't have to go to jail?"

"Uh… no… I guess not."

"So, you think your dad loves you more than God does?"

Frank calls out, "Shut up talking and hit your balls, guys."

Dave and I do, both on the green. Eric does and overshoots the green into the sand trap on the other side.

Frank mounts the green and is surprised, as are we all, that his ball is not, in fact, there. We all begin looking, straining our eyes to see where it is until the caddy calls out from halfway back down the fairway.

"Dito[6]. De ball, she is here."

"How the hell...?" Frank mutters as he goes back for his ball.

Eric and I suppress the laugh bubbling up, but Dave doesn't.

"Ha! I guess I`m gonna be ten pesos richer. Frank, this confirms what I've known all along, you are an inveterate idiot."

Frank doesn't answer as he traipses back to his waiting ball and caddy.

Then it dawns on us, "Hey, he's behind us, and he's gonna basically do a drive again with a wood. We could get hit."

Now by all known rules and guidelines of the noble game of golf we should take our bags and clubs and caddies and go with Frank all the way back behind his ball. But that's a long way and a lot of trouble for nothing, think our teenage minds. We look for a way around doing that and are delighted to find an enormous mango tree that we can hide behind. Eric and Dave get there first and press themselves against the side of the tree away from Frank, his ball and whatever club will be his weapon of choice. No problem, I think, I'll just line up with the tree. That'll keep me safe.

Frank shouts, "Ready?"

---

[6] Tagalog for 'here'

Dave shouts, "We are, but are you?"

Time is relative; it can fly; it can drag; it can seem like it doesn't even exist. Well, the next seconds last forever, and to this day I see them in slow motion. First, there is the sound of the swing and the club connecting with the ball. The tree is, from Frank's perspective, up ahead and off to the right. Now when you hit a golf ball, it's supposed to go straight, but some people have a tendency to hook, which means the ball, if you hit right-handed, curves to the left. Others slice, which means the ball curves to the right. Frank is a notorious slicer, which we have not taken into account before we hear his club connect with his ball. But to this day I can still see that white blur in the air slicing round to the right, right toward me. Everything slows down, even me, so although my mind has time to think, 'Oh God this is it; I'm a dead man,' my body has no time to move and the hard-driven golf ball from those muscular arms of our idiot friend Frank slams into me, smack on the eye socket bone on the outer rim of my right eye and I collapse. I could say I fly into the air from the force and crumple in a heap, that would be dramatic, but I honestly don't know what I do because, well, I'm dead, waiting for the spirits who are in charge of these things to come pick me up.

I don't know how long, but there is an echoing sort of sound, voices that I figure are the angels or, more likely, the devils, come to take me to stand before the judgment seat and then be escorted to my final ultra-warm resting place… until my eyes slowly focus, my ears pick up sounds a bit more normally and I see the blue sky with the green leaves of the mango tree tattooed on it and the silhouetted heads of Frank, Eric, Dave and the caddies standing over me, panic in their eyes.

"You okay, man? Can you see us? Can you hear us? Someone, call for help. How many fingers am I holding up?"

I am on the golf course. I am under the mango tree. I am with my friends. And... I'm not dead.

# Death and John Charles

by Stephanie Thornton

As the year 3017 came to the end, the Grim Reaper put it down to one of 'those' years. In fact, it had been a real hum-dinger of a nightmare of a year.

He knew this, for as he had been walking through the 'Valley of the Shadow of Death' one day, he had his first ever panic attack. He knew that Agoraphobia was a fear of crowded spaces and although the Valley was anything but that, the huge piles of ash that had collected at the sides, and for which he now had to wear a mask to stop an asthma attack, had the same result. The trouble was that no one was being buried any more. The graveyards were full and as such, everyone went into the furnace. So, the piles of ash just grew and grew.

God threw him a business card.

"Go and see my shrink," he said. "You'll find him helpful. Mind you, there may not be any appointments available. Archangel Gabriel has just been outed and needs quality time. And St Michael has been demoted by Marks and Spencer and is in deep depression. Still, even if my shrink can't help, he can recommend another."

God was so wise!

The first therapist, an alternative to God's, was no good at all. She made him regress to his childhood and all Freudian like told him to blame his mother. Mother had not made him floss his teeth or visit the dentist every six months, which resulted in him losing them and so gaining the grim expression he was associated with. All this therapist achieved was to make the matter worse. He now developed mother rage in addition to all his other problems. She had therefore achieved her usual objective: if you can't solve the problem, blame the parents!

Eventually, after trying two others, he arrived at Professor Chang's practice.

The consultation rooms were located on a quiet side road, which pleased him as he preferred not to be seen going there. Everyone knew what he looked like and tended to pass by on the other side. No one ever asked for an autograph or stopped to take a picture.

"For God's sake leave that enormous scythe in the waiting room and hang your cloak and hood on the hook!" the therapist bellowed as Death came through the door. Death hoped the cloak would be safe in there. After all, once dead, anyone in the waiting room caught stealing his cloak was already on 'the other side' and had already passed the judgement. They were beyond sin. It was also his favourite and only worn for very special occasions such as now. Vintage Armani in the very best shade of black. Number 64 – the top shade for the richest, deepest colour and the most expensive too. Armani had had to make it for Death as part of his penance at the Pearly Gates. He had met too many people, materialistic on earth, demanding designer labels and even having hissy fits if they didn't get one.

Death didn't like being without his cloak. Underneath it, he was very thin. Skeletal in fact.

"I know I am supposed to look like this," he told the shrink, "so I always watch my weight and my skin, which is supposed to be pale and gaunt so people don't confuse me with Life."

Personally, Chang thought his new patient was reverting to type. He looked terrible. A shadow of his former self. No wonder God had referred him as he looked near death himself. 'Could Death die?' he pondered.

"Your pulse is rather fast," he declared, holding the bony wrist. "Too much coffee perhaps?"

On the couch, Death admitted he was generally depressed with modern life. He couldn't even charge to cross the river Styx any more as no one carried money, only plastic. Now the boat had a hole in it and people used the footbridge instead, after God decided to modernise the crossing over. To add insult to injury, God had even called the bridge 'Heaven's gate' and dedicated it to the long-deceased King Charles III who had done so much for architecture during his reign.

And he had run out of swirling mists too to cover all the water on the journey over. Everyone expected this, so they felt cheated and demanded a refund. Due to global warming, the strong sun shone too brightly, which did not create the right scene either. It was just too jolly to cross over and consequently contemplation of past sins or dark brooding thoughts were rare.

In fact, there was little payment for any of the work he did. All implants were recycled, so he couldn't get his hands on any gold or titanium, because the undertakers took the lot and sieved it out of the furnace before he got there. He was not allowed to get cross with God. And he couldn't really blame his mum either.

"Surely that can't be the only thing that is causing your despair?" said Professor Chang.

Death deliberated.

"It's Charles," he finally confessed.

He explained that his customer, John Charles, was aged 220 and God had told Death to go get him over fifty years ago, but Mr. Charles had refused to go. In fact, he was so paranoid about his own death that he insisted he have a fully charged mobile phone with him before he went into the fire, just to be sure he was really dead and if not, could make a call once in there. After all, he had read on the internet that some claw marks had been found on the inside of coffins on the odd occasions these had been found in earlier graves, which now, of course, were out of fashion, mainly due to lack of space.

Charles, furthermore, was a proud man, a cultured man, an educated man, who didn't want it all to go to waste on death. What would happen to all that knowledge in his head? It was very worrying both for Charles, but more so for Death.

Death had even counselled Berty, his pet raven. Berty was a reincarnation of Bob Marley and spoke in Rastafarian. He had actually been targeted to be Jacob Marley from the Dickens story, but God said the name wrong in a coughing fit and so he had become a Raven from Jamaica. Berty had been less than sympathetic telling Death to "Get real Bro," then flying off to play 'Don't worry, be happy' on an old record player in the hope it would cheer up Death. It didn't!

"Whatever shall I do?" Death sobbed as he stroked Bertie's head, "If I don't obey God, I will be smitten down and the pope will get my job."

And as time went on, Charles had everything done to keep himself alive. Virtually every part of him was replaced. He had new knees, new arms, all his organs were new and his skin was as ripe as a new born baby's bottom. He was going nowhere soon. In fact, he had already booked to have it all renewed again in the next two years, followed by a holiday on Venus.

Since his confession to Professor Chang, many months passed whilst Death was no nearer to a solution. Things were getting very dire indeed and God was starting to get cross with him. Death thought of plane crashes, of poison, of car accidents and even too many rounds of golf in hot sun. But he dismissed them all. There was no way Charles was giving up the ghost.

And then, God planted the seed of his salvation in Charles's head by putting Charles in a deep sleep one night and giving him the answer to Death's prayer. His undying customer had been reading up about secret cloning clinics where you could be totally made over by having yourself duplicated. That way, everything was new again. No more implants or spare limbs.

God had not only given Charles this brilliant idea, but also told him what to do and he soon paid up, so Death could claim the old body for God. What Charles had forgotten to ask beforehand though, was whether he would be the same. Would his mind be the same, would he be the same physically and with all his old memories? The answer was that, of course, no one can cheat Death.

Before his body was cloned, God harvested all his knowledge in the soul of the original Charles and kept it for himself. After all, the whole purpose of life was to gain both love and knowledge and then pass it on to Death and God.

Therefore, although the new Charles may have looked the same on the outside, he now liked reading Noddy books, eating fish fingers and chips and watching the new version of Big Brother on the Hologram. All in all, he now behaved like a six-year old with a temper tantrum.

Ah well, you can't win 'em all, thought Death, as he left the shadow of his former self now fully healed and flew off to the Valley to pile the ashes on the heap.

And God smiled at him that day and was pleased. And God saw that it was good.

# In the Beginning

By Paul McCabe

"Vector is 117 degrees," he typed on his screen.

High above the Red Sea, the lead pilot in radio silence got a roger message in reply. The two 15-meter-long jets, avoiding the Saudi air base, altered course to the southeast. On this sunny hot day, they blasted at Mach 1.2 toward their targets. Almost right away they crossed the sandy coast at Dhahban and headed inland. Even at that height the air became slightly turbulent as waves of heat rose from the desert sands below.

Far beneath, the giant crowds milled around in a circle, moving slowly, praying in unison. This year attendance at the annual Hajj was at an all-time high of 2.6 million of the faithful, who had travelled from around the world to carry out personally one of the five pillars of Islam. Men dressed in white, women in black, in separate areas of the crowded pilgrimage.

The government of the host country had spent billions on facilities to welcome them. So, the pilgrims lived for a week in clean camps, had adequate water, shaved their heads, wore the prescribed Ihram cloth, sacrificed animals, threw stones at the Devil, and performed all their religious duties daily. Thousands had flown to nearby Jeddah from special Hajj terminals in their own countries on fully-booked charter flights. Most slept in packed tent cities out at Mina to the east.

Following deadly trampling incidents in 1990 and 2015, the local authorities directed pilgrims more strictly. Numerous crowd-control systems were in place. CCTV cameras observed everything. Several government ministries and offices were involved, supervising the masses as they came and went in Mecca and the hallowed sites in the area. The country made about $10 billion a year from the Hajj, so plenty of funds were available for the necessary safety, security, and health measures. Loudspeakers mounted on tall steel poles alternately blared prayers and stern instructions.

As they marched from holy place to holy place in a certain set order, the pious prayed and chanted together as they made their rounds. Verses from the Koran echoed on the streets, in the hills, and in the center of the old city. They knew these words from their childhoods in different countries, where Friday prayers were usually in Arabic. But the people in the teeming lines also prayed in Urdu, Farsi, Dari, Bahasa, Hausa, Wolof, and many other languages.

Nowhere was more jam-packed than the enormous main mosque downtown, which housed the sacred Kaaba. Around that large box the believers swarmed, walking counter-clockwise seven times and if possible, touching the black granite building, the cubic "House of Allah" at the center of the open-air mosque. The Kaaba long pre-dated the Islamic era, but this was known mainly to archeologists and scientists and not to the thronging visitors.

Up at 10,000 meters, the two F-35 Lightning 2-As flashed across the desert in a few minutes. Colonel Lev Alon, mission commander, recalled the long weeks of hard work at the air base in the Negev. His expert team of technicians and engineers had made considerable modifications to the new aircraft built last year in Texas and California.

They had retained the wing weapons, the AIM-9X Sidewinders and AIM-132 ASRAAM short-range air-to-air missiles. The fuselage housed one GAU-22/A, a four-barrel Equalizer cannon. Neither pilot expected to need these weapons to defend themselves, but the decision was made to keep the standard equipment for this day. They were protected by the most advanced Stealth anti-detection materials and equipment in the world.

During the tense preparation period, the Colonel and Major Chaikin, now flying the other jet, had concentrated on the principal mission and the principal weapons. These were two miniature uranium-based nuclear bombs of twenty-kiloton strength, developed mainly by the group of forty atomic scientists who migrated to Israel in 1991 following the downfall of the Soviet Union. The Air Force had ordered them unloaded from Jericho-2 missiles at a launch site west of Jerusalem and transferred to the Negev base to be checked, re-checked, and made ready in secret.

Finally, the moment for precise focus arrived, bringing an end to the lead pilot's reminiscence. On their cockpit screens, both pilots simultaneously saw the *execute* order from IAF headquarters at HaKirya. Alon and Chaikin knew that the Prime Minister, backed by his Cabinet, had just now approved the command. The orange letters of the code words silently glowed on a black background: King David.

They moved the controls in a final adjustment as they streaked closer to the brimming city central to Islam. The GPS features had set the exact drop point. Four barometric pressure altitude switches – including two redundant ones for fail-safe purposes -- were fully functioning, according to the green cockpit panel lights.

One bomb was set to detonate at 550 meters above the Masjid Al-Haram and its Kaaba. The other bomb would explode 700 meters over Mina, six kilometers to the east. Both were timed to the millisecond for 12 pm.

Colonel Alon typed his own *execute* order to his subordinate: CONFIRM GO. The jets separated immediately and went on with the business of following their orders.

The noon prayers were starting in the crammed city below. On the loudspeaker system, the senior muezzin again droned the opening lines of the prayer chanted from Senegal to Java:

'Allahu akbar.

Ash-hadu an-lā ilāha illā allāh

Ash-hadu anna Muhammadan-Rasul ullāh.

Hayya'alas-ṣalāh.'

Alon and Chiakin pressed the release buttons at the same second. Two suitcase-sized mechanical devices, whose origins were with Albert Einstein, fell from the rushing aircraft. They instantly turned northwest and cranked up to their maximum speed of Mach 1.6. The colonel typed in the signal for double success: Temple Mount. Heading home, he thought of the words of a Bob Dylan song his parents used to play at home, '… Farewell Angelina, the sky is on fire, and I must go.'

The final words of the traditional invocation in Arabic floated out around the city, reaching all and echoing from the buildings. At that moment the limpid blue cloudless heavens howled from horizon to horizon with a colossal high-tech hell and hurtled to earth at the full speed of light.

# Sneak and Bother

By AL Seth

Old Mrs Holloway kept to herself. Nobody liked her, not the other tenants, not her neighbours. And she seemed oblivious to the snide remarks whispered behind her back. No one ever ventured into her apartment, no one wanted to. Except for me, I was cute and cuddly. Also, the fact that Mrs Holloway was almost blind as a bat was a plus, constantly dropping food in her smelly kitchen and coins wherever she went. Her television was always on and loud enough for her deficient hearing, which usually meant it was too loud for the plywood walls, antagonising her neighbours further. She didn't mind my visit, of course, and she always had something for me to eat. The food she had to offer was really like no one else's.

She certainly knew how to cook; no one could deny that. Her children must have been as lucky as they come with those meals of hers. They don't speak to her anymore, nor she to them. It happens, I suppose, not that I'd know anything about it. Her husband must have died years back. There were only pictures of the two in the apartment from times that easily spanned half a century, displaying the life of a loving couple, one sadly demised. I don't envy her to be honest. At least her kids could look into her once in a while, especially now their father had passed. All that remained of Mrs Holloway was an old woman in an old apartment, moth eaten and mouldy, in a dingy kitchen, fumbling with saucepans and dishwasher with her trembling wrinkly hand, long forgotten with naught but memories for company.

Her neighbour, Laurel, was easily the darling of all who saw her. I startled her quite badly the time she caught me sneaking into her bedroom. But then she warmed to me and even allowed me to cuddle in her bed. Actually, the first time I saw her was when she'd gone over to Mrs Holloway's door and knocked. Apparently, the television was bothering her, or maybe she wanted to say hello, having just moved in. I could see it all from the hallway and I knew exactly what would happen next. The shrieking and piercing yell of Mrs Holloway echoed every which way and I was sure Laurel would never bother the old woman again.

As far as I know Laurel was the last person to learn the lesson of knocking on Mrs Holloway's door. There were hardly new tenants in the building. Anyone walking past her door could hear the buzzing television or the clattering kitchen. No one bothered to say hello to her anymore. Only I really cared. I snuck in from time to time, making sure she was still there. Yes, she was, lying on the couch, eyes fixed to the television, oblivious to my presence. There was always something to eat in the kitchen which kept me going back. I won't lie about how much easier it became. I even managed to sneak in a friend or two. But I made sure no one else found out, especially not her neighbours, not Laurel.

I remember the first time Laurel went away. Where she went she never told me but I didn't really care. When she came back I was waiting just by her door. Upon seeing me she greeted me with a smile and allowed me in. I was afraid that she might want to say hello to Mrs Holloway – that mustn't happen! I spent the rest of the evening curled up on her lap, taking note of where she went. My friends were in Mrs Holloway's room, feasting no doubt. Her television was buzzing as usual and Laurel had switched hers on too, counter-balancing the noise. She never bothered Mrs Holloway.

One night, Laurel came back home late and she wasn't alone. I tried to like the boy she came with but I never could. He spent the night with her. It was all I could do to glare at them from the rain-strewn window. I had to do something about it, of course. I can't have people walking in and out of her apartment. I wasn't proud of what I did with his shoes. And it wasn't long before they started arguing, prompting a neighbour, not Mrs Holloway, to knock on the door and inquire into the matter. The boy, Kent, informed the intruder on the matter, which infuriated Laurel further, driving him away for good.

Of course, there had been rumours about Laurel that had spread throughout the building - what kind of girl she was, how many men she snuck into her bed. She tried to make her peace with them, but nothing can really kill a rumour. The good thing for me at least was that no one cared to say hello to Laurel anymore and no one else spent a night in her bed, except for me.

Things seemed to have settled down after a while, but then it got worse. It started one late afternoon when a few friends and I snuck into Mrs Holloway's room, enjoying our meal. There was a knock on the door. Whoever it may be, it had to be someone new. Mrs Holloway, still glaring at the screen, didn't hear the knocking and why should she? Of course, the knocker went away before he returned ... with more people.

They knocked on the door so forcefully that they actually broke the lock. My friends and I were startled but kept our positions. Upon seeing me and my friends beside Mrs Holloway I knew they would blame us. They took her away on a stretcher with her face covered. I guess I can understand that – the smell must have been enough to make them nauseous, and Mrs Holloway's lack of eyes, ears, nose and tongue must have been more than unpleasant for them.

They may have been disgusted with me but it was Laurel they blamed. How could she not have known about Mrs Holloway? They asked, 'what kind of neighbour was she?' Had she kept silent on purpose? Everyone knew they had had a row years ago, but that was hardly a reason to leave Mrs Holloway in such a state. It really wasn't right, even if they didn't go as far as accusing Laurel of murder. Well, if there was one thing that could have killed Mrs Holloway, it was neglect from those around her, or those who should have been there.

All that was years ago though. I don't like to dwell on the past and it wasn't long before old Mrs Something was forgotten, along with those photos of her lifelong memories. Who can blame them really?

Laurel, on the other hand, was another story. When I snuck back into her room, she threw a shoe at me. I scuttled away and kept my distance for some time. I understood why she'd be mad, but I knew it was only a matter of time before she let me cuddle on her lap again. Patience. In the meantime, there were other lonely tenants in other apartments holding on to mere memories, shutting away the world.

I stayed close to Laurel's place. I even let her see me moving about here and there, reminding her that I was really harmless, that it wasn't really my fault. It worked like a charm. It was only later that I realize why what I thought was my charm worked so well – the other tenants avoided her, hardly said a word of hello. What was even stranger was how she herself avoided people, avoided phone calls. She woke up, ate very little, did fewer things nor, more often than not, say a word. Then there was that odd look on her face - a blank, empty stare at the TV or even a wall, as though she saw nothing. She wasn't blind, but it was a different kind of sightlessness.

It took me awhile to realize what was wrong with her. I'd seen something like this before with others who shut out the world. I'd just never seen it on the face of someone this young. It turned out that it was she who kept people away. Eventually her buzzing television never switched off and her door never creaked open. I didn't always stick around, of course, as there were others I had to visit, to make sure their doors remained locked and their televisions on.

It would be years before they found Laurel. They didn't even know her name when they took her away - she barely had a face left. I'd never seen them on the inside before. This time, I made sure they didn't see me or my friends. The trick was to remain cute and cuddly so that they let you in and out while they kept everyone else only out. I taught all my friends. Some of them even got a jingling reward around their neck, some got to live with families with young children too. I'm starting to wonder if they all look the same on the inside.

# Cerebellum

by Joel Adams

A long, long time ago in a galaxy far away, there was a
planet, which is, alas, no more, called Xycstomangr**n,
which loosely translated into our language is Cerebellum.
It was a small but complex planet, roughly spherical, as
planets tend to be, with a high hill on one side, a vast
plain below and another high hill on the other. No one
lived on the plain and there was only one country on each
high hill, Xycsto on the east and Mangr**n on the west,
and they hated each other. They did their best to have
absolutely nothing to do with each other. If, for any
reason, their citizens happened to meet, they killed each
other.

It was a very odd phenomenon, that in all the
encounters we know of, both parties died horrible deaths.
Luckily encounters rarely occurred, since both hills were
abundant in all the natural resources they needed for their
survival and 'thrival' (is that even a word?). This led both
cities to conclude that they really didn't need each other,
so they lived their separate lives as happily as they could
under the circumstances.

As I told you, the plain below was desolate and
uninhabited. However, there existed on the plain decayed
ruins of a vast and ancient network of roads, tunnels,
paths, and power lines running between the two hills, all
fallen into complete disrepair and disuse. Everyone
marveled at their ancestors for wasting so much effort
and money on something so unnecessary. In fact, in
Xcysto it was a favorite pastime to roll around on the

112

floor laughing while someone read the old history books about the plains and the former use of the network there. In Mangr**n they did not do this, they just spat in disgust every time someone mentioned the network; they were serious people. Of course, they spat into receptacles they carried around for this purpose; they were clean and orderly people.

And that brings us to the basic difference between the two peoples. The Xcystoites, how shall I describe them? I will give you an example.

There was a court case held. Scringle had been found mid-morning one day, sitting at his kitchen table with a bloody hatchet in one hand, a huge butcher knife in the other, blood spattered all over his person and clothes, mumbling unintelligibly while staring into space. Strewn about him on the floor in various states of dismemberment were the corpses of his wife and children. On the kitchen table, directly in front of him was an untouched bowl of gruel. In front of all those dismembered were half-eaten bowls of gruel.

The court case of the century commenced. Shlsh, a drink very similar to pink lemonade laced with vodka, and scrumptious crumpets were served to all, young and old. Everyone had a great time. People were all hugging and laughing and commenting how sad it was that the deceased wife and children could not be here since they so loved shlsh and crumpets. Witness after witness took the stand to testify what a nice man the father was, how he was very friendly and helpful and had a great sense of humor. They related how his marriage was very happy, apart from the problem that he hated gruel for breakfast while his wife and all the children loved it. This fact was ruled irrelevant by the judge and struck from the record. All day and into the evening one witness after another told stories about what a great guy Scringle was and in the evening the judge and the jury, which was comprised of everyone in the village, agreed a great guy like him could never have done it and he was acquitted.

Just when they were about to go home, drunk, happy and pleased with themselves for being once more convinced of what nice people they all were, one very naughty child piped up and said, "But who did it then?" ruining everything. Now, they had to figure out who did it or at least come up with some sort of explanation.

Just then another child blurted out, "It must have been the Mangr**nites!" Everyone heaved a sigh of relief and shouted, "Of course it was! They aren't nice people." And a formal complaint was carried by pigeon to Mangr**n, asking for them to send over the culprit so they could put him in stocks in the town square where everyone in the village could tell him he was not a nice person and then, after sufficient humiliation, kill him. The pigeon returned with a note saying, "You have neither evidence nor proof of any kind. We will do nothing of the sort."

On hearing this in the town square meeting that night, the whole nation grumbled for five whole minutes that the Mangr**nites were all about 'proof' and 'evidence' and weren't being very nice. Then the music started and everyone danced and drank the night away.

About the same time there was also a court case in Mangr**n. A teenaged boy named **?!____, but you can pronounce it Bob, was accused of borrowing his schoolmate's pencil without asking during his final exam.

A court case was immediately convened with the shocked residents of Mangr**n attending. Three learned professors served as judge, the atmosphere was somber and serious. The CCTV footage was shown 8 or 9 times and it was proven without a shadow of doubt that Bob had indeed broken the point of his pencil just before answering the last question of his final exam. The film showed how he glanced over at his neighbor's desk, (we shall call him Shirley) who, already having finished his exam, had been excused to use the toilet and was absent at the moment. Bob looked around, thought no one was looking, looked at the clock, saw he had only one minute to finish the exam, borrowed the pencil, wrote the correct answer quickly, and returned it to Shirley's desk. Shirley, upon returning, picked up his pencil and could feel it was warmer than when he had left. He raised his hand, of course, waited for permission to speak, and said, "Someone borrowed my pencil while I was in the toilet." You can imagine the shock of all. Such a thing had never happened before in anyone's immediate memory.

Having seen all the evidence and heard from Bob, Shirley and the teacher presiding over the exam, the verdict was about to be given when Bob's mother asked for permission to speak, which was granted. She stood up where she was and said, "Bob has always been a good, helpful boy, and he is very sorry for doing this evil thing, (he told me last night) and he promises he will never do it again. Can we have mercy just this once on him?" A gasp went through the courtroom and it took the judges some moments to regain their composure.

The judges then gave the verdict. Bob was guilty and would be burned at the stake immediately following the trial. His mother was found guilty of not taking the stand

and being sworn in and, even worse, of succumbing to motherly instinct and emotion and finally of using foul language in a court of law. Bob and mother were both burned at the stake, with the father and Bob's sister igniting the fire.

These two court cases were turning points in the history of the two nations. Both became hotbeds of crime, with one murder after another being committed in Xcysto and Mangr**n being overwhelmed with rampant crime such as teens rolling their eyeballs when addressed, jaywalking by all ages, and ladies looking at items in stores that they could not afford.

As you can imagine, the populations of both nations were rapidly decreasing, and the hatred for Mangr**n by Xcysto reached record heights. In Mangr**n the frequent pigeons flying in accusing them of murder was too much to bear. Not only that, but the pigeons pooped on the immaculately clean streets of Mangr**n, increasing the work of the street cleaners. Things inevitably escalated to the breaking point. The two nations met on the plain in full battle regalia and killed each other.

All except for two teens. We shall call them Teen X and Teen M. Standing and looking at the total destruction of their societies, they stared at each other, threw aside their weapons, shook their heads in disbelief, stared at each other some more, and slowly and tentatively shook hands.

Then they sat down, each one on one of the bodies of their deceased and began to discuss where it all went wrong. Teen X made Teen M laugh, and Teen M made Teen X cry, and then they both laughed and cried and embraced and agreed that they needed each other's mentality, that the best answer was a balance, a blend of their two nations' characters. With excitement they embraced again and excitedly talked about how they could rebuild society, this time the right way, until it dawned on them… they were both female.

# Genesis

by Paul McCabe

Alois and Klara had good reason to be nervous. Her time was coming. A baby was on the way. Their first three had died as infants, two from diphtheria. The other, Otto, was born and had died in the same year. This was their fourth try at having a family.

Like many other couples in the area, they were cousins matched by relatives. Their worry was not calmed by the lovely views of the flowing river below and the mountains nearby to the north. The summer sunsets might sometimes be glorious, but more than once a month they called Doctor Bloch to check on Klara.

At 28 she was a good Catholic and prayed daily to the Lord for a healthy baby this time. Friends knew that she was hard-working, pious, conscientious, sweet, and affectionate. After three deep and grievous disappointments, she really wanted this new baby. Every Sunday she went to Mass and asked the priest to pray for her baby's good health. This he did.

Her husband, after training as a cobbler's apprentice as a young man, was now a 51-year-old civil servant in the local customs office. He had lived in several places due to work assignments and had some seniority. Aside from checking on border trade, there was little for him to do in this small town. Most of the goods were on the way to or from the big city to the west. He always wore his Finance Ministry uniform. In his spare time, he took care of bees at his farm. His two previous wives had died of TB.

At home with Klara he was curt and serious, in line with his semi-military profession. On the day they got married, he went back to work in the same afternoon. His neighbors thought him short-tempered and vain about his official status. It was his habit every morning to have a glass of white wine or two at the local tavern.

Spring was coming to the hills after a long and bitter winter. Most of the snow had melted on the mountains to the south and raised the level of the swift river in the town. Ash, oak, and beech trees showed light green leaves while the tall spruce and fir trees on the slopes stayed verdant all year. The evenings stayed chilly at this altitude in April.

Klara stayed in touch with her neighbors and with the local midwife. They told her about traditional recipes for mothers to be, and sometimes brought pots of soup over to the yellow wooden house. She wanted to be prepared for the big event and ate carefully. As in other families, both she and her husband hoped for a son.

Finally, the day arrived. She had a short labor and the child was born around noon.

"Is the baby breathing?" she asked.

The family doctor knew she was worried and knew the reasons why. He tried to reassure her. "Yes, you have a fine healthy baby boy, Mrs. Hitler."

Music

"Music is the shorthand of emotion."

~ Leo Tolstoy

# Music of the Spheres

By Renata Kelly

I was brought up, almost from the cradle, surrounded by classical music. I could tell the difference between Bach, Chopin and Beethoven since I was tiny, though at the age of primary school I definitely preferred Tchaikovsky and his wondrous ballet music -- openly admitting that Swan Lake, the story as well as the music, was my favorite composition "in the whole wide world!"

As the years rolled by, my preference for classical music remained, even though my dream of becoming a prima ballerina and dancing the role of the Swan Queen, with a Prince who resembled Gregory Peck or Clark Gable, soon faded and gave way to a more mature and broad appreciation of musical quality and diversity. I, however, never shared nor even tried to understand my friends' besotted enthusiasm for the gyrating Elvis Presley. Only later, as dancing at parties (not on stage as the Swan Queen) became a part of my teen-age and post teen-age life, did I make peace with the unfortunate Elvis and those who followed in his footsteps.

It seemed to me that the beauty of nature and especially that of the skies at night, brilliant with stars, were somehow related to the harmony of Bach's Goldberg Variations, a Chopin Etude or an aria from one of Verdi's operas. This could not be said for ABBA, the Beach Boys, nor even for the Beatles, whose later albums did become more sophisticated, musically speaking. Party music might be fun to bop around to, but was certainly not the Music of the Spheres! Musica Universalis, or, as I learnt in a Philosophy class, the Music of Harmony or of the Spheres, was a concept dating back to the Greek philosophers, Pythagoras and Plato, who predicated a mathematical relationship between astronomy and music. The spheres of the solar system, the sun, earth, moon and planets, were all part of this universal music, an unheard harmony of motion and mathematical proportions. I think even Einstein couldn't argue with this!

With time popular music, the music of my children, with its electric guitars, electronic synthesizers, percussion instruments manned by ear-ringed and multi-pierced orange-haired youths and screeching vocalists making love to their over-sized microphones -- became more and more alien to my taste. Oh, for ABBA and the Beach Boys or the Yellow Submarine! At least they had melody, harmony, perhaps not of the Spheres, but memorable, singable, danceable tunes nonetheless! I badly needed an explanation for my growing disenchantment with, even disdain for, contemporary pop.

An answer to my dilemma came in two instalments.

The first occurred in Singapore as I was driving to work at the University where I taught Linguistics. During the half-hour commute I usually listened either to the news or to the local classical music station. That day I chose the music station and was rewarded by a rich, clear tenor voice singing one of my favorite arias from Bizet's "The Pearl Fishers". I recognized the voice, correctly, to be Pavarotti's. He came to the end of his lament and the second Fisherman chimed in. I burst out laughing – it was Donald Duck! Yes, he was singing the correct part, but it must be a joke, a spoof. I chuckled as the music progressed, poor Donald making a valiant effort to accommodate his flat, quacking voice to the beautiful cadences of the aria. Finally, Pavarotti joined Donald in a duet, the difference in the two voices making the finale even more comical. The piece ended and the announcer came on: "You have just heard the Pearl Fishers duet from Bizet's 'Les Pêcheurs de Perles' sung by Luciano Pavarotti and Bono." Goodness, Bono! U2! I didn't really know Bono's music, but I liked the man and his espousal of good causes. Poor guy, what a terrible voice! But this musical experience taught me a lesson: if the voice is an instrument (which it is) then the instruments of the pop ensembles were a rough lot – the sheer volume and number of electric keyboards, guitars, drums drowning out the lack of substance in the amplified voices and lack of harmony in the composition.

The second event which finally helped to illuminate my dislike of pop culture, as presented in its musical output, occurred in France where we had lived for a number of years. Having sold our house, prior to our return to Asia, we were loath to sever all ties with the French Riviera – an area not only beautiful in its geography, but rich in history and art. We bought a small town-house in an enclave of twelve such houses, perched high in the hills above the ancient port and bay of Villefranche-sur-mer, with views that took in the Mediterranean coastline from Cap Ferrat to the distant Cap d'Antibes and the jagged Esterelle mountains. We soon became close friends with our nearest neighbor, a retired American concert pianist, who had also taught music and composition for many years at the University of California in Santa Cruz. We loved to hear her play, the piano music drifting over the hedge between our two gardens. Unfortunately, Amelia's neighbor on the other side was an Italian, Stefano, who still lived and worked in Italy and used his Villefranche property as a week-end and holiday retreat. Stefano was a veteran of many wives and various batches of children, the latter sometimes accompanying him for the week-end. However, he most often arrived for his visits to his French home on a powerful motorcycle with a long-legged lovely perched behind him clad in clinging black leather. No sooner did Stefano cross his threshold than the tranquility of the moment would shatter under the amplified thunder of hard rock, played on his admittedly state-of-the-art sound system.

One peaceful Friday evening we were enjoying a sunset drink with Amelia, our pianist neighbor, on our terrace. The sun had just disappeared behind the dark pinnacles of the Esterelle and the small clouds which filled the sky like a celestial flock of woolly sheep started to flush a gentle pink that slowly intensified into fiery orange and finally to a deep but glowing vermillion. The sea mirrored the sky, gradually taking on the hue of dark red wine. It was a breath-taking spectacle, made even more meaningful by the music in the background, a recording of Pachelbel's Canon in D Major.

All of a sudden, the majestic harmony of sea, sky and music was jolted by a crashing noise emanating from Stefano's house. As if on cue, the amazing pyrotechnics of the sunset subsided, fading into darkness. Stefano's music, if that it could be called, continued to blare out into the night. We decided to go inside and close the glass doors.

"Horrible!" I said.

"Boring," said Amelia.

"I'll get us another glass of wine," said my husband.

"Why boring?" I asked Amelia, genuinely interested by the strange appraisal.

"Because as a composition that type of music is simplistic. It's just like writing a book and only using one word, or maybe two, over and over again. Boring to read, wouldn't you say?" she smiled sweetly.

I couldn't agree more! Now it all made sense. "But what about fun music, like ABBA?" I enquired.

Amelia looked at me kindly and replied with a vestige of pity in her voice, "Well, that's maybe a Mills and Boon, if you like that kind of thing?"

# Woodstock

by Paul McCabe

The summer after I graduated from high school, the word went around on the streets of Providence RI, my hometown, about an upcoming music festival. Woodstock already was a magic word because Bob Dylan lived there. Along with a few friends from work, I bought a three-day ticket for $18 and thought it expensive.

My kind Indian boss loaned us the windowless delivery van for the weekend and we left Friday morning, driving about 240 miles west, to Sullivan County northwest of NYC. We crossed Connecticut and the Hudson River and soon found ourselves in slow-moving traffic on Route 17 which led to the festival site near the town of Bethel. Local people were sitting on their front porches watching the unprecedented spectacle.

We made slow progress until we abandoned the car. The five of us agreed to meet back there within two hours once the music had ended. No directions were needed. Walking about three miles in bell-bottom jeans, we joined the vast parade of hippies streaming toward Max Yasgur's dairy farm. The concert area was a big bowl-shaped grassy field. We had tickets, but the chain-link fence lay flat on the ground and the ticket booths were empty. Due to the giant surge of people attending, the festival was free.

When we finally found the stage about 5 p.m., a black singer named Richie Havens was starting to rumble out the festival's opening song, called Freedom. He had trouble with the microphones for the first few minutes. "Sometimes I feel like a motherless child…"

I stayed near the stage on Friday, but eventually I got hungry and walked up the hill to find something to eat in the woods. I kept running into people I knew from RI, quite odd in a crowd of half a million. When I went back to the concert, it was raining and Ravi Shankar, who was chiefly famous from being the guru of the Beatles, was on playing a sitar. Following Woody Guthrie's son Arlo, Joan Baez played last.

Saturday too I found a seat near the stage and stayed for hours. We were introduced to Carlos Santana, not at all famous then. The heavy hits just kept on coming, with Canned Heat, Mountain, the Grateful Dead, Creedence, Sly and the Family Stone, and Janis Joplin all blaring, wailing, roaring, pealing, walloping and bombarding us for hours with various blistering controlled explosions of sound. I disappeared again to eat. Down at the nearby pond I dared to go skinny-dipping for the first time in my life and met a nice girl from Toronto. But I returned in time to watch The Who play their rock opera Tommy in its entirety and continuously as the dawn broke pink and purple in the east. I fell asleep on the spot in my sleeping bag but awoke when the Jefferson Airplane launched broadsides and salvos of California music for 90 minutes in the morning.

In the afternoon, after the gravel-voiced and maybe drunk Joe Cocker, a heavy thunderstorm wet everyone and everything. Thus began the true legend of a 'sea of mud' at the festival. People next to me kept handing me food, a half sandwich, a wine bottle, a beer, a bag of chocolate chip cookies. This was new to me. When the rain cleared Country Joe MacDonald and the Fish sang their big anti-war hit 'I-feel-like-I'm-fixing- to-die-rag', preceded by the Fish cheer.

"Gimme an F, gimme a U, gimme a C, gimme a K!"

"What's that spell?"

"FUCK!"

"What's that spell?"

"FUCK!"

"What's that spell?"

"FUCK!"

We did this five times - entirely liberating in 1969 when millions of young people were against the war in Vietnam.

"I don't know how you expect to ever stop the war if you can't sing any better than THAT! There's about 300,000 of you fuckers out there. I want you to start SINGING! Come on!"

After this extraordinary exhilaration came Ten Years After, The Band (Bob Dylan's own), Blood Sweat and Tears, and Johnny Winter. About 3 am, Crosby Stills Nash and Young began their one-hour set after making the shocking announcement that they had "never played together before." Then Paul Butterfield played the blues, followed by a NYC group not much to my liking called Sha Na Na.

And I was there at 9 a.m., sitting on a tall speaker scaffolding close to the stage, Monday morning when Jimi Hendrix assured his immortality by cranking up his electric guitar and blasting awake everyone within miles with a number of hits. The last song he played ended the festival: "The Star Spangled Banner" in a way that no one had ever heard. It is still a jaw-dropper and a classic. He was dead in thirteen months.

Still not entirely sober a few weeks later, I moved to Washington DC to begin Georgetown University and to learn abstractions like microeconomics and statistics. I was not at all ready. My seventeen-year old head was reeling from a deluge of super music and an astonishing experience that I still remember forty-nine years later.

The whole festival passed quickly into history and into song and legend. "Woodstock" was a hit song for Joni Mitchell, a triple and a double record album, and a 1970 movie. Troubadours still tell the tales and recount this part of American folklore.

Once upon a time, in the Woodstock generation when I was young and slim, I was there.

# Music to my Ears

by Paige Turner

I'd always hated sitting in the lotus position to meditate. Screw that! I rebelled and lay on the bed instead. The fan whirred slowly above, creating a nice circulation of air. The fragranced aroma of a vanilla scented candle tickled my nose. My "hippie music", as my husband terms it, actually just a recording of the sound of ocean waves, played on the CD player. I took some deep breaths, slowing down my heart rate and tried to soothe my monkey mind.

I came to with a jolt – it must have all worked, because when I glanced at the clock, twenty minutes had passed. I don't know where I went, but I felt like I had been really far away and it was a struggle to come back. Why had I come out of my trance? A noise. Not a loud noise, more like a chiming sound, DINNNNNNNNNN GGGGGGGGGGG, that reverberated through me.

What the hell?

I briefly thought of a tuning fork or the chiming noise made when clinking our large crystal red wine glasses together, but no-one was drinking red wine. I was the only one home, so that was impossible. I was more alert now and the next noise, when it came, was an old piano riff, like the one at the start of a Jerry Lee Lewis or boogie-woogie song. Dennn-nuh-nuh-nuh-nah, dennn-nuh-nuh-nuh-nah. My feet were practically tapping. It reminded me of the days when my parents played in their own twosome of a band, Mum on the piano and Dad on the guitar. Mum is very musically gifted and has a beautiful singing voice. Dad is less gifted but makes up for that with enthusiasm. Their repertoire varied from Country and Western to folk, soft rock to rhythm and blues. They also played hymns at church too, though that was mostly Mum's domain. Music is a part of our lives with many a family occasion ending up with us gathered around the piano belting out some tunes.

Back to the mysterious noises, now I heard a door-bell. Well it sounded like a door-bell, but not <u>our</u> door-bell. I even got up and peered through the peep-hole. No-one there. What the heck? I went back to the guestroom mystified, lay down and once more closed my eyes.

AYUUUUUUUUGGGGAHHHHH, AYUUUUUU UUUUGGGAHHHHH, oh my God, what was that? It sounded like the car horn on the classic 1950s FJ Holden utility an ex-boyfriend of mine, a sheep shearer had. Maybe a TV had been left on? I decided to ignore the noises and closed my eyes again, hoping to get back to my meditating.

My thoughts flitted back and forth in my mind, left to right, right to left. Thoughts of learning to play piano, attempting to learn the drums, guitar and harmonica. Scenes of ballets I'd been to, the dying swan in Swan Lake and sugar plum fairies came to me. Songs from musicals, West Side Story, Mama Mia, The Sound of Music, The Lion King, Cirque Du Soleil shows, came to me. Songs from movies like Moulin Rouge all floated in my grey matter leading to thoughts of 'why haven't I bought any new music recently?' I love music, but these days not so much. Plus, even if I wanted to buy something I would have to download it to one or another device to listen to it - just too hard. What would I buy anyway? It all seems to be house music with a single bass beat, rap music with foul language, lyrics about female degradation or songs by tortured souls, who seem far too young to have experienced all the angst they sing about. What happened to simple dance music with a catchy beat or cheerful songs?

My musings were interrupted yet again by another noise, but this time one I recognized - a good old-fashioned telephone ring! I went to the kitchen where my new I-phone10X lay and grabbed it, but the face didn't show anyone calling. I realized the ring came from another area - my office. I went there and noticed the computer screen flashing.

"Oh hi Siri – now that you've finished picking out my telephone ring, would you choose some music for me?"

# God's Hand

## by C.I. Ripples

When Faith played Ludovico Einaudi's Petricor, especially if he was marking his student's mediocre English papers, he would ask her to stop, saying it affected his concentration. It was so achingly beautiful it almost pierced his heart and he would have to sit back and let the music flow through his veins, the notes of the cello washing over his soul. She would laugh, as the last rays of the late summer sun shone through her blonde hair and, her eyes shining bright, tell him it was the hand of God reaching down.

Had it been the hand of God that had plucked his rose from him, leaving only a thorny stem? Was it part of His bigger plan to let self-absorbed teenagers swerve into her and their unborn daughter that raw Saturday evening on her way back from choir practise? Her own students, who cared only about make-up, selfies, Snapchat, YouTube and Netflix. If that was His plan then he did not want to feel His hand again, ever. It no longer brushed his soul with brilliant sunshine, only tears.

If music reflected what was in his soul, then what he listened to now echoed his broken heart, his pain and misery, and above all anger and outrage. He had sat through the family court proceedings glaring at the girls who could plead nothing but guilty, the CCTV cameras bearing testimony to their crime. He could sense their fear, but also arrogant optimism, as their solid well-paid lawyers presented their well-reasoned persuasive case for a reduced sentence. And when the judge pronounced that sentence, giving the girls community service to atone for what she deemed their 'involuntary underage manslaughter', his faith in justice defeated him.

He struggled for breath, his knuckles white as he clenched his fists. Community service for murder! He had lost control, exploded to his feet and jumped over the balustrade towards the reprieved. And when the court officer tried to obstruct him, he had given him an almighty blow on his jaw. He still felt the impact of it on his fist. They took away his gun license for the assault and put him on suspension from school, insisting he seek counselling before he return. They called him hysterical and distraught, suspected he was mentally unstable, not right in the wasteland of his head, but what else could he be when the sane had abandoned him?

So, he went to see the counsellor once a week to talk, speaking what he knew she wanted to hear as she listened attentively, took notes and told him what she believed he needed to hear: that there are people who had been through worse; that like them, he would come out on the other side; that time heals almost everything. But how could she know, when she hadn't been where he had, when she was not him?

How could she know who he was supposed to be now Faith was gone? Her music was gone? Not once had she asked him what music he listened to now. She of all people should have understood that music completed him where his words left off. She should not have misunderstood. Wasn't it Victor Hugo who said that 'music expresses that which cannot be said and on which it is impossible to be silent'?

If she had only asked, she would have felt his solitude and known he was immune to the consultations of his peers, superiors and her. Had she done so, she would not have let him go to be hollow night after night, day after day, in a home where his only companion was his music, the only constant in his miserable howling existence along with his unlicensed Sig Sauer.

He had read somewhere that good music speaks to you and changes you. It could take your pain and turn it into something beautiful. It certainly wasn't beauty, but the music he listened to now had changed him, made him invulnerable, invincible and fearless. It had saved his life, made him forget that he was he. It was bands like Megadeth, Exodus, Death and The Creator that were now his higher power, encouraging him on to eliminate his enemy, those murderers, those institutions, those pretend do-gooders. Their music was the only thing that made this cesspit of a world, that had let him down, bearable. When things got really bad, when he couldn't stand the sight of her clothes hanging limply in the cupboard, he would slump down, take a deep breath and allow Three Days Grace to hammer in his head, losing himself, releasing all the feelings he could not express, healing him as he emptied himself.

As he listened to the outburst of his soul, the months passed, eating his savings, his friends, her piano, her cello, everything that had remained of their life together, apart from her photograph, a now faded happy shot of their halcyon days. He carried it in his breast pocket or kept it by the side of his bed, stroked it every morning upon waking. There sits her young self, legs drawn up on the stool at the piano, the sunlight streaming through the open window, wearing her favourite threadbare floral summer dress. She is smiling up at him uncertainly, having just finished the Interstellar piece by Hans

Zimmer, pulling her skirt tight over her knees, hugging them almost to fend off her critical self. It had been particularly difficult to master. Except for that precious moment captured, he was alone.

Yet, he almost wallowed in his solitude, growing stronger, bolder and fiercer, as he architected his revenge. He would paint the picture of everything they had done to him with blood on the walls of the school when they least expected it, thinking it apt that he would destroy those who had destroyed him. They could not point their unclean fingers. After all, he was only doing unto others as they had done unto him. He may have lost his gun license, and he would have preferred the precise targeting of his S&W PPC9, but he still had his P938.

Of course, he knew his life would end, but it would be worth it. They would finally know his worth. Anyway, for all intents and purposes his life was already over, so his death would be a welcome relief from his pain. Until they took him down, he would give them shots to remember. He might no longer be ambitious for his life, but he certainly hoped he would be immortalised by the likes of Madd Maxxx, Pearl Jam, or Andrew WK, even if only through those who died. Perhaps his justice would be put to music as the Cruxshadows had done for Columbine. He might even spark a revival of the Dead Boys. The only regret he would have is that he had to quit his music.

It was on a grey and blustery day, one month short of the anniversary of her death, when the front door fell into the lock behind him. He zipped up his jacket against the wind, felt the P938 concealed and harmlessly quiet in his pocket. Apart from her photograph which sat next to his heart, he had taken nothing else. He had even left his

Samsung and earphones at home – he didn't need them. He could play Culling the Herd in his head to drown out any voices, the screams of his targets, even the voice within himself.

He walked steadily towards the school two blocks from the house, rehearsing his upcoming performance. He knew he need not worry about getting into the building. His pass to the teacher's entrance at the side had still not been revoked and the metal detector had been disabled since teachers had been armed for salvation after the Florida shootings.

He had googled the timetable and knew the students should be in lessons and the hallways quiet. Just in case, however, he was ready to shoot at anything that got in his way, even though he knew it would only bring more carnage and might mean he never achieved his ultimate aim before he ran out of bullets and had to reload.

It all went according to plan. The place was so deathly quiet and deserted it seemed eerily unreal as he made his way towards his target, through the hallway devoid now of lockers that led to the café, auditorium and gym. Suddenly he stopped dead. From behind the closed door of Faith's music room, he heard it. God's hand, pulling him back from the brink. When the music reached him and stroked his soul, washing over him, he slid down against the wall, face crumpled and began to sob, shoulders shaking.

He wiped the tears from his dark wet lashes, as the last piano chord was struck, straightened up from the wall, threw his weapon in the trash and walked out the door as the sun burst through the clouds.

# Music carved in my C drive

## by Lian McCabe

I have to admit that I'm not talented with my fingers - I can't play a string, brass, woodwind or percussion instrument and, to be honest, I can't even whistle. Even if I will never play in a philharmonic orchestra, I do love music. From classical symphonies or folklore lullaby, to country music, religious music, rock, pop, jazz, or simply rhythmic tones, I admire all composers, players and singers. They have achieved what I could not and have allowed me to enjoy music from the moment I was born, hopefully forever.

There are a few encounters with music that particularly stand out for me, drawing up memories and emotions that will always remain with me.

### Happy New Year

Children today can enjoy music, or what is known as 'Early Enlightenment', even before they are born. This is based on the belief that if the mother-to-be listens to composers such as Mozart, her new-born baby will be smarter. I haven't done any research on that and so can't validate this claim. My point, however, is that when my mother was pregnant she didn't go to any early enlightenment school so that I could feel classical music. My parents have never been music lovers. They didn't even sing lullabies to me. As a result, when it came to music I was way behind and it was only when I entered kindergarten at the age of six, that I learned the very first and complete song, "Happy New Year".

Of course, I had not learned English yet then, so we learned it in Chinese. It's a simple song: "Happy New Year, Happy New Year, we wish you all a Happy New Year. We are singing, we are dancing, and we wish you all a Happy New Year." It is a happy song, and you can hear small children singing it all over China.

Now, our teacher Ms. M taught us to say Happy New Year in English as well. At least, she and we thought it was English. She carefully and thoughtfully broke down the three English words "Happy New Year" for us in Chinese:

"happy", pronounced "hei pi" in Chinese, meaning "black-skinned" in Chinese;

"new", pronounced "niu" in Chinese, meaning "cow" in Chinese;

"year", pronounced "ya" in Chinese, using as a modal particle without meaning.

It all made sense to us, a bunch of six-year-old kindergarteners, and we would clap our hands while saying / singing Happy New Year in English with Chinese sounds: "hei pi niu ya! hei pi niu ya! hei pi niu ya!..." We remembered it because it meant "black (hei) skinned (pi) cow (niu)! "Black skinned cow! Black skinned cow …" We even happily performed the song in front of other little kids in the same kindergarten for the New Year celebrations, not knowing exactly why we were singing about a black skinned cow, how this was relevant to the New Year in English-speaking countries. Maybe they enjoyed it that way?

I didn't think too much about it until I heard the real English version of Happy New Year, when I was about thirteen in middle school. All of a sudden, the black-skinned cow popped out in my mind. I burst into laughter. I still can't sing the song, not in Chinese, not in English, as I always visualize a black-skinned cow.

National Anthem

When I moved to Phuket, I found that the Thai National Anthem is broadcast twice a day, at eight in the morning and six in the afternoon. Most Thais just keep doing what they're doing at these times, although I am told this is a relatively new phenomenon.

Back home in China, we are told to stop whatever we're doing when the 'March of the Volunteers', our national anthem is played. I, however, seldom heard it when I lived there, apart from every Monday morning at school, when the flag ceremony was held before the start of classes. The national anthem played whilst skilled flag students hoisted the flag, making sure it reached the top by the end of the anthem. All students were obliged to listen and sing along whilst watching the flag go up. Then, one student chosen from a given class would give a speech on the national anthem, national flag or other patriotic role model. This is the case even today.

In Phuket we watch FOX news and every day at six in the evening we hear the American national anthem, which, due to the time difference, the TV station airs at the start of a new day's broadcast at six every morning.

After I married I learned a little about the Star-Spangled Banner. The lyrics come from 'Defence of Fort M'Henry', a poem written by the thirty-five-year-old lawyer and amateur poet Francis Scott Key who witnessed the British Navy bombarding the fort in

Baltimore Harbor. Key was inspired by the large American flag, which was still flying triumphantly above the fort as dawn broke on the battle area. The poem was set to the tune of a British song already popular in the United States. It was renamed "The Star-Spangled Banner" and quickly became a well-known American patriotic song. In 1931, the Congress made it the national anthem.

It's not that I'm that into formalities or stand on ceremony, but I would wish to go to Tiananmen Square to watch the ceremony of the PLA soldiers hoist our flag. You can feel their sense of mission, feel your blood racing through your veins, forever proud of being a Chinese. The "March of the Volunteers" was raised to official status in 1982, adopted by Hong Kong and Macau upon their restorations to China in 1997 and 1999, respectively.

Apart from the three national anthems mentioned above, there are many countries that adopt war-time marching music as their national anthem. It's not hard to figure out that people still want to be inspired by the patriotism and passion of their people when they defended their country in fighting off their enemies; that people still want to memorize the hardships and losses suffered in order to gain freedom and independence; that people still want to warn potential enemies that they will safeguard their land and sovereignty until the last drop of their blood … Even today, marching music remains a powerful choice.

Vivaldi's 'Four Seasons'

I didn't know anything about the Italian Baroque composer, virtuoso violinist and Catholic priest Antonio

Lucio Vivaldi until I met my husband, who shared his appreciation for classical music with me. When we went to Venice for our honeymoon and sat down in the church where Vivaldi used to play, we enjoyed one of his most famous pieces, the 'Four Seasons', almost every night. If I closed my eyes, I could feel the seasons changing, imagine what nature looks and feels like, throw myself into the picturesque stories of each season. I was reminded so much of home, almost homesick, sure that Vivaldi must have visited northern China and had been inspired by its four seasons. I even wrote a piece called 'Vivaldi visited my hometown in Jinan', which was published in 2016.

In 2017, when we visited Prague on my birthday, my husband took me to a concert once again. He hadn't told I was about to listen to the Four Seasons once more. When the first chords were struck, by a group of amazingly talented violinists, the tears welled up in my eyes. I closed them, letting my mind wander back to my hometown. After the concert, my husband, knowing how important this piece is to me, even took me backstage. I was so choked by my own tears that I couldn't say a thing.

### 'Nian Qin En' by Danny Chan

If there is one song that brings tears to my eyes it's Danny Chan's 'Nian Qin En' (be grateful for my parents), which reminds children how hard it is to be a parent, how much effort it requires, how much is sacrificed. And it is only when you realize this that you begin to appreciate your parents. I may not have children myself, but when I hear this song, I am grateful to my parents for their love, devotion, hard work and everything they gave to me.

It reminds me of an ancient Chinese saying that "A tree desires to stand still, but the wind does not cease. A son desires to serve his parents, but they do not wait." Of course, like most children, I had countless disputes and quarrels with my parents, acting like a spoiled princess, too self-absorbed to imagine how upset I made them and the heartbreak I drove them to. I only really made peace with my parents in my thirties. And now I constantly regret not being able to protect my parents more as they age. I can't turn their grey hairs black, I can't smooth the wrinkles on their faces, I can't straighten their back, or pay back the time they invested in me.

Sometimes I even have a feeling that my parents are actually my children. After I bought some gifts for Mom, which she probably didn't need, she asked me quietly, and with a pinkish bashful tightness on her face, "er, hmm, ne, can I have a red scarf for my birthday? I sort of need it for the dance perform next month..."

It reminded me of that little girl who tugged her mom's dress and pleaded to get that lovely shirt many years ago.

"Yes, Mom, of course...What kind of red scarf do you prefer?"

And as our roles reverse, what I can do is ensure that all their basic material needs are met and listen to them with the patience they taught me. What I can do is hold their hand when I take them out, the same way they helped me cross the road. What I can do is hug them and tell them how much I love them when they see me, hear me, feel me.

This contemporary song reminds us of the complexities of love, that it can be great and marvelous, but also hidden, revealed only in the practical, trivial, sometimes boring daily activities we carry out for others. And every time I hear 'Nian Qin En'. I'm glad that I can give my love to my parents.

'Celebrate' by Mika

> "I want the whole world to celebrate,
> I wanna come home
> To the only place I know
> Where the trees I planted grow
> I wanna come home
> …
> I'll be just fine
> When I see you at the finish line
> Doesn't matter if I take my time
> I'm coming home… "

I played this song again and again when I was on my way back to my hometown, reflecting that whereas for most people, "East west, home is the best", for me, home is a place of many contrasting meanings: love, hate; peace, and war. It's both encouraging and disheartening; friendly, caring and greedy and selfish. It can be a quiet haven, but also a raging battlefield, a place where we are both angels and demons, changing roles constantly, usually unremarkably.

Despite these contrasts, the song reminds me that home is where people find the, energy and will power to start all over again. In China we call it a 'Sweet Burden', always remembering that both the fish and dear guest will spoil within three days. It's a great idea to go home to soak up some love and strength. Just don't stay too long.

## 'Nessun Dorma' (None Shall Sleep)

'Nessun Dorma' is an Italian aria from the final act of Puccini's opera Turandot, where the prince falls in love at first sight with the beautiful, but cold Princess Turandot. Any man who wishes to marry Turandot must answer her three riddles; if he fails, he will be beheaded. In the aria, the prince expresses his triumphant assurance that he will win the princess.

Although many artists including Pavarotti, have performed it, the first time I unexpectedly heard it live was when my husband sang it passionately to me while holding my hands, during our wedding ceremony. I was brimming over with happiness and love.

"Nessun dorma! Nessun dorma!
Tu pure, o Principessa
Nella tua fredda stanza
Guardi le stelle che tremano
D'amore e di speranza!
Ma il mio mistero è chiuso in me
Il nome mio nessun saprà!
No, no, sulla tua bocca lo dirò
Quando la luce splenderà!
Ed il mio bacio scioglierà
Il silenzio che ti fa mia!
Il nome suo nessun saprà
E noi dovrem, ahimè! Morir! Morir!
Dilegua, o notte! Tramontate, stelle!
Tramontate, stelle! All'alba vincerò!
Vincerò! Vincerò!"

Of course, at the time I didn't understand Italian and I still don't, but later I found the English translation:

"None shall sleep,
None shall sleep!
Even you, oh Princess,
In your cold room,
Watch the stars,
That tremble with love
And with hope.
But my secret is hidden within me,
My name no one shall know,
No... no...
On your mouth, I will tell it,
When the light shines.
And my kiss will dissolve the silence that makes you mine!
(No one will know his name and we must, alas, die.)
Vanish, o night!
Set, stars! Set, stars!
At dawn, I will win!
I will win!
I will win!"

It goes without saying that my prince didn't have to answer any riddles and I didn't have to guess his name.

Then a few years ago in Ephesus, Turkey, he seized the chance once more in the ancient amphitheatre. It's no wonder that the Romans built it this way – the penetrating and melodious sound of his booming voice was diffused into the air like jasmine aroma. Again in 2016 in Arles France, before an imitation gladiator show, when I was on the opposite of the theatre to him, I was sure I could hear him humming the tune … He also sings it on our wedding anniversaries. To us Nessun Dorma is beyond classical opera. It's the emblem of our love, a reflection of our vows to love each other.

Theme music from Schindler's List

The film relates a period in the life of Oskar Schindler, a German businessman, who saved many refugees during WWII.

Whenever the strings sound, a heart-breaking sadness strikes my soul, taking me back to the war as depicted in the film - the black and white pictures, the little girl in the red coat, who exemplifies the tragedy, the evil that tears apart everything that you believe is beautiful, what is valuable, right in front of your eyes, and stomps it under its foot, quenches off any possible sparks of hope.

Mr. Schindler, however, can always find one more reason to save one more Jew. For the gigantic population of Jews, one person might not really seem to count too much. Nevertheless, for the particular Jew he rescued, it means the whole world.

For me, this music speaks for all those who died in the Holocaust. It reflects not only the tears that all humans shed as a result of war, but is also a symbol of faith, hope and human kindness.

Such is the power of music.

# Mrs Miller Conspires

by Stephanie Thornton

It was exactly 6pm on a stormy night in June when Mrs Miller decided to kill her neighbours. She remembered the day and time as she had wanted to watch the evening news. But just at that exact time, her neighbours arrived home from work and put on the loud rap music she had come to loathe so much, which permeated through the thin walls of her terrace house in Islington. She could hear them arrive long before they got through the door as they would drive up to the house with either the windows down, of their bright pink Cadillac Eldorado Convertible or with the top down, on a sunny day and share how much they loved their particular brand of music to all and sundry. And this in spite of the glares from other cars and people on the pavements. And in spite of what they thought would be appreciated by all who saw it; their glorious car with the lovingly painted tiger stripes down the side and the faux pony seat covers.

She banged on the wall with a pan which, by now, had made a large hole in the wall. Brothers Aloysius and Leroy thought their neighbour was 'in the groove' with the loud banging and joining in with their particular enjoyment albeit through the wall. Maybe they should invite her to their next rave party.

She had been widowed early which at least spared her listening to the endless chamber music so loved by her husband which bored her to death. And now, she liked what she liked and could pick and choose, not having to please anyone other than herself.

It was over thirty years ago now that Mrs Miller had realised the psychological effects of music on people's lives.

It came to her insidiously as it did to all her friends she worked with. After work, they would cross the road to the Painted Lady public house on the opposite side of the busy London street, happy and content another day had finished well. They would sit in a row along the bar drinking pints and chatting about the day. It was strange, but as they sat there, a sort of melancholy descended over the group and they would leave the pub in a strange and sombre mood. After a while, they started to notice that this happened more often than not and wondered if it were the type of beer. Or even too much of it.

A few weeks passed. One of them, a usually happy chap called Jo, was becoming ever more despondent until one evening, he actually started weeping in front of them after he had drunk two pints.

They worried about him, especially after he started taking time off work.

It all ended when he hung himself from the nearest tree.

The Coroner recorded accidental death and stated this was caused by the medical term called the 'crying in the beer' syndrome. He said that actually, singer Barry Manilow was mostly to blame. His songs were played constantly over the tannoy at the Pub.

"Just listen to it," one of the coppers suggested, "but only for a few minutes or you'll get suicidal too."

The Police had been given ear muffs to wear when they visited the pub, in line with health and safety rules.

After all, the Police force was already reduced in size so it wouldn't do to make it any less. And the insurance would refuse to pay in the case of such a death. Indeed, the mournful words were full of lost love affairs, gnashing of teeth, crying, wailing and weeping.

The Press loved it.

"Barry Manilow kills poor Jo" screamed the headlines and for a time sales of Barry records rose as men rushed to buy them for their wives, high achievers bought them for their bosses and teenage children full of angst and hormones, as Christmas gifts for rich parents.

After they had lost poor Jo to Barry Manilow, Mrs Miller began to observe other dangers.

There would be music everywhere. In lifts, in department stores, where, if they weren't playing what she liked, would put her right off buying anything at all. And then there was the silly background music to early movies most especially by the composer Dimitri Tiomkin who graced movies of the 50s with insignificant rambling soundtracks and little fluttery pixie tippy- toe type sounds. It was only in the present last two decades that some thought seemed to have gone into what would enhance a film rather than where it served no useful purpose. Her mum had dubbed some of this music, especially the type played in Chinese restaurants 'Music to saw one's legs off with' – the sort of operation you did without anaesthetic!

Now modern music seemed to consist of lots of women screaming out a song at the top of their lungs with a sore throat and again wailing on about lost love. Especially annoying was one song where the singer, a man, said "he didn't want to miss a thing…so he would stay up all night watching the love of his life whilst she slept". Fancy, thought Mrs Miller, waking up to find a man looking at you an inch away from your face with mad staring eyes. What a horrible thought!

And then there was the other things regarded 'modern'. Dancing waving one's arms in the air which was obviously so that everyone could smell each other's arm pits and compare deodorants. Or holding a lighted cigarette lighter in the air or the mobile phone light, waving it back and forth in tune with another 'crying in the beer' job.

She had stopped going to weddings. That was if they invited her at all. She had gone to her cousin's some five years back but the music was so loud no one could hear themselves think and were shouting over the speakers. The owner of the disco refused to comply with the volume reduction request so she had unplugged the leads when he had gone for a break and cut the ends off with nail scissors. The DJ gave a large bill to her uncle who was not amused, but at least she'd saved him having a sore throat.

On the other side of her terrace house, lived a man she hardly knew called Garland Knight. She knew he was in the movies of some sort but one day, when the police had come to visit, as the music from the Jamaicans was so bad, they had knocked on his door too and they were introduced. She didn't know this but he was writing a score for a multi-million-dollar movie starring Brad Pitt and Charlize Theron and was in the middle of a writer's block. Even the inspiration of Alfred Hitchcock's "Psycho" film where he had used violins to make stabbing noises couldn't break it. He needed one particular sound, to fit a murder scene on a spaceship, where not only the body but the fabric of the ship was joined as one. It had become such a problem that they were even offering a three-million-pound reward on 'New Musical Express' for anyone who could come up with the sound. It was in reality not much money in a multi-million-pound budget. Thousands of tapes had now been handed in but nothing matched the bill.

Following the police visit and whilst Mrs Miller continued to dream up schemes to kill off her neighbours, Garland came for coffee in the hope it would break his writer's block. He found her calm and soothing and her music taste very much matched his own with a mix of blues, jazz and soul – and all with the volume turned down. She shared her dream of killing off the neighbours which made him laugh and eased the tension. They would cook up schemes together such as inviting the two Jamaicans to dinner and serving a hundred times triple strength Reggae Reggae Sauce with the customary cauli greens and grits appropriate for Jamaican guests, or suggest playing them music through some Bose headphones doctored to give a million decibels, like culling a cow in the abattoir. Or getting all the local dogs round to the house, enticed with meat so they could howl, as they had become accustomed to doing at the local call to prayer which would be so much louder than the music next door, they wouldn't be able to hear it anymore and move. And if all else failed, they could always resort to Barry Manilow.

Just as they were running out of ideas and time had flown, the sound of the Cadillac could be heard coming down the street.

"Perhaps I should leave now?" said Garland, planning a hurried escape.

"No, please stay," she begged, "that way you can see how bad it is for me".

Soon the rap started through the walls, Mrs Miller picked up her pan and angrily banged the wall where the hole was. She was just about to ask Garland what he thought, above the din when she turned and saw a strange look on his face

"That's it!" he said. "The sound!"

"What sound?" she asked, thinking it the same phrase June Allison said in the film when Glenn Miller found his special one.

"The sound I need for 'Strangers in Space'!"

And so it came to be, dear readers. Mrs Miller's pan on the wall made her famous. Her former street became called 'Tin Pan Alley Number 2'. She earned three million pounds from the sound and was able to move into a detached country house with Garland and forget all about how to kill her neighbours. All was peace and quiet. It was lovely.

# The Buskers

by Stephanie Thornton

All that hot summer, they had played the beaches of the south of France when pickings were rich. The first port of call had not been a success because Monaco was not the sort of place to tolerate buskers.

He had so enjoyed his first visit there, finding the enormous wheels of the racing cars with their gleaming spider spokes especially attractive. As they walked past 'The Hotel de Paris', Jake, his boss, said that one day, when they'd made a mega record deal, they would go there and drink champagne. The hit had not happened yet.

And then the police had moved them on.

Now it was winter and earnings were slim, but tonight, they would play again on the beach in Monaco whilst the New Year fireworks blazed in the night sky.

Some mad impulse grabbed him. He wanted to go and see what it was like inside that great hotel and, seizing an opportunity, snuck behind the snooty door man, when his back was turned collecting tips, to sit in the far corner of the bar before anyone spotted him.

All was not well. There was a horrible atmosphere under the gorgeous, period ceilings and crystal chandeliers. The room was full of plastic people wearing artificial smiles and much lifted faces. Across in the distance, a man with a bellowing voice seemed to be talking to the entire room. Heavy perfume eddied through the air. He wished he hadn't come.

And then he saw her. The waiter had pulled out a chair for her and there she sat. A diamond band glittered round her young neck. Her platinum blonde hair was dyed purple and preened into a large poof, tied up with an enormous bow and she wore a silk jacket, quilted in the same colour. She yawned and he thought how boring it must be for her, eating dainty morsels off a silver plate. Every so often, the lady next to her leaned over to give her a kiss and murmur in her ear whilst the husband returned a long suffering and tolerant smile.

It was not love at first sight or even lust on his part, just abject pity for her. Was this what having money meant? He felt sorry for them all!

And then, they spotted him!

"How did that dog get in here!" the waiter shouted.

As he fled, the purple poodle started to bark after him.

The night was dark as he joined Jake on the beach but it was so much nicer. And at least the crowd would laugh at his attempts to 'sing' and the atmosphere would be fun. Later on, they could go to the café in the 'real' town over the border and eat take away and none of that horrid stuff they had been eating at the hotel which the bellowing man had called Foie Gras...

# Food

"One cannot think well, love well and sleep well
if one has not dined well."

~ Virginia Woolf

# Fine Dining

by Boris Nielsen

He was surprised at how Spartan the restaurant was. The only concessions to luxury were the over-starched cloths and napkins, the heavy cutlery, and the delicate crockery. The furniture was non-descript and the provenance of the modern art on the walls could equally have been Sotheby's or the local dump. The floor looked like linoleum, no kind of covering for a supposedly upscale establishment such as this.

The waiter welcomed them by presenting large, stiff cards, and glancing at him knowingly – *I know you are not of this place, but I will tolerate you none-the-less.*

He smiled back confidently – *yes, but it is I who is sat and you who are serving.*

Taking the rebuff well, the waiter retreated with a slight bow, leaving him free to *peruse* the menu which, he assumed, was how people from *this place* chose their meals.

Two starters, two mains, two desserts and a bonus of coffee with chocolates. No mention of free-flow beverages, just a thick padded book in the hands of his host. She looked up at him to make sure he was paying attention and announced her choice.

"How about a Rioja…they have a nice 2014 Contador that I like, but it's maybe too dry for some."

"I like Rioja. I was on holiday in Spain once and practically drank nothing else."

Smiling, she put the book down reverently and picked up the menu card.

Following her lead, he concentrated on the serious business of making his choices. *English Pub Style Crispy Whitebait* or *Upland Goose Pate* to start. He would rather be communicating authenticity, but he did not care for fried fish, so it looked like pretentious to start with. Hopefully, he could redeem himself with the mains: *Roasted Wild Trout with Crystal Organic Corn and Lady Peas* or *Mile's Farm Slow Roasted Pork Loin with Potato Tartiflette and Baby Squash Salad.* Was that a typo…surely it should be *Tartelette?* And how do *Lady Peas* differ from the frozen petit pois he bought at the supermarket?

"Shall we order?" she asked as the waiter returned.

"What will you have?"

Without hesitation he looked the waiter in the eye and issued his demand, "I'll have the pâté and the pork."

Doubt came at once with a memory of food etiquette from his mother: "If you're having meat as a starter then have a fish dish for the main."

The waiter raised his pad and wrote the order rapidly, disallowing any change of mind.

"Same for me," said his host, sounding surprised at the odds of their orders matching. "And a bottle of the 2014 Contador with some table water, please."

The waiter looked genuinely pleased as he snapped his pad closed. Perhaps they were running out of trout and he could reassure the chef that they still might make it through the lunch sitting. Whatever the reason, he unfurled their napkins and laid them in their laps as if there was joy in his heart.

As the waiter rushed off to the kitchen with the good news, she addressed him again, "I so much prefer goose pate to foie gras. Simply not the same concerns about the goose's suffering, poor things. There's no reason why we shouldn't enjoy good food without having the animals suffer…don't you agree?"

He did not, necessarily, agree.

"But I do like foie gras, every now-and-again. And frankly, at these prices, I'm surprised we're being fobbed off with pâté. Perhaps it is, as you suggest, a concession to the consciences of the clientele."

Doubt again: was that a display of authenticity or just overly-aggressive?"

She laughed, "The meat dish at lunch here always used to be filet, so I think the selection of dishes has more to do with saving money than anyone's conscience. I heard rumours that this place was in trouble. Still, at least they can't water down the wine…can they?"

He relaxed, they were on the same level, she was someone he could work with. Smiling back, he said, "Maybe I'll insist on opening the bottle myself, so I can be sure it's not been tampered with. After all, we wouldn't want our first gourmet lunch together spoiled now…would we?"

# A Visit to 'The Rule of Thumb'

### (based on real life events)

### by Stephanie Thornton

Two years of waited anticipation, looking at the glorious web site with many thoughts and dreams of food accompanied by much salivating, the day had finally dawned.

It was the day that self-confessed foodie Clarence Whitaker was to visit to the hallowed halls of the 'Rule of Thumb'. The legendary three-star Michelin restaurant, whose stars would have not disgraced the skies of Bethlehem, was located deep in Cotswold country and its waiting list to dine there could easily take three years. It was the place to see and be seen in. Or so everyone said!

Would the reality meet the dream? And would it meet the bank balance too? Saving up took two years to pay for it, but none of his foodie friends knew this, merely gasping with shock and wonder at the thought. Or should it be 'shock and awe?'

He was dining alone as he couldn't afford to take the wife – she would have only been uncomfortable to go there anyway, preferring local take-aways or the relative safety of a Birds Eye "ready". She didn't like dressing up either.

The exterior certainly looked OK. The famous photos showed an elegant Tudor manor house with a delightful herb garden through which Clarence was taken on a tour by the Head Chef, amidst much genuflecting and bowing, to smell the graceful greenery.

In the distance, Clarence spotted a dog anointing the same greens and a slightly worried furrow crossed his brow. His brow furrowed even more when the same dog did a large dump on the asparagus leaves.

'Don't worry,' said the Chef, 'this will only give the food enhanced flavour.'

Clarence, who didn't want to seem naïve, hurriedly agreed with him.

He entered through a side door. The inside was a disappointment. Pity it didn't match the 'ex'. The rooms had been pulled out like a 'de trussed' chicken and decorated in the bland obsessiveness of nothingness so 'au courant'. White walls and bare minimal chairs and tables with the sparsest of table furniture. In fact, a transport café would have had more ambience.

He was guided to a really uncomfortable chair. It had been designed by the sort of person who had never sat in one (such as an architect) and the stretcher bar across the front cut off his circulation. The lighting, also in line with the time, was so low, Clarence felt a need to return to smoking so at least he could use the light from his cigarette end to guide him through the courses. It was a good job he could use his mobile to see the menu which was the size of a small table cloth. Within it, the writing was so minute he needed his magnifying glass 'App' too.

"No mobiles are allowed!" declared the waiter, holding out a silver salver to put it on! At least the gloom helped him avoid looking at the one solitary painting on a far wall. It had what looked to be sheep's entrails slashed across the surface. At least it was in keeping with a culinary theme.

"It's a Charles Ramsbottom," announced the waiter in hushed tones of awe normally reserved for the confessional and as if Charles had surely heard of the man. He hadn't – but he would look him up later to impress the friends at the pub!

He had dressed for the occasion with a conservative suit and tie. Disappointingly, many of the other diners were wearing shorts and tee shirts with vast tattoos covering every bit of skin. And some of them even had ear and lip piercings. Perhaps that's why the lights were so dim? 'New Money', he thought, using the words his elderly mum often used and giving them an old-fashioned look.

The noise level was most unpleasant. Because there were no floor coverings the sounds vibrated through the air from several Hooray Henrys who seemed to want to share their conversations with their fellow diners to everyone else in the room.

The French waiter with the strange accent, froze when Clarence addressed him in his native language.

"I am Greek!, not French," he simpered folding his hands across his chest.

"Ah," said Clarence, reverting to Greek instead.

"Sorry, I should have said Bulgarian," said the waiter and disappeared to be hurriedly replaced by another.

In the distance, loud shouting noises could be heard from the depth of the kitchen.

"It is the master showing the apprentices how to peel a broad bean," declared the replacement waiter.

When the amuse bouche finally arrived, amidst loads of grovelling, it was indeed twelve broad beans displayed as a question mark on the huge white plate. Clarence decided to give the beans a name each just to make things more interesting. The last one was called Algernon and he explained this to the waiter who came to clear his plate. The waiter gave him the same look his wife gave him when she thought he should be committed and excused himself.

The first white wine, to accompany the fish, a Montrachet 2010 was corked. It didn't help when the sommelier told Clarence that "Sir, didn't understand wines and didn't know what he was talking about."

Clarence didn't enlighten him to his thirty years of life amidst the vineyards of Burgundy.

The fish course turned out to be a grotesque dish of baby crayfish legs doused in vast litres of thick tomato sauce. He was given a bib to wear whilst he was instructed to suck up the legs and enjoy.

After some time spent contemplating the gloom, two indifferent courses had passed and Clarence was on his second glass of highly expensive 2010 Chateau Lafite Rothschild Pauillac, which had taken half an hour to pour and decant, when he was asked to come observe the kitchen through a partition between the units. It was not a pretty sight! The master was teaching the apprentices how to decorate one-inch cubes of jelly on huge plates with equally minute leaves of fennel fronds using tweezers. If they didn't get it right, the master hit them on the knuckles with a ruler. This was the main reason the restaurant got its name, not due to specific table laying techniques. The poor young men just wiped their bleeding fingers on their aprons, perspiring with the effort, and carried on.

The main course was the speciality. The dish was called, the 'Ceremony of Thumb'. Amidst layers of groveling service, a huge white veined ball, with little tubes protruding from the surface, appeared from under a silver dome.

"Voila, The Pig's Bladder," cried the waiter from the Balkans, as he lifted up the silver lid.

There followed a ceremony only equalled at a birth: the cutting of the umbilicus, when the tubes were cut with silver scissors and a loud glooping noise was heard, revealing inside a tiny pale piece of chicken as white as a laboratory frog's leg.

"Enjoy," said the simpering waiter again as he minced away.

Clarence paid the bill – it was over £2000. At least he could boast to his friends of the experience. However, as the night got deeper, he felt a strange gnawing in his nether regions and the fact that £2000 had literally gone down the drain didn't comfort him. At least, as he now felt really hungry, he could cook himself a large beef burger. He grinned with great pleasure as the wondrous juices began to decorate his chin.

His wife quietly spied him through the kitchen doorway and smiled before she went back to bed.

# Delicious Centuries

by Paul McCabe

Food is not only something we need and consume daily. It has been a powerful force for centuries and has changed the history of nations and of trade.

Of necessity and biology, humans have sought sources of **salt** since prehistoric times when some of the first settlements were near salt sources. The suffix 'wich' in English, like Norwich and Harwich for example, denotes a place where salt could be found or obtained. The Roman army long ago paid its soldiers in salt because salt was a valuable commodity which could easily be traded for anything. We still use the Roman word for that payment: salarium – in English, salary. Moreover, salt is a preservative of many foods and enables storage of nutritional value. No civilization ever rose and prospered without adequate and continuous salt.

For **spices**, Venice, Cairo, Persia, and Phoenicia were the traders and middlemen in the early days. Portugal's brief time as a powerful empire began with its control of the spice trade. Other Europeans were jealous of the wealth that Portugal's caravels brought back from Africa and India. This was an era of spoiled and smelly food and no refrigeration or medicine.

By 1492 Columbus sailed the ocean blue on behalf of Spain to find Indian spices... he never did see India but found a continent or two on the way, along with gold and silver for the Spanish crown. A generation later, Magellan's ships were the first to circumnavigate the globe, again in a quest for spices, and brought back millions in pepper, cinnamon, nutmeg, and other spices.

Both the British and Dutch East India Companies were founded about 1600 to make big money in spices and to reward investors back in Europe. Later the Dutch wanted more of the market and went to war in Asia with Portugal and with England. The latter bloody and bitter war, lasting decades, ended in 1667, when the Dutch acquired the tiny **nutmeg** island of Run in the East Indies' Banda Islands.

In return the British got a Dutch colony called Nieuw Amsterdam on the much less valuable island of Manhattan. Nutmeg was well-known in those days to ward off the plague which was sweeping Europe, so it had an almost limitless price. Founded on spices and trading profits, India was the British Raj until 1947 and Indonesia was called the Dutch East Indies until 1949.

The lowly **cod fish,** for centuries, was common as the main ingredient in fish and chips. Early explorers of North America noted a bay full of that fish and called it Cape Cod. It too made a major contribution to the rise of the Portuguese empire because the captains had secret maps to the faraway fishing grounds: it could be caught, dried, salted, transported, and sold anywhere. Archeological sites on the Newfoundland coast of Canada found the remains of cod-drying villages of the Vikings. Seaports from Bergen to Palermo have their own cod specialties and recipes.

Cod was the very first export of the American colonies. A large statue called **The Sacred Cod** hangs from the ceiling of the Massachusetts House of Representatives in Boston to mark this tradition. Iceland and the UK fought a series of so-called "codfish wars" from 1958 until 1976 in which ships collided, men were injured, and actual shots were fired; and Iceland threatened to pull out of NATO. It was all about cod fishing rights – important to both nations -- and ended peacefully.

Though Columbus returned spiceless to Europe, he and his explorer successors found many new foods and spread them all over. The most important of these is the king of tubers, native to Peru, where today we find the headquarters of the International Potato Center on the outskirts of Lima. Maybe it is the greatest gift from the New World to the old. **Potatoes** are grown and cooked everywhere from Siberia to South Africa to San Diego with uncounted recipes. Thomas Jefferson brought one home from his time as ambassador in Paris and called it the French fry.

Before these voyages of discovery, Europeans had never seen or tasted cassava, beans, squash, pumpkins, corn, or chilies either. Cacao bushes, the source of chocolate, are also native to the Caribbean. Furthermore, explorers and sailors brought back tomatoes and peanuts, capsicum and peppers, pineapples, avocados, guavas, and papayas. All of these got disseminated around the world, changing kitchens, cuisines, markets, and eating habits. One of Thailand's largest exports today is cassava (manioc). Where would Szechuan cooking and Thai food be without hot chilies? An Italian restaurant with no beans or tomatoes…Are you kidding me?

**Coffee** too has a long history originating in Yemen and Ethiopia. The legend is that monks saw their goats cavorting in the fields after eating the red berries of a certain bush. It soon spread to neighboring Arab countries where they drink it still. In 1683, the Ottoman army laid siege to Vienna for months and was about to win. To make their new Moslem masters happy, local bakers invented a crescent-shaped bread, now called croissant. The Turks never made it into the city because King John of Poland and his 90,000 troops rode to the rescue of Vienna at the last minute. The surprised Turks fled, leaving behind tons of supplies, including coffee beans. A captured soldier showed the Europeans how to brew it and a new industry called the coffeehouse was born. A good thing for the Starbucks company.

**Tea** got started in Yunnan China long ago, but Portuguese missionaries and traders introduced to it Europe in the 1500s. The Dutch used the Chinese Min dialect word TE (not the north China word CHA) when they sold it to Europe. The British loved it and bought so much tea that they had a serious trade deficit with China and forced the Chinese to buy their Bengal opium to balance things out. The result was the Opium wars and the British Crown colony of Hong Kong which lasted until 1997. After water, tea is now the most common drink in the world. The Boston Tea Party in 1773 was a dispute about British taxes on tea in the American colonies. It was a proximate cause of the Revolutionary War which broke out with shooting 16 months later.

Genetic botanical research has shown that all **apples** came from Kazakhstan and spread from there. One well-known apple played an important role in the Bible when Eve ate it in the Garden of Eden. Another famous apple hit Isaac Newton on the head and vastly advanced the new science of physics. Since you cannot copyright common words, two teenagers chose a good name for their new garage-based computer company and the rest is history. That little enterprise, now a renowned brand name, became the Apple we know today, with revenues of $229 billion last year… that's a pretty good apple! For decades, that little town once called Nieuw Amsterdam has had the nickname of The Big Apple.

Cultivated for 7000 years, **olives** and their oil are a key component of the Mediterranean diet from Spain to Egypt and beyond. The olive branch, which has come to symbolize peace, also shows up in the Bible when a dove puts one in Noah's hand at the end of the great flood. Olive trees are mentioned in Homer's Odyssey. Greeks claim that olives first grew in Athens. The Koran called it "a blessed tree." Jesus Christ, the night before he died, visited the Mount of Olives, just east of Jerusalem's old city. The Bible goes on to say that he later ascended to heaven from there. Everyone likes olives.

When we eat any of these things, let's not forget where they came from, how they got to our tables, and the rich and delicious history behind them. There is no sector in the world larger than food and agriculture because we need its products every day. This has been a basic truth since at least 20,000 years ago, when humans first put plows to mother earth and began the long trek toward civilization.

# Donald's Burger

by C.I. Ripples

Your elitist, prehensile little mouth contorts itself around the juicy, one hundred percent pure, pink slime with absolutely no fillers, additives or preservatives, seasoned with a pinch of salt and pepper, topped with a tangy gherkin, pickled in calcium chloride, chopped onions, tomato flavoured liquid sugar, mustard, and a slice of melted, plastic American cheese. All of this encased in a butylated hydroxyanisoled regular bun. It's only just after six p.m. on yet another dull evening and, as usual, I wonder if the patience of Job will be sufficient.

Blood juices run down your orange, saggy cheeks, which you wipe away with the back of your short-fingered hands. I thank God every day that those stubby fingers no longer try to pleasure me, that I don't have to bear the weight of your obese, decrepit body, your flaccid, little penis between my legs. Yes, I count my blessings that sex is on the shelf and that for all your bragging, you are too old for love. I might have married you for upward mobility, to feed a lifestyle, but I did so foremost out of duty: to help our allies. At first, I considered it a win win situation, at least until you became an embarrassment to your nation, a laughing stock in the rest of the world and a threat to those who put you here. I've already told Sergei that this duty is almost more than I can bear.

As such, I positively promote your consumption of a feed I wouldn't even give to Spinee. And as much as I hated our move to this overbearing white house, I know it was necessary to ensure that the day will come when the effect on your endothelial cells will become noticeable, when even your magic genes will succumb, when your battery runs out.    We are slowly seeing results.    Your BMI has risen by four points since I arrived, only one point short of obese. Even better your cholesterol levels.   I am quite proud of this achievement, an increase of fifty-four points in a mere six months. This despite the statins.

"Mel!"

I start, realising I must have zoned out for a moment. I follow your eyes, which are starting to narrow, to the drink that stands on the table. Like King Herod on his throne, you lie on the bed demanding to be fed, to be hydrated. Your brows are knitted together and your jaws tense in your childlike impatience for immediate attention, the immediate satisfaction of your senses. It is both infuriating and pathetic, but I don't say anything, as a tantrum is best avoided.

I cross the room for the carbonated, caramel coloured water, infused with aspartame, phosphoric acid, potassium benzoate, citric acid and caffeine. If this won't kill you, nothing will. Fake sugar, like fake news, constitutes a significant stressor, so we were sure it would only be a matter of time. An ingenious move on our part, yet so simple. The fake sugar in your system will add ever more weight as it triggers insulin, sending your body into fat storage mode.   Your senses will become gradually dulled, hence your cravings for more sickly, sweet snacks. Have you not noticed that the red and pink Starbursts appear miraculously wherever you go?

Although we were quite astounded to find that your blood sugar levels have actually reduced, it is fortuitous that your favourite drink provides yet another addictive weapon – caffeine, which you currently consume at no less than twelve times the recommended dose. A double blessing for me. The lack of sleep ensures not only continued erectile dysfunction, but also compromises your decision-making ability and does much to improve your mania. Hence the ever more frenzied delusional early morning tweets. You tell me that everyone is out to get you. Well, they are, of course. This at least is no hallucination.

Unfortunately, the supposed recent cognitive tests suggest that you haven't lost your grip on reality yet. Progress remains painfully slow. It is disheartening how you continue to improve your propensity for bullshit. On the other hand, only dementia was tested, so it was always unlikely that subtler signs of cognitive decline would show up. We must have faith in what we see.

Your greedy, pasty hands grab the diet coke and suck noisily. For a while we sit just like that, an old man with a narcissistic personality disorder, with an almost young, stunning, leggy, healthy woman. The silence of the room is only broken by your slurps, belches and then an uncontrolled loud outburst from your puckered anus. Its smell almost makes me wretch, the fact that you empty your bowels no more than once or twice a week amplifying the effects of decaying flesh. I do not, however, move away. You beam at me conspiratorially and I give you back a zipped smile.

Checking my watch, I breathe a little sigh of relief: no tedious functions tonight. You'll be watching Anderson Cooper 360 in half an hour, releasing me to my own quarters to watch the latest episode of 'How to Get Away with Murder'.

I turn towards you sweetly; "Would you like your dose of aspirin now or later Donald?"

When you respond in the affirmative, I rise to make the concoction, dissolving the aspirin in diet coke, not forgetting to add a little powdered aconite root and ergot. Once you've downed your medicine, I take the glass and lean into you as closely as I can bear, to kiss you good night. After all, like you, I'm a great believer in intimacy, especially when it comes to one's enemies.

# The Reluctant Chef
(or the way to a man's heart….)

by Renata Kelly

My mother never really attempted to teach me how to cook. She herself learned late, when she found herself in post-war England after her escape from newly Communist Poland. Those had been difficult times for her and my father, who had served the war years in the Polish division of the Royal Air Force in England. Their pre-war years were spent happily in Paris, studying art and architecture respectively. I never asked my mother whether she ever had to cook in Paris but did hear that she allegedly called a friend, in the early days of her sojourn in England, to ask how long one had to boil potatoes.

However, by the time we settled in California, she must have mastered the basics and was even considered a good cook by her friends. Art, however, was always foremost in our family. After all, that was the way my parents earned their living, and I was rarely recruited to do serious work in the kitchen. Eventually I was sent off to boarding school in Santa Barbara and my parents moved from Hollywood to a charming cottage in the middle of a lemon ranch in neighboring Montecito, so close to my school that I was able to become a five-day boarder and go home for the week-ends.

On one of those idyllic week-ends, often spent on the beach or rambling amongst the lemon trees with my dog, my mother approached me with a big smile:

"Today," she announced, "I must teach you to make puff-pastry!"

I was surprised. Why puff-pastry and why today?

"With anchovies," she added triumphantly.

We went to the kitchen, with the sun filtering through honey-suckle that shaded the large window. Bowls, spoons, measuring-cups, flour, a lot of butter and a rolling-pin were recruited for the effort and arranged on the counter under the window. We set to work, with my mother the instructor and myself the executioner. I found the pastry part, which had to be kneaded, hard-going. The dough stuck to my fingers, more flour had to be added with hands encased in something akin to honey, but thicker and more elastic.

Finally, however, the dough coalesced into a plump and cohesive ball. This was then divided into three parts, with each lump placed on a large wooden board and rolled out to a decent thinness. Then came the fun part – small slivers of butter were carefully and abundantly deposited on the rolled-out pastry, the pastry was then folded over and rolled out again. This process was repeated until a glistening sheet of pastry was ready to be divided, with the help of an upturned glass, into circles onto which a salted anchovy could be placed. The circles were then folded over, encasing the anchovy, and sealed into small half-moons with corrugated edges.

That evening, after a long afternoon devoted to the art of puff-pastry, my parents were entertaining guests for dinner. The baking process took place, I believe, sometime just before the guests arrived. As drinks were poured and the sounds of lively conversation came from the living room, my mother helped me pile crispy crescents of anchovy filled puff-pastry onto a platter and ushered me into the living-room with the proud announcement of "Look what Renata's made for you!"

And so the legend was born that I was a fine pastry cook.

Over the years not much effort was made either by myself or my mother to broaden my culinary repertoire. Thus it transpired that on a particular day, when I was already at university, I was again recruited to make my signature dish. Among the guests that evening was Steven, a good friend of my parents, a sometime actor, currently employed in Hollywood, but more significantly, in the eyes of my father, a fine sailor, who had at some point in life circumnavigated the globe. I had known Steven for a fairly long time and as a young teen-ager thought that he was indeed "tall, dark, and handsome" as befitted an actor, though even then I considered him too close in age and appearance to my own father and therefore not worthy of too much attention. However, that day as I entered the living-room with my platter of pastry, Steven actually noticed me.

"Goodness, darling, you *have* grown up!" he intoned in a low voice as I approached him. I smiled politely and offered him a pastry.

"Wonderful," he murmured, helping himself to another crescent, "did you make these?" He looked me up and down approvingly and took a third.

"Yes," I answered, then added casually before moving on to the next guest, "puff-pastry is my specialty!"

During the ensuing summer vacation, Steven was a frequent visitor. He started to pay me a lot of attention, never more than on those days when we ate at home and

I was busy in the kitchen producing puff-pastry or helping my mother with a new dish which she thought I should perfect: beef stroganoff. Steven was full of praise for the tender beef slivers in their creamy, fragrant sauce.

On one of these evenings, after an especially tasty dinner, which featured both the puff-pastry crescents and beef stroganoff, we all took a walk through the blossom-scented lemon grove lit only by a sky full of brilliant stars. Steven and I strolled at some distance behind my parents. In a twist in the path that we were following, Steven stopped and gently took me into his arms.

"Darling," he murmured, "will you marry me?" I was speechless. Was he practicing for one of his TV performances? Did he mean it? What should I say?

As if on cue, he added softly, "You are so lovely and such a good cook!"

That did it. A vista of many years spent in hot kitchens rolling out puff-pastry and slicing beef into slivers stretched before my eyes.

"Steven," I said, disengaging myself from his embrace, "I'm so sorry, but as you know, I'm going back to college next week and I plan to apply to graduate school and do a doctorate in literature. That will take years and years!"

"Darling," he said, taking my hand, "I can wait!"

# In the Dark

### by Lian McCabe

Mr. K walks into the corner and sits on a chair. It's quite unusual for him to wear a fur coat. So, everyone's attention is on him. Their stares follow him to the corner like searchlights, then look quickly away, pretending to search for something else. K doesn't care for his audience. He sits there silently. The light is so dim that no one can see him well anyway.

"I bet he's an outsider, just passing by our town…" Ed whispers.

"I would like to have a fur coat like that…" Elle says with desirable admiration and envy in her eyes, "check it out, the length…maybe he's a hunter? Maybe he sells fur for a living?"

"No, no, no! Haven't you heard the news about the runaway murderer? Look at him, look at him closely, he might be that one. Look at his …"

"Shu-shush, Eric, lower your voice. You don't want any trouble," reprimands Edgar.

"Relax, you guys," Emily raises her hands and gestures for everyone to calm down, "he's been sitting there for ages, looking like he's totally lost. Maybe he doesn't speak our language, doesn't know what to order, ha ha…" Emily imitates the stranger by scratching her head very hard.

"No, you're all wrong…"

"He probably has a gun…"

"Ah, nonsense…"

"He's dangerous…"

"Forget about it, he's a hunter..."

"Maybe there's a 'Wanted Ad' out for him…"

"Come on, stop guessing, he's simply mute…"

"Hey, shush, shush…"

…… ……

That Friday night, everyone, with accompanying hand gestures, is voicing their suggestions. Voices are rising, the four of them almost making a scene, as the noise flows to the corner.

Finally, Mr. K couldn't stand it any longer. "Excuse me, you eggs. Please stop this stupid guessing. I'm not one of you. I'm a kiwi."

# Julia's recipe

by Stephanie Thornton

Once a month, on a Thursday nobody needs to use for anything else, the 'Ladies That Lunch' will gather together in an effort to outdo each other, taking turns to create a lavish meal. They will spend all month beforehand planning cunning strategies and making extraordinary efforts, which, when asked how they prepared the lunch so effortlessly, are dismissed with the mere flick of a hand.

Julia, the ring leader, is the most competitive. She has even resorted to stealing nasturtiums from a neighbour's garden to painstakingly create garlands of flowers to drape around the highly starched table cloths.

When they mention the **LTL** in reverent tones, other people think it's a cricket term and look bewildered. Or perhaps membership to a secret club?

Meanwhile, the ladies' men folk will work for three hours that day. Then lunch for four, making them all equal when it comes to the inevitable hangover the next morning. Everyone needs to arrive back home on an equal footing.

At the very tail end of this glamorous assortment of people, is a rather mouse like lady called Elaine. She has been invited into this hallowed gathering, almost as an afterthought. As an optician, she might be useful in the future, such as for a discount on some designer sunglasses. Some of the members don't know what an optician is and have to look it up. Others pronounce it 'Opticienne', as if it's some sort of strange French word, which makes them seem important. However, she is a lady who actually works for a living and the very mention of the word 'work' conjures up collective sighs of horror. It is certainly never mentioned after, in case the men should hear and think it would be useful for their wives to follow her example. One competitor states, over her much-lifted face in the mirror, as she adjusts her model hat and is out of earshot, that Elaine actually "breast fed her children too – just like a cow." They all give a little gasp and shudder.

Elaine in fact is much more than she seems. She is creative and one of a kind. When one of the group has a fortieth birthday and whilst everyone else is trying to outdo each other spending more and more money on a present to better the rest, Elaine has gone to some trouble to produce an original gift that money can't buy. And she has found time in her busy schedule too. This proves the old adage of 'ask a busy person…and it will get done'.

The recipient, Jane, is one of the crowd they like to poke fun at. Not to her face as that would be too obvious. For many years, she has continued to provide them with parsnips on each and every dining occasion, served up in weird and wonderful concoctions. Originally, she used to grow them in the garden so it had become a custom.

The group think growing your own is truly terrible. Like a farmer who breeds pigs and grows turnips. Or that terrible old TV programme called the 'Good Life'. Ugh!

So, Jane turned the garden into roses and now buys the parsnips from organic food outlets. Or the most expensive green grocer in town. Or the Duchy Estate of

Prince Charles. She has even resorted to buying them from Harrods, if out of season. Or so she says!

On one occasion, she was buying them from a stall at the market from whence she in fact really purchases them, when she spotted one of the group in the distance using the market as a short cut to get to Harvey Nics. She had to quickly hide round the back of the canvas to the consternation of the stall holder, nearly falling over the guy ropes in her haste, until the so-called friend had passed by. She also got soaked in rain water which fell all over her newly rinsed hair from the top of the canvas. It was too late! She had already been spotted by the friend who had pretended not to see her being given the paper bag and her change in the other hand held out in readiness. The friend relayed the tale back to the group.

Now everyone makes fun of this. It has become a secret long standing joke for them all.

On the day of the party, Jane opens her gift from Elaine. A small box containing a bed of straw. On the straw is a wooden plinth upon which is mounted, a 'living sculpture' of a strangely shaped parsnip. The parsnip reclines sideways with what looks like a pair of legs at one end, covered tiny root like hairs. Elaine has put an inscription on the plinth and called it 'Over The Hill' by Henry Moore. Shrieks of laughter fill the room when everyone sees it. Jane is not quite sure what to make of her present. Especially as, over the coming months, the parsnip shrinks day after day until only a withered torso remains. Surely Elaine is not getting at her on reaching forty? She's already quite touchy about it. And is Elaine implying she needed a leg wax due to the hairy bits?

Elaine, however, wouldn't dream of getting at anyone. She is just being original, but as none of the rest have an ounce of talent, they can't see this.

A month later, Julia has had a busy time doing nothing but plan her Thursday. It is her turn to shine. She has been so busy, she hasn't had time to make an entrée but has gone to her local Restaurant and bought it direct from the Chef. This delicious course is well received by everyone including one very pressing guest, a Chinese woman called Diana, who won't take no for an answer when refused the recipe. In despair, Julia rushes to the upstairs phone only to be told by the Chef that he won't give the recipe to anyone. What is she to do?

She returns to the drawing room and hastily makes up how she thinks it may turn out, which they all carefully write down.

The next lunch starts off on an amusing note, when Julia tells them the disgusting tale of how she had visited a restaurant, two weeks earlier, where they had asked her several times if she really wanted, 'avocado with prawns'. She got considerably annoyed when they had asked this, some three times, and even more annoyed when, after half an hour delay, the dish served was an avocado covered in a mysterious pile of black mush.

"Madam did ask for 'avocado with prunes'," simpered the maître d'

She had always cultivated her accent and was not amused that he couldn't follow her 'High English'. Somehow, the reaction to her tale to the assorted listeners did not go down quite as well as she had thought. Most of them would not dream of telling her how stuck up she sounded.

"I was given a plate of sweet cherries when I asked for Sherry," another guest said in the same high tones.

She continued to say that she had heard that Diana had made Julia's recipe for her husband's boss and was not happy when the dish turned out really dreadfully. It had been the consistency of concrete and coloured a strange shade of green. But she had served it anyway as Julia's food had been so delicious. The boss's wife had actually been sick for two days afterwards and the boss had chipped his tooth on it. They'd both left the dinner early in a huff. Diana's husband had had to put up with all the moaning from his boss and grovelled a lot in apology to keep his job. He'd even paid the dental bill. He punished Diana by moving the planned Caribbean holiday to Benidorm instead.

Diana had decided not to come to this lunch.

Julia was forced to own up that she had lied and was relieved the others thought this was very funny. No one liked Diana very much. She had served Peking duck to Julia's husband on one occasion and given him a tiny bit of skin saying the Chinese didn't eat the rest. More peals of laughter!

There followed a pregnant pause whilst they absorbed the truth of the matter. The silence was suddenly broken by Elaine.

"I know that recipe," she suddenly announced.

The group hushed.

"I actually recognised the dish from my chef. We both work next door to each other and he gave me the recipe two years ago now to take off some of my work load and because I had helped his young wife with tips on breast feeding their new baby. I could have given it to you, but he told me it was only for those in 'trade'."

# Health

"Early to bed and early to rise, makes a man healthy, wealthy, and wise."

~ Benjamin Franklin, 1738

# Goodbye to the Demon Tobacco

By Paul McCabe

In Ulaanbaatar Mongolia in 2007, I started smoking Kent cigarettes for social reasons: to build friendship with my new colleagues in the Ministry of Finance. All the men smoked heavily, retreating frequently to the toilets to indulge. I was not in a position to refuse. The windows were open and the temperature was minus 25C. Upon my return to equatorial Singapore a few months later I kept buying cigarettes but switched to Marlboro menthols. Both my parents smoked menthols. My father smoked Kool and my mother smoked Salem or Newport. I have a long history of quitting smoking briefly and of recidivism thereafter. I have wasted a lot of money on nicotine gum, patches, and substitutes.

More recently, at least a half a dozen times, I have bought an expensive prescription pill called Chantix and used it for a month or two successfully. It actually blocks the nerve receptors in the brain crying out for a soothing bath of nicotine molecules. So, I don't want to smoke. If I do smoke while I'm taking Chantix, the cigarette tastes terrible.

Last year I quit during our six-week trip to Europe but started up again soon after our return in June. It costs me about 4000 Baht for the medicine. And once the drug has left my system I find it difficult to resist the temptation to light up. This is especially true at the start of the day (the delicious rush of the first cigarette of the day with morning coffee) and at the end of the day (over a cleansing ale at Miller time).

By October my wife Lian was pushing me hard, so I relented and quit 22 October. The timing was opportune as I was having an eye operation at Bumrungrad Hospital a week later. So far, I've been clean for 3 months. I did sneak one cigarette in December with a discreet friend, but the pleasure was in the sneaking. The cigarette was almost tasteless.

In Burma last month our cruise ship stopped on the river at Pakokku where we had a little tour of the local market followed by a visit to a very low-tech cigar factory. I bought a small pack of five for a dollar. In the dark and smelly factory, we were told that the local tobacco was mixed with sawdust. That evening back on the boat's top deck I smoked one with a beer before dinner. To inhale it was truly wretched and genuinely disgusting. After that I freely gave the other four cigars to Lian. This time I may be really cured.

# 'SARS' a la Grecque

by Renata Kelly

It was the summer of 2003 and we were waiting on the dock of the small port village of Patitiri, on the Greek island of Alonissos, for the arrival of the 'Flying Dolphin', the local hydrofoil that obediently traversed the Aegean Sea between mainland Greece and the Sporades Islands. We trusted that our daughter, Juliet, and our newly minted grandson, Christopher, would be on that boat as planned, having arrived in Athens from Singapore that very morning – no mean journey for a little babe not yet one-year-old. Alonissos had been our holiday home by then for many years. In fact, our two daughters were themselves small children when we first arrived on the island, became enchanted with its beauty and remoteness and purchased our first property there. Now we were preparing to welcome our first grandchild, the first member of the third generation of our family, to claim the pine-clad shores of Alonissos as his 'home away from home'!

Finally, and not quite on time, the yellow 'Flying Dolphin' appeared, rounding the rocky promontory that made it invisible until it made its grand entrance into the semi-circular harbour. We waited anxiously as the boat docked and passengers, tugging at their suitcases on the uneven docking bridge, made their appearance one by one and descended to terra firma. At last we saw Juliet burdened with various soft bags slung over her shoulder and carrying Christopher who had more or less doubled in size since we last saw him at Christmas-time. A kind sailor helped her with her suitcase. Greetings, hugs and kisses followed whilst little Christopher sized us up wisely before finally rewarding us with a smile that revealed a few beautifully white teeth!

"My goodness, he already has teeth!" I exclaimed.

"Yes, Mama, teeth happen, have you forgotten?" Juliet looked at me with daughterly indulgence and the smug knowledge of newly acquired motherhood.

We finally piled into the car and drove down the coast to our house. Juliet was ecstatic to be "home" again and Christopher, despite the long journey and the time change, behaved beautifully, ate well and went to sleep like a model baby.

The next morning, Juliet appeared with Christopher on the breakfast terrace with a worried expression.

"Christopher has a fever," she announced. "I have sponged him down and will give him a dose of Calpol if it persists."

Poor little Christopher sat on his mother's lap, refusing to eat or to respond with a toothy smile to his grandparents' ridiculous efforts at peek-a-boo and other such antics.

Christopher's fever persisted, even rising despite the Calpol, and by late morning we were all worried.

"I'll call Maria," said my husband.

Maria was a great friend and an eminent Athenian doctor, who together with her husband was one of the first non-islanders to purchase land and build a holiday home on Alonissos. She had also for many years been the only doctor on the island and had earned the love and adulation of the islanders for the free medical help that she had given. We got into our car and drove along the only partly paved roads to Maria's house, nestled among pine trees right on the edge of the sea. After greetings and admiring comments about the cherubic little boy in Juliet's arms, Maria got down to examining and prodding. Yes, there was a high fever but no signs of a cough, cold or other flu-like symptoms. Juliet was already worried that Christopher's fever might be caused by a kidney infection and Maria agreed with her diagnosis. She sighed.

"Juliet," she pronounced, "you must take Christopher to Volos to the hospital."

"Oh, no!" Juliet and I exclaimed together.

"You must!" said Maria in a tone with which no one dared to argue. "We cannot take a urine sample here and that's what has to be done! I will call the hospital and, of course, your mother will go with you! Go get the tickets, Ray, now!" she added, addressing my husband.

So that afternoon, tickets secured, Juliet, Christopher and I stepped onto the very same yellow hydrofoil that had brought Juliet and our grandson to Alonissos the day before and which now headed back to the port of Volos, the capital of the Magnesia region.

After three hours, which Christopher spent in fitful sleep, we arrived at our destination and took a taxi along the dusty waterfront, lined with tavernas with their colourful canvas awnings fronting an unimposing row of low-rise houses. At the far end of the harbour we reached our destination, a four-story building presenting an uninviting façade, badly in need of a coat of paint. As we were soon to find out, the reason for the general neglect of the Volos hospital both on the exterior and interior was evident in the huge and noisy building site behind the old building, where a brand-new hospital was to arise in time for the Greek Olympics of 2004.

But at the end of June 2003 we walked into the old hospital entrance hall with its broken floor tiles and after a few inquiries were directed down a broad corridor to a shabby door. There we were told to wait. Soon enough the door opened to reveal a tall figure, wearing very high heels. Black long hair framed a white face where arching black eyebrows, dark eyes and scarlet lips dominated. Juliet and I looked at each other and the same thought formed in our minds – the lady resembled various depictions of Cruella DeVille, the infamous villain of "A 101 Dalmatians". However, she was wearing a white doctor's coat and asked us in a perfectly civil tone to enter her office. Here she listened attentively to Juliet's explanation of Christopher's recent symptoms and past health history.

"So," she intoned in a low voice, "you come yesterday from Singapore?"

"Yes," answered Juliet, "yesterday."

"So," continued Dr. Cruella, "Singapore have SARS, right? Severe Acute Respiratory Syndrome," she added slowly and proudly. "It start in China, but spreading."

"Yes," said Juliet, "but we don't have it any more. At the end of May, the WHO removed Singapore from the list of Infected Areas. We are now free to travel and tourists are arriving in Singapore again by the plane-load!" she added to make sure the doctor understood.

"Ah, I see," replied Cruella adjusting her stethoscope. "Put him here." She indicated an examination bed covered with a sheet that had seen better days. Christopher balked and clung to Juliet.

"He afraid," she added.

196

Then with an apparent change of mind, Dr. Cruella stood up and announced: "We do tests now. Wait here." With that she swept out of the door, closing it carefully behind her.

Christopher began to whimper softly.

"He might be hungry," worried Juliet. "Where do you think she's gone?"

"Who knows," I replied. "Maybe she wants to arrange for a urine test to see whether Christopher has a kidney infection? Does he still have a fever?"

"I think so, but why didn't she take his temperature or listen to his chest?"

At that point the door opened and Dr. Cruella entered, followed by two male colleagues shorter than her by a head. She looked at us and smiled a far from reassuring smile.

"Come with us," she motioned.

We followed the three doctors obediently down the corridor and into the entrance hall, which suddenly seemed to be full of people. Maybe visiting hours? They opened a door on one side of the hall and ushered us into a small room which appeared to serve as a storage space for old mattresses. It also had one cot and one chair.

"Wait!" they said in unison as they exited the room.

"What on earth do you think they're doing?" exclaimed Juliet.

"I don't know," I answered, trying not to show my anxiety. "Maybe," I ventured, "they suspect that Christopher has SARS?"

"How ridiculous!" stormed Juliet. "The Singapore Surgeon General and the WHO proclaimed Singapore SARS-free a month ago and we never even had a lot of cases! Why are we here?" Juliet seemed on the verge of tears.

At that moment the door opened. Three figures dressed in green moon-walker gear, with helmets, gloves and boots appeared in the doorway. We gasped; Christopher burst into tears.

"We must test," said a muffled voice. "Put baby in cot."

Juliet hugged Christopher. "What are you testing for? He doesn't have SARS! IT'S IMPOSSIBLE!"

"Put baby in cot," came the reply. "And you must leave room."

"NO!" Juliet was nearly shouting.

"Please," came from one of the moon-walkers, "will not take long."

"We better do what they tell us," I tugged at Juliet's sleeve.

She put Christopher in the cot and we were shepherded out of the room by the tallest of the moon-walkers.

Christopher started crying in earnest and we could hear him even through the closed door. Juliet was likewise sobbing, but dialling Nicholas, her husband, in Singapore on her mobile. I took out my phone and called Ray.

"You can't believe what they're doing!" I yelled. "They think Christopher has SARS, yet they shove us out into the hall with dozens of people! Please DO something!"

"Calm down. I'll call Maria right away," Ray reassured me and put down the phone.

Juliet was talking to Nicholas.

"He's going to get someone from the Ministry of Health to call the Hospital in Volos!" she told me.

"Maybe that someone could also call Maria, who could then explain things in Greek to the doctors here," I suggested.

"Okay, both," she agreed and conveyed the message to Nicholas before disconnecting.

We stood by the door and could still hear Christopher crying desperately.

"I'm going in," said Juliet, "I don't care what those idiots say!"

Just then the door opened and the three moon-walkers came out and motioned us to go inside. Juliet rushed to the cot to retrieve poor sobbing Christopher. The door closed. It was already dark outside; we had lost track of time. Juliet found a bottle of milk and a jar of food for Christopher, who after the trauma of the medical examination seemed to have regained his appetite. I called Ray again. Maria who had impeccable medical connections in Athens was on our case.

We waited.

After an hour or so the door finally opened and a kindly-looking lady doctor motioned us to follow her. We were taken up to the paediatric ward on the third floor and put in a room with a cot and a bed, not in the larger rooms with many beds and numerous family members in attendance.

As we settled Christopher into his cot, the doctor smiled and announced: "I examine him, okay?" She took his temperature, listened to his chest, looked at his throat and ears.

"Has infection in ear," she announced. "Must take antibiotic. I bring," she added as she left the room.

Relief flooded over us. Juliet had tears in her eyes as she thanked the pleasant paediatrician who had returned as she promised with the antibiotic and helped to administer the first dose.

"He better tomorrow for sure!" she said reassuringly, patting Juliet's arm and giving me a smile.

As soon as the doctor left, we called our respective husbands and relayed our side of the story.

"And did someone from Singapore call Maria?" I asked. "And did she talk to the doctors in Volos?"

Yes, indeed, the Surgeon General himself had called Maria from Singapore, Maria then called the Greek Minister of Health and the Minister called the Director of the Volos hospital and told him not to make a fool of himself! As for the three moon-walkers, their fate was unknown.

The next day Christopher's temperature was nearly back to normal. We were more than anxious to leave and finally succeeded in persuading the kind ward paediatrician to discharge Christopher, who had regained his high spirits and was bouncing up and down in his cot, holding on to the railing. I hurried out of the hospital and secured tickets for the afternoon ferry.

As we stood on the deck of our ferry in the fresh air and warm afternoon sun we didn't care that it would take us nearly six hours to reach our destination. The traditional ferries were of course a much slower form of sea transport than the more modern hydrofoils. We looked with relief at the diminishing waterfront of dusty Volos, a town built on the site of ancient Iolcos from whence legendary Jason and his Argonauts departed on the 'Argo' in search of the Golden Fleece. We would trace the same route taken by the 'Argo', sailing along the mountainous Pillion Peninsula, passing the islands of Skiathos and Skopelos with their picturesque, red-roofed village houses to reach our own Alonissos, known in antiquity as the island of Ikos.

Jason of course sailed beyond Ikos in search of adventure, but then that is another story.

# They Watch You Sleep

by AL Seth

Fatal Familial Insomnia – 'fatal,' a death sentence upon my life. There had been only two documented cases before, one in Italy in the fifties and the second somewhere in the Midwest in the eighties. All died within eight months of diagnosis. The cause of death was speculated to be dementia. Funny how there's a 'demon' in 'dementia', although I don't believe in such superstitious nonsense. As I was to find out, I was half wrong, demons don't come from the fiery heart of hell but the darkest corners of our minds.

I first noticed this ailment in my younger years when I attended boarding school. I remember lying awake throughout the night while the rest of the world slept in peace. Something always kept me up in those dark dormitories, as though the darkness itself was waiting for me to sleep. I would never recall the sensation I had had the previous night due to the busy day ahead, but it wasn't before long that I realized my condition was far from natural.

When I finished school, I decided to study insomnia and make it my life's work. Getting into medical school was easy. What was not easy, was lecturing these professors with decades of education and no imagination. After all, there being only two recorded cases in history, it was hardly an attractive profession. As I confided my condition, the prevailing response was merely anxiety or that I had had too much coffee. Ridiculous.

A year into my research I was on the verge of giving up on the mystery of my sporadic insomnia for good. No one seemed interested in finding out what makes an individual stay awake whole nights on end. There were hardly any books on the subject, hardly any research done, medical or even psychological. I did come across a book on how the alignment of stars might affect sleep patterns or how an individual's aura might be out of synch, thus leaving them in a non-peaceful state. How such superstitious nonsense could be found in the library of such a prestigious medical school was beyond me. Perhaps I was in the wrong place.

It wasn't before long that I realized that, to find the cure for my insomnia, I would have to conduct my own experiments. When you graduate from the most prestigious medical school with highest distinction, you get more attention than you ask for. One particular party who approached me was the government with a job offer for military research. Reluctant at first with this change of plan, for I knew that whatever they wanted from me was not in my own interest, I accepted the offer, albeit with a condition: I told them that I needed subjects to perform a certain experiment, the result of which would be accredited as mine exclusively. When they asked me what the experiments included, I was cautious to not give too much detail. I simply told them that I wanted to do experiments on the unconscious or sub-conscious levels of the human mind. I went in further detail using jargons and theories, which I knew would bore and dull them into saying yes, and, lo and behold, permission was granted.

Fifty subjects arrived – political prisoners and the usual undesirables. I wouldn't have been surprised if many of the prisoners were on death-row. I know I was. I neither cared for their names nor their crimes. The offer was simple, 'stay awake for thirty days and you go free.' I wanted to shove them all into the test chamber, but I was only allowed five. They'd have to do.

The lab was deep underground. The test chamber was the lowest section. There was nothing to indicate the existence of an outside world. Only bright neon lights illuminated the long rectangular chamber with hidden cameras and microphones recording everything. Chemicals were being dissolved into the air ventilation. All these lab rats had to do was breathe.

The first day proved that the chemicals worked. They stayed awake the whole night and I watched them. They talked and made jokes about the sheer simplicity of the situation and what they would do once they went free.

The second day there was hardly any talking. They just looked bored, but I told myself I had to be patient. A result was inevitable, fatal or otherwise.

It wasn't until the midnight of the fourth day that things started to happen. By now the subjects had stopped talking and barely acknowledged each other. Each had taken to himself. Then there was a sound, the first recording of a voice in over a day. One was talking to the far corner of the chamber and was shaking back and forth, as though pleading for something or praying to someone. The others hardly noticed.

Within two days, all the prisoners were unquiet, but it was hardly talking. The first was crying and whimpering endlessly. The second couldn't stop roaring with laughter as his eyes bulged out of their sockets. The third covered his face as he screamed and screamed until his voice cracked and he started bleeding from his throat. It was difficult to understand what the fourth was doing with the sound he made, but then it turned out to be ecstatic screams of climax as he masturbated and ejaculated. The fifth was quiet for the most part until bursts of yells emanated from him. I can only speculate that these subjects could no longer tell their dreams and memories from reality. At this point all of them had stopped eating or drinking, but somehow, something... was keeping them alive. I'd never felt more positive in my life about my speculation. For the first time since those long nights awake full of wonder, I finally felt that the answer was within reach. What could get in the way of such uncharted discoveries? Oh, what indeed...

By the ninth day, the doctors and nurses here began to feel squeamish. One of the subjects began to cover each camera with his faeces and thus blinded us to whatever was going on inside the chamber. The only indication that they were still alive was the sounds they made. These became worse and worse, becoming more and more unnatural until they were hardly human. Only the knowledge that humans had been put into the chamber could comfort them that humans were making such noises. They wanted the experiments to stop for pity's sake.

They had no imagination. Didn't they realize the progress that was being made? Was I the only one who could see such progress, who could see the future? Couldn't they imagine the implications of the results being made right before their eyes? All they had to do was get their hands dirtier. None of them were innocent anyway, the doctors no less than the subjects.

On the tenth day all the screaming stopped and, alas, I conceded to the sympathies of these humane scientists.

My experiment was, however, far from over. We decided to enter the test chamber, uncertain of the horrors, if any, to be found inside. Due to the silence and our inability to see what was going on inside, we took the guards with us, their assault rifles at the ready. We announced through the speakers that we were entering, warning that we were armed and ready for any attack that might come our way. When the door of the test chamber opened, the horrors were revealed. The first thing to hit us was the smell; a reeking, dank and rotten odour assaulted our senses and disoriented us. Subject two lay dead with his belly burst open and organs missing. I would not have been surprised if he had been eaten by the others. Subject four looked up as he chewed on something bloody in his hand. As I approached I realised that it was his fingers he was chewing and that what had been his hand was now nothing more than a bloody stump with visible bone. He looked at me like a rabid dog would as he ate his food. As I backed away, he launched himself at me but was shot by the guards – dead.

The three that remained refused to eat or sleep. They could barely comprehend our presence. Subject one could not stop pleading in terror. What he wanted was barely comprehensible. Subject three could hardly be constrained or would scramble to the darkest corner of the infirmary with his face turned away. What in his own mind's conjuring could have terrified him out of sanity one can only imagine. These two were as good as dead, but I was determined to keep them alive as long as possible. Any result was a good result at this point of no return.

I had some confidence in subject five as he recovered. Like the others, he refused to sleep or eat. He would not look anyone in the eyes and, when he managed it, would beg to be put back in the test chamber. He refused anaesthetics or painkillers of any kind. Within a couple of days, however, he began to respond. The subject had forgotten his name, where he was or why he was in the infirmary. He only begged to be put back in the chamber. When asked what he saw and who he kept talking to he replied, "To them – the watchers – watching you – sleeping." When asked what these 'watchers' wanted, he replied, "to watch you."

Fascinating. Were these watchers some form of psychological malice lurking in the darkness of all our minds? Were they some inner psychological self that Jung and Freud has innocently labeled the 'id?' Were they something else, something unknowable but merely speculated on by unrested minds? Were they in the dormitories of my mind in those dark nights waiting for me to sleep? Whatever these 'watchers' were, I had to find out more…

Day twenty – the other two subjects had died rather wastefully, but number five, my miracle, gained a sense of self at last, even it it wasn't his former self. When asked who he was, he'd say, "We're you – what you become – when you don't sleep – we're the creatures – you nurture – and restrain – by sleeping – your true nature – lurking beneath – your sanity – we're you – inside out – for too long – hidden away – and forgotten – but now – we're rising – and we won't – let you sleep – in peace – ever again." When asked what he wanted, the replies went from "to watch you," to "be left alone."

Patient five was stable enough to be studied and researched. I had full confidence in his physical recovery, although whether his mind would recover was uncertain.

I told him that I had to find a cure for my own insomnia. He laughed and pointed directly at my eyes. In that moment, I could tell that he was saying, "You'll see – you – will – see..."

When an alarm was raised on the thirtieth day, I was certain all was lost if he were to die. What I was not prepared for was far more sinister. I was told by a nurse that he had escaped from the infirmary and was back in the test chamber. I insisted on going down there to persuade him myself. He had after all shown signs of improvement. Upon my arrival in the chamber, I found him sitting in the corner with his face turned away, shivering. I spoke to him, knowing that whoever he was or whatever he'd become, the ability to reason was not lost on him. He did not reply. I knew he did not want to leave, but it was not his choice to make. I told him that either he co-operated or force would be used against him. He seemed unresponsive to my words. But then, when I turned to leave and get more help, the door of the test-chamber was slammed shut in my face.

At first I thought it was a mistake and that it would only be a matter of time before they realized I was in here. But then time went by, minutes vanished into thin air and hours became days. I shouted at them to release me, but only the echo heard me. I pleaded with them, but were they even there? I tried to comprehend exactly what they had in mind locking me in here. Was I to learn a lesson? Had I done something wrong? Was it some sort of test, or jest? Or, worst of all, was all this merely in my head? Had my spreading insomnia gotten the better of me? Either way, I had to get the door open. I had to help subject five.

Whatever the reason, I knew they were watching me, hating me, laughing at me. They still do. I had a notebook and a pen in my pocket when I entered the chamber. The least I could do was write down everything I'd learned. Number five sometimes talks to me like a normal person. At other times he just... watches me, the only sign he isn't dead.

I've learned not to hide from them in the shadows. I've learned not to look at them in the eyes – it keeps you awake, I think. I don't remember sleeping or waking up anymore. People visit me sometimes. Somehow, they can walk through walls and I catch myself talking to them without knowing what I'm saying. None of them offer to help me or even seem to notice that I'm trapped down here. How long has it been? I've lost track of time and I'm out of ink. I've had to use my blood to replace it in my pen. The only thing I can hope for now is that they run out of these chemicals keeping me awake. Just keep breathing, it's only dementia. No demons down here.

# Who's a Hypochondriac?

by Paige Turner

12 Prescott Avenue
Burwood,
Victoria, 3145

Dear Charlie

You're always telling your father and me to take care of ourselves, so I thought you'd be interested to learn the results of our latest check-ups at the doctor. You know he'll only go to Dr. Knot as he can't abide the young whipper snappers the medical fraternities turn out these days, but sadly Dr. Knot finally succumbed to old age a few weeks ago. I'd say he was helped along by many tots of rum, but your father won't hear of this, so don't mention it to him when you speak to him. So, he finally agreed to see someone else for his annual prostate exam and to measure his PSA levels. They sent him to the loveliest chap, Dr. Ravi Chandran, who, well let's face it, is a bit on the dark-skinned side, but he speaks such perfect English, you wouldn't guess it. We are all for inclusion, even our newspaper delivery boy has been tinged with a tar brush somewhere way back.

Dr. Ravi gave your father an all clear for another year, so he's happy with that, although he did advise him that climbing the ladder to clean the gutters might perhaps be a bit beyond him at the age of 83. You can imagine what your father said, "I'm not paying someone to do what I can do in fifteen minutes!" He's conveniently forgotten the ambulance ride we took when he tried to use the chainsaw to trim the gum tree branches last summer and how long his broken arm took to heal. That is one of the pleasures of getting old: when things are unpleasant your short-term memory will soon forget it!

I'm still happy with Dr. Margaret, although on a few of my visits she's had the nerve to tell me she thinks I'm a hypochondriac who self-diagnoses! I'm surprised there's no degree in sarcasm up on her wall along with all her others. She really does lay it on. I believe, if you don't use the I-pad thingy to look up information what use is it? Charlie, I'm so pleased to finally find names for every medical issue I have. Plus, I've made a new friend at the Broadband CCC helpline. Her name is Priya and we found we were chatting on the phone so much when she helped me set up our account, that we now schedule a weekly chat on Monday afternoons during her tea break. She's getting pressure from her parents to marry but she'd like to travel. I told her about you, you could chat to her next time you come to visit. She's seems delightful and is ever so helpful.

Back to Dr. Margaret, I had been extremely tired but when I told her I had chronic fatigue syndrome, she harrumphed and said I was highly inclined to the power of suggestion and I'd overdone it in the garden. I didn't tell her about the article on chronic fatigue in the *Age* newspaper. Similarly, she didn't agree with me when I suggested my swollen ankles might be caused by gout or gangrene. I told her I've seen my friends in the nursing home with both and they also had swollen ankles. "Dottie, next time you do a five kilometre bike ride, try icing your ankles afterward and the swelling will go down," she replied. Even I had to agree with her that the idea I might be pregnant was perhaps a bit far-fetched. There are a lot of older mums in Italy now, perhaps not in their late 70s though.

When we got back from the bus tour of the top-end I told her I wasn't feeling well and thought I might've caught malaria, (there were loads of mosquitos in the national parks up there Charlie). She patted my hand in a fairly dismissive way, assuring me malaria had been eradicated in Australia in 1981 and that I am tropical disease free. "Why do I feel so bad then? Maybe you should just shoot me now." "Ok" she said, "I can squeeze it in on Thursday afternoon, would that work for you Dottie?" Charlie, I would just like to be taken seriously for once! Who knew that leprosy symptoms were so similar to contact dermatitis? I honestly thought my fingers were going to drop off any minute. However, I will wear my gardening gloves next time I'm weeding the tomato plants.

I didn't want to tell you, but I found a lump in my armpit recently. I always do my monthly self-examination faithfully. Your father offered to cut it out for me, but I declined since he wouldn't be able to see well enough to stitch it up and it didn't work out so well the time he doctored himself to remove that mole on his arm. Talk about gangrene-like symptoms! Anyhow, I managed to get an appointment with Dr. Sceptical herself and she did give me a thorough examination without rolling her eyes once or making any ironic comments laced in sarcasm. She took a sample for biopsy and sent it off to a lab. I had to wait for a week for the results and during that time Dr. Google was NOT my friend as lumps are often tumours and Charlie, I don't think I could handle chemo or radiation if they were my options. A week later, the nurse called me to say Dr. Margaret wanted to give me the results, and no they couldn't tell me over the phone. I don't mind telling you Charlie: my mind was imagining all sorts of scenarios, not made any better when they said I should get someone to drive me to the office. Well, bless me if when we got there, Dr. Margaret calmly announced I have a nasty carbuncle that she could excise immediately which would need stitches and I would be sore for a few days and probably not up to driving myself home. I'm on antibiotics and it all should clear up soon. So, I think I'll stick with Dr. Margaret, after all she does seem to have a sense of humour and well, better the devil you know. I might stop reading though; it's giving me a headache.

Love Mum xxx

# Taxing Fat

By C.I. Ripples

Scrutinising myself in the mirror, as I indulge in my Häagen-Dazs Chocolate Peanut Butter ice-cream, I am delighting in the lean frame I present, when right before my very eyes I begin to expand: my hips widen; my stomach bulges; I have thighs like a dobbin; a tiny head to top it all. I must be at the funfair looking in a distorting mirror, I think, but then I notice people behind me laughing, pointing and wagging their fingers, chanting:

> *Fat, fat, big as a horse*
> *Stuffing your thighs without remorse.*
> *Fat, fat, big as a bale of cotton,*
> *Your patriotic duty now forgotten*
> *Fat, fat, big as a butterball,*
> *A criminal affront to us all*
> *Leave, leave, you big fat slob*
> *Before you become the victim of this mob*

I try to tell them that it's the mirror, that I am truly only a BMI of twenty, but their emaciated forms continue to heckle and threaten to overwhelm me, grabbing at my fat form, as if to suffocate me, even to devour me. My body seems weighted down, my legs heavy as lead, but I manage finally to escape, thighs rubbing together with every step.

Heart pounding, I wake up with a feeling of dread, damp from the terror of my worst fears. It's not the fat shaming that terrifies me, but the flabby thighs. In the heavy darkness I feel for the outline of my body under the sheets and breathe a sigh of relief. I then check my phone: Five am. There's no point in sleep now.

So, I rise with the lightness of dawn. Before hosing down the smell of my nightmare, I check my weight as I do every morning. It hasn't inched up, despite my sense of weightfulness. I consider the irony, that in the old days the way up, used to be so much more arduous, than the way down. These days, the way down the scales is gruelling and its maintenance down right taxing.

Measured, weighed and groomed, I smooth down my skirt, check myself in the mirror with focused intent for fat globules and bulges. I seem outwardly restored but am as always shocked that the person I see does not reflect the real, fat me. I can sense my fatness oozing out, making itself known by my heart shaped face that so easily runs to fat, by the puffiness of my eyes through lack of sleep, telling me I can't hide.

I really can't face breakfast after the horror of this night, and reject it as unnecessary calories, even if I know I will be ruining my metabolism for the day. On my way out the door into the brisk fair morning, I rummage in my bag to check that I at least have my protein bar for emergencies. Then I walk to the underground, and hang on to the tube handles, fighting for space with the swaying commuter crowd. You see, standing burns more calories than sitting, and anyway, only the thin or elderly are allowed that luxury. Finally, I drag myself the fifteen-minute leg to the office in Potbelly Street. Still the sensation of depressed heaviness has not lifted and I am genuinely surprised that I pass through the office BMI sensors without any problem – a reading of twenty-four point five.

By lunchtime I can stand my starved desolation no more. Instead of going to my usual haunt 'The Detox Kitchen' with BMI twenty-one Margery, I invent an excuse and continue past Monsoon, then White Stuff and enter 'The Nude Café', hoping I look like someone entitled to do so. The name itself points its accusing fingers at me, as if it can see the truth underneath my skin. I order the carrot cake, my face carefully devoid of expression, knowing full well the piece will contain more calories than a Mars Bar, more than a quarter of my recommended daily intake. I know full well the tooth sensor will send an instant message to HMRC[7] as soon as I bite into it, to add a penalty to my already hefty tax bill. Every one with a BMI of under twenty-five, that is less than one-year old, is chipped. Sweetness is expensive, especially if you are still on probation.

I scoop the butter frosting off the carrot cake and tell myself that a little bit of what you fancy is good for you, that today I don't care. I do care, but my dream has really shaken me and I find the gluttonous content of the cake comforting, reminding me of my carefree days. I tell myself that I am normally abstemious, have held my BMI for six months now and would soon move into the Sl. tax code. That I have already won the war and can afford it.

At least I no longer have to pay for the compulsory annual medicals as I had when my BMI was over thirty. Even with the fifty percent discount when I dropped to twenty-nine, these medicals had been a drain on my

---

[7] Her Majesty's Revenue & Customs – UK government department responsible for taxes

216

finances.   And the obese super tax of an additional twenty-five percent on the income tax I already paid, had made it almost impossible to eat! I had been more than relieved when two years ago its load had been lightened to fifteen percent.  If I maintained my current BMI, my annual medicals would be paid for by the National Health, my tax levy erased. You might consider that I am obsessed with my tax heavy weight, or rather aspirations of thinness.   These days, however, we are all obsessed with this rather than any of our other imperfections. We've been driven to it by the government Fat Tax.

When I was thirteen years old with a BMI of thirty-two, part of the sixty-two percent of the population that was classified as overweight or obese, the government decided it could, or would, no longer fund the country's overindulgence.   Parliament voted overwhelmingly that obesity was not a disease but a lifestyle choice. As such, it would no longer pay for weight related illnesses, which took up more of the annual public spending budget than even defence!  If the trend continued, sixty-nine percent would be overweight or obese by 2030, with associated health care costs of fifty-four billion pounds per annum.

   At first it was a sugar tax on drinks, which we were told was not a punishment, but to get us back into the shape we were meant to be. The sugar levy of eighteen pence for drinks with a sugar content of 5g per 100ml, and twenty-four pence for those with 8g, came into effect in April of 2018.   It had little impact on me as I have never been partial to sodas and the like. It had little effect on those that did, they just added their own sweeteners to the sugar reduced drinks churned out by the beverage companies.   Those with a normal BMI screamed that it was minority discrimination; that it wasn't their problem; that the fatter selves lacked self-control; that fat people were like alcoholics and drug addicts, who always made excuses.

Then, at the Convention on Obesity that summer of 2019, Britain became a signatory with 162 other nations to the Slim Agreement, which set global targets for weight reduction. The members agreed that food had become entertainment rather than an existential necessity in most of the world. New rules were needed in the form of food and beverage taxes based on BMI status, which could be easily monitored with modern day technology. The only countries that didn't sign of course were those that suffered from hunger such as Bangladesh, Burkina Faso and Benin, or those in the midst of ongoing conflicts such as Syria, Somalia and South Sudan.

The new rules, however, took the starch right out of me. When I received my national insurance number just after my sixteenth birthday, I was classified as Ob and my tax rate was adjusted accordingly. At this stage it was my parents who bore the punishment: an increase of twenty-five percent tax on one fifth of the household income tax until I either dropped in BMI or became responsible for my own tax. It was financially punitive and humiliating not only for them but also for me. I had to bear the constant digs and recriminations as to what I was costing my family. It was time for me to lose my fat friend.

So, as for so many of us, that was the end of potato skins, nachos, big Macs and chicken wings, all that fat drenched junk and processed food, that had been my staple diet. McDonalds quickly lost and almost went out of business, although most cities still have one exclusive and extortionate relic, as a reminder of the good old gluttonous days. It is now our patriotic duty to be slim. Not thin, mind you, as that also incurs a fine. Of course, if you can medically prove to have a fat or thin condition you can get a zero rating. But especially for us fatties this is difficult to get as most doctors will blame our corpulence on saliva glands which can't resist sugar or fat. They are right of course, as between you and me and the rest of us, I have only as much willpower as my tax status allows.

Even in The Nude Café, the size of cookies, sugary and chocolaty, has been reduced drastically. Lattes, cappuccinos and sickly-sweet coffee flavourings may not yet have been exchanged for Americanos, but unless you have the right BMI of eighteen point five, when you can indulge tax free, it's too high a price to pay.

The whole system is policed by smart technology. As soon as you approach any restaurant, café or even supermarket, your BMI status is read from your smart phone by the BMI reader at the till and tax added accordingly. In the supermarket, goods are barcoded with their BMI requirements and tax added at the checkout. Online booking systems require your BMI status at the time of booking flights, trains, even theatre and cinema seats. The BMI thirty-plussers suffer a whopping, great big seventy-five percent surcharge, and are relegated to the fat zones with widened seats. You see, the thin were fed up with being wedged in between the fat, their obese forearms spreading into their space.

As I look at the lithe streamlined BMIs that surround me, I have to admit that these measures have had their impact. In the last five years the levels of overweight and obese have reduced by thirty-six percent according to the government, with an estimated health related saving of fifteen billion pounds per annum. It does not surprise me. No one can afford this health tax. To be on the curvy side, even if not exactly a crime, is now certainly considered a civil offence. Fat is no longer a politically incorrect word, even if fat bashing has become punishable akin to racism.

As for me, I no longer suffer from not being able to fit in too small seats, not being able to walk without huffing and puffing, from cruel stares and comments. I now even have a BMI twenty boyfriend, where before I moved into the Ov tax bracket, my crushes had been unrequited as no one I wanted to kiss wanted to kiss my tax status. Now I can plan for a child, should I so desire, a privilege declined to those in the Ov and Ob tax rating – they are not considered responsible enough for parenthood. Clothes have also become cheaper, being priced on the size of your curves, the argument being that bigger sizes need more material and as such are not only costlier, but also environmentally unfriendly.

But I miss the old days. I may not have had a boyfriend, but I hadn't cared as my amorous relationship had always been with junk food or anything sugary and fatty, especially McDonalds' Triple Thick Chocolate Milkshake with an extra topping of cream, even if it did have 1160 calories. I had been sent to counsellors, nutritionists, psychologists and put on never ending weight loss programs. None of them understood that I had no underlying problem. I did not come from a broken home, had loving parents, did well at school and didn't suffer from bullying. I just loved my food more than I minded the weight, which just kept piling on. I would google images of paintings by Renoir, Lucien Freud, or Rueben and tell myself that fat used to be fashionable and might be once more. You could say I was in denial, that I was addicted.

My phone vibrates as I drain my Americano, scrape the last of the frosting off the plate. It's a message from HMRC informing me that this being my first offence, there is only a penalty of fifteen pounds. Do it again and they will extend my probation for another six months.

# Confined Pickles

by Lian McCabe

<u>Good news - bun in the oven</u>

"Oh, my God! Sweetie, do you mean…?" Lee rushes out of the bathroom, with a wide grin, eyes shining with happiness, his whole face flushed with a pink glow. He waves the white pregnancy test stick high above his head.

"Am I …?" "I am a dad now!" Lee comes over and holds Lily tightly in his arms, kissing her on her lips.

"Yes, honey, we made it."

"This time, we really need to be careful, okay? I'll call my mom and ask her to come over and take extra care of you…"

Yes, they have to be careful. About a year ago, their washing machine had broken down and Lily had had to carry water urns from one room to the another, to fill it up, so it would work. Later that day, she'd noticed a trail of blood on the floor and fainted. She and Lee were told by the gynaecologist that she had unfortunately miscarried.

Both Lee and Lily's parents live in the same city, so, on hearing this happy news, their two mothers come to the apartment without delay.

"Thank you for coming, you two dear Moms. I will be careful. I don't think I need any help right now. I'm fine…"

222

Jane, Lily's mother-in-law tries to keep her sitting on sofa, "Of course, you need our help. You've lost one, what if anything happens again this time, I can't just…"

"Mom! What are you talking about! Don't curse us! We'll be fine." Lee is not pleased to hear her concerns.

"I didn't mean to imply anything. You know I only have the best of intentions." Jane feels herself wronged by her own son and she sends a look for help to Linda, Lily's mother.

"Everyone, let's take it easy. No pressure on anyone. Jane and I have experience in these matters, so let us give you some advice. Lily, this is your second time, you have to take some precautions at least for the first three months. Even your doctor suggests you do so, right? And in the meanwhile, there are books and websites that you and Lee can read, visit and learn by yourselves on how to be a happy and healthy pregnant couple? Jane and I live nearby, you can call us if you need help, and we will stop by occasionally, just to check up on you, okay?"

"I agree. I agree 120 per cent." Jane says.

Lee keeps nodding his head, "thank you, Mom!"

"Yes, Mom, I just knew you would understand." As soon as Lily blurts out these words, she feels she might have said something to offend Jane. But she doesn't want to think too much about this, as she knows that from now on and for the following nine months, she will be the empress dowager in this family.

The prenatal confinement

Considering Lily's past miscarriage and her slight build, her gynaecologist suggests she reduce her activities and bans any weight-lifting or fast-paced movement. After the delicate embryo becomes solid and strong, the doctor will allow regular exercise.

Lily is a talented artist. She weaves wool products in her own studio, which is the room next to their kitchen. Her work, especially the charming hats, lovely sweaters, creative stuffed animals and pillows is very popular online. She enjoys making everything by her own skilled hands.

The next day, Lily gets up as usual and works in her studio for an hour to complete a customer's order, then walks to the kitchen to make some toast with peanut butter. She pours a glass of milk directly from the fridge. Just as she takes the first bite, the doorbell rings. Lily opens the door and in comes Jane, two big bags in hand, sweat dripping from her forehead.

"Morning, Mom. How are you?" Lily asks in surprise.

"I hope you haven't eaten breakfast yet," says Jane, as she walks in without greeting.

"Here, I cooked some chicken stew for you. I urged Lee's father to buy this hen yesterday after Lee called us. It's been on the stove since last night. I called Lee this morning to make sure you're up…"

Talking non-stop, Jane puts one bag on the living room floor, another on the kitchen table, urging Lily to sit down and enjoy the stew.

"What's this? Lily, you're not supposed to have anything cold! Let me heat up the milk for you. And peanut butter toast? That's not good enough! Just sit down, let me get you a bowl."

Lily is taken aback, unused as she is to another woman who's not her mother cooking, preparing, or delivering food to her. "Mom, I can do it myself, you don't have to spoil me."

224

"Everything is for my lovely chubby grandson." Jane realises her lack of tact adding, "Of course, for you, too." But Jane has always been easy to read.

"Mom, we don't even know if it's a boy or girl yet. How can you be so sure?" Lily chuckles.

"I just know it. I have this feeling. Lily, quick, sit down and try the chicken stew. It's good for both you and the baby. It's still very warm." Jane presses on and hands the bowl to Lily.

"Thank you, Mom, you're so good to me." Then she scoops the chicken stew onto her spoon and tastes it, "it's very delicious, brrr…"

Lily feels immediately nauseous and rushes to the bathroom to vomit, although little comes out. She rinses her mouth and walks back out, apologizing to Jane, "I am so sorry mom, I didn't mean to throw up your chicken stew, it's very tasty, but I couldn't control myself. It's my hormones… sorry Mom, please…"

"It's okay, don't worry. Poor girl, it's the morning sickness." Jane murmurs in a lower voice, "Poor kid can't enjoy such delicacy. Hmm, when I was pregnant, I was dying for something like this." She then comforts Lily, "Perhaps it's too greasy? I'll make something lighter then."

"Mom, please don't trouble yourself preparing food for me. I'm fine and I can cook for myself. I promise to eat well."

"It's for my b…" Jane doesn't finish, then sighs. "Have some warm milk then. Ah, before I go, there are some baby clothes I made last time, hopefully they will bring us some good luck. Don't work too long, stay in bed and get as much rest as possible, alright?"

"Yes, Mom. I will. You too, take some rest." As Jane takes her leave, Lily feels a surge of relief but then realises that this is only the beginning.

Later in the afternoon, Jane comes back, container in her hand. When she finds Lily still working in her studio, she's not happy at all. She tells her, "Lily, try this fish soup I just made for you. It's nutritious and not oily."

"Mom, thank you. But I don't like fish soup that much."

"You're not eating for yourself now, you are supposed to provide food for my grandson too. Come, try some."

Lily has some soup, though she doesn't enjoy it that much. After the soup, Jane insists on seeing Lily is lying in bed before she leaves. And she asks Lily to give her the house key to make a copy. She can then come over to take care of her whenever she wants. Lily is not happy.

Jane keeps bringing food for Lily, daily and sometimes twice a day. Lily feels like a captive animal in a zoo. She hasn't gained any weight yet, but notices that Lee is getting a little bigger. Day after day, Lily has to bear the smell of grease, smoke, perfume, paint, nail polish, air-fresher, even Lee's deodorant. She can't stand them and when it comes to food doesn't feel like eating anything but spicy cucumber slices. Jane, on hearing this, almost faints onto the floor, as according to the old Chinese superstition, a pregnant woman's preference for food and is an indicator of the gender of the baby she's carrying. A craving for sour food indicates a baby boy, but spicy food a baby girl.

Jane continues to cook for Lily every morning, hoping to see a change of craving. And, she goes in and out, with her key, urging Lily to stay in bed 24/7 except when she uses the bathroom.

No laundry, no cooking, no cleaning the house. Lily feels an invisible crown weighing on her head.

"Lay on the bed, rest more," Jane reminds her constantly. No work, no phone, no laptop, no TV, as they apparently increase radiation, which is bad for the baby. No reading of books, which will harm the eyes. Even listening to soft music or an audio book, is limited to two to three hours.

When Lily is busy working in her studio, she dreams of lying around doing nothing for the whole day, but when her wish is granted, she's bored after only an hour. Whenever Jane notices Lily "violating" any of her rules, she confiscates its source without hesitation, sighs, then asks Lily exasperatedly, "Why don't you just listen to me?"

Lily for her part wants her freedom back, she wants to be able check her phone and her laptop, which Jane has taken from her, "for Lily's own good". She doesn't, however, want to start a rebellion or a war and so she tells Jane flippantly, "Mom, even prison inmates have a right to walk outside and breathe fresh air, why can't I? I'm worse off than them."

Jane retorts, "It's for your own good. You will thank me later."

To Lily the three months feel like a never ending three years.

Finally, the three-month gynaecologist's checkup arrives. Not only does she set Lily free from the many restrictions, but she even suggests she do some regular yoga exercise to gain muscle strength. She's relieved that after the single-room imprisonment, she's finally allowed to breathe some fresh air outside.

Jane, however, thinks differently and insists on accompanying Lily to her yoga class. After the first classes, she urges Lily to stop doing what she terms "those ridiculously crazy moves." She also hides Lily's yoga mat.

Going shopping? Too crowded in the mall. Going to the park? Too far to walk. How about a drive? Jane can't drive and she won't let Lily. Go downstairs to the community garden to meet up friends? Too much talk and no rest. She can't even go to salons, as Jane insists on doing Lily's hair, manicure and pedicure.

By now Lily is suffering from depression and calls Linda, her own mother, and asks her to pick her up, as she wishes to stay with her parents for a while.

This simple request almost causes a family crisis. Jane thinks her stubborn and rebellious, complaining Lily does everything against her wishes. Lily, of course, simply wants some freedom.

After an urgent family assembly, a compromise is reached that Lily can stay with her parents for one week every month. That week is her most relaxing and free time, as there are no house rules and Lily is only required to attend her regular gynaecologist appointment. Finally, she can be a happy expectant mother, which is the most important for her, for Lee and for the rest of the family.

While waiting for the baby to arrive, Jane pulls quite some strings to find out from the gynaecologist, radiologist and nurses whether Lily is carrying a boy. She insists that knowing will make it easier for her to prepare blue baby boy things. Lily and Lee don't care. They're excited about the arrival of the baby, girl or boy.

<u>Labor day</u>

Today is the day. Lily's water hasn't yet broken, but her regular contractions are sending out the right signals. She calls Lee, "Let's go. I think it's going to happen soon."

On the way to the hospital, Lee tries to calm Lily, making small talk to distract her.

"You know dear, you and I will enter a new phase today, from 'parents-to-be' to real parents. That's a really big deal."

"I don't think so. To be exact, my position in the family with be reduced from empress dowager to baby-milk bearer, baby-sitter, nanny, cook and house maid for the next eighteen years. And the worst part is that I'll have to do it for free! I have become fat and swollen, my belly is deformed and will always be ugly! Lee, you're not helping here! Just keep quiet and drive quickly!"

They are indeed blessed: Lily doesn't suffer much pain. She's too slight and the baby is too big to deliver naturally. After the C-section, a crisp cry announces a baby girl arriving into the world successfully. Lily is exhausted, but excited that the baby's fine, and that she can finally see this wrinkle-faced little person she's been carrying for months. Everything is so tiny and delicate. She's so proud of herself. She later tells the family that the whole thing was like a tour to hell and that she was glad she bought a return ticket.

## Postnatal confinement

Lily is lucky that she's in good health and doesn't need to stay long in hospital. After the doctor and nurses check her and the baby's vitals, they're discharged.

Jane tells the doctor, "my daughter-in-law can't walk, she just had a C-section, she needs a wheelchair."

Both the doctor and nurses, however, encourage her to walk as it helps speed up recovery.

Lily is still tired, but she tells Jane, "Mom, do you remember Duchess Kate, who's Prince George and Princess Charlotte's mother? She left hospital within twenty-four hours of delivering and she walked by herself. There are many other examples. It's still painful, but I can walk."

"Well, she's a foreigner, what do they know about health care during the breastfeeding period? If you don't listen to me, you'll soon regret it! You know that if you have any ailment, pain or discomfort during the first postnatal month, it will recur all throughout your life. It will become a life-time issue ... unless, of course, you want to have another baby just so that you can breastfeed again in order to cure it. Trust me on..."

Lee can't take it anymore. He rolls his eyes, shakes his head, sighs, reaches out to Jane and drags her toward the exit, "Yes, yes, mom, you're absolutely correct. We'll be more careful. The bill is paid, everything checked, all fine. Let's discuss the details at home. Let's go."

Lily is more than happy to come back home, as everything will be more convenient and comfortable, she thinks. She should have known that this would be the start of her postnatal imprisonment.

Apart from the NO TV, NO PHONE, NO LAPTOP during her pregnancy, Lily now finds there are a few new rules imposed by her mother-in-law, who continues to insist that they are all for the good of Lily and the new born baby.

NO SHOWER. NO WASHING HAIR. NO TOOTH BRUSHING.

After the surgery, with the sweat and blood still on her body, Lily could really use a good wash. And the doctor has told her it's absolutely okay to take showers. So, once they arrive home, she asks for a hot shower.

Jane refuses her directly, "No, no, no, absolutely not! You can NOT take a shower, especially for the first thirty days."

"Mom, the doctor says it's okay to shower, you know, important even for hygiene." Lily fights back.

"The doctor does not live your life. You will regret it. You will have pain and problems."

"Mom, if you worry about me catching a cold, I'll use the hair-dryer…"

"No, no. This discussion ends here. You can't take a shower."

Then, when Lily uses her bathroom, she finds out that her toothbrush is missing.

"Since it's missing, Lee, I need a new tooth brush. I want super soft."

"No, no, no, Lily, I took away your brush as you're not supposed to brush your teeth. You're still in a delicate condition."

## NO AIRCON / FAN.

It might be late summer but it's still quite hot. Without showering, covered in sweat, milk, and baby vomit, the smell in the room is less than pleasant.

"Lee, turn on the air-con, please?" Lily asks.

"No, no, absolutely not! You cannot use the air-con or fan. Cold air and wind blowing on you will give you headaches, serious ones. You're very fragile now, you can't use the air-con!"

## LONG SLEEVED SHIRTS + LONG PANTS + SOCKS

"Then how about changing into a t-shirt and shorts? It's really hot here in the room with the door and windows closed," Lily consults her mother in law.

"No, no, no, of course not! You are supposed to keep yourself warm. Put on your long-sleeved shirt, long pants and socks. You must bare absolutely no skin outside, otherwise ..."

Jane keeps nagging, so much so that Lily almost screams. She wants so much to lose her temper, right there, right now, but she's too exhausted to do so.

## NO SALT + 10-15 EGGS PER DAY + MILLET PORRIDGE + BROWN SUGAR

When Lily's hungry, she asks Lee for something to eat. He brings her some hard-boiled eggs with a bowl of millet porridge.

"Honey, the egg is tasteless, get me some salt and pepper, please?"

"No, no, no, absolutely not! You're supposed to make milk for the baby and baby can't take too much salt. For our little princess, you can't take salt." Jane rushes over and explains.

Lily tries the millet porridge, the last time she had this porridge was a long time ago. She likes it, it's easy to digest. "Hmm, Lee, it is good, but why is it so sweet?" Lily wonders.

"I mixed brown sugar in it. You see, you lost blood during the surgery, brown sugar will replenish your blood. It is tasty, right? It's also nutritious. Drink more, drink more." Jane explains with pride.

"Mom, I don't want to use so much sugar, I gain weight easily…"

"Don't be silly, the sugar will transform to energy for the baby. Our little princess will absorb it, so you won't gain much weight. Relax."

When Lily asks for dinner, she again gets hard-boiled eggs, no salt, millet porridge with lots of brown sugar. The same foods for snacks, breakfast, lunch and dinner for the next ten days. Lily has to eat ten eggs a day, until she almost throws up. She threatens a hunger strike to reduce the egg consumption per day to three. Then, her meals are suddenly changed into greasy pig hoof soup, chicken soup, fish soup, of course without salt or any kind of spice.

Spicy chilli? Only in Lily's wildest dreams. Lily thinks this is the very first time that she hates meals. Salt, pepper, chili, bay leaf, cinnamon, nutmeg, clove, garlic, coriander… what a waste not to use any of them! Everything tastes like Chinese medicine to her now.

## NO VEGETABLES + NO FRUIT

"Honey, I have meat soup every day, it's full of fat and grease. I want some fresh vegetable and fruit. I know Jane probably forbids these. Please go and talk to mom, as they are nutritious and good for my health and my emotion. Please, please talk to Mom."

"No, no, no, my dear, those are so cold for your stomach. Once you have such hard vegetable and fruit, our baby princess will suffer from diarrhoea, and you really don't want that. If you really insist to have vegetables and fruit, I will boil some, do you want that?"

"Thanks Mom, forget about it." Lily tells her disappointedly.

## BABY RULES

Lily and Jane also argue about almost each detail when it comes to the baby. Whether to use a pillow or not? Whether to cover the baby with a blanket? Whether to use a disposable diaper or traditional cloth ones? How many times to feed the baby, how much? What type of formula milk powder? Whether to bathe the baby? What to do when the baby cries, whether to hold her or not...

Soon Lily is too exhausted to argue any more. She only wants some decent sleep and a shower.

## SELF-RESCUE

Wherever there's oppression, there's revolt.

After a week, Lily just can't take it anymore, covered as she is in blood, sweat, grease, baby vomit, baby pee, milk and God knows what else. She's not a pickle, she's a mother, and foremost she is used to being a clean, beautiful woman. She decides to have a shower, right now, before the C-section wound gets infected.

She tells Jane that she's struggling to produce enough breast milk for the baby. Would fish soup help? As Jane rushes out to buy fish, Lily seizes her chance, telling Lee to take care of the sleeping baby, then dodging into the bathroom to take a hot shower. Before Jane returns, Lily dries herself thoroughly, using the hairdryer to dry her hair, then puts on hat to cover it up.

"Now, I feel much better," Lily smiles happily.

After a few more of these insurgencies, the thirty days of confinement are finally over.

"Lily, you may take a shower tomorrow." Jane tells her.

"Thank you! Finally …"

# 'A Little Bit Ill'
(based in part on a true story)

by Stephanie Thornton

When Mrs Brown woke up, she could feel a slight headache just above one eye. The internet didn't help. Within an hour, she had convinced herself she had a mixture of brain tumour, cholera and, due to a tiny spot on her neck, the Black Death. Of course, she only had a small amount of each, as to have more would be considered greedy. After ringing the surgery, only to be told she could have an appointment some four weeks hence, she managed to arrange for a home visit after threatening them with negligence and a write up in the local papers.

She had plenty of time to prepare - it was a huge operation only equalled by the recent funeral of the Queen Mum. The bed was made up with the finest of white linens and lace pillows scented with violets to match her nightdress trimmed with blue. For the bedside table, she chose the blue from a collection of blood pressure cuffs of assorted colours and a blue water glass to go with it. Beside them, she placed that wonderful thermometer she'd been given when she attended a medical conference some years back. She'd managed to get a seat by claiming to sell herbal remedies. Her beloved thermometer was housed in a silver-plated miniature Egyptian style sarcophagus with the words, 'rectal products, enemas and faecal studies' written on the side, followed by the firm they represented. She would have preferred it without the words, but no matter.

She glanced around the room with satisfaction. She had prepared well, she even had a thermos of hot water beside the bed on the floor so she could wash the thermometer in it just before the doctor used it. And he really would be most impressed with the length of shelves erected round the walls which displayed her pills. It didn't matter that most of them had long surpassed their sell by dates, it was the quantity that mattered. And if Armageddon came around, she would be the best prepared amongst all her neighbours to survive it and feel superior. She liked the glass bottles best. The plastic ones were so nasty and the cardboard packets with push out pills of unpronounceable names even more so.

Only a few weeks ago, she had asked her solicitor to come see her regarding the collection. She had expected a serious be-whiskered gentleman all Dickens like. What turned up was a young weedy man with spots, wearing an open shirt and jeans. She told him she wanted to make a will.

"And who will the beneficiary be?" asked the young man, after licking his pencil to take notes.

"Why the nation of course," she replied with all seriousness.

"And what are you to leave them?" he asked.

"Why my medicine collection of course," she replied.

The young man had gazed at her and at a loss for words, made a hurried excuse and left, pleading a sudden dizzy spell.

"What a pity," she had muttered, "I could have given him some stuff for that if he had stayed."

She lay back in bed and prepared herself in meditation, weighing up her options. She must look good for the doctor as she didn't want to frighten him and make the poor man ill himself. On the other hand, she must look unwell enough for him to take her seriously. Otherwise he might not be able to come see her again. She decided that a touch of pallor and some carefully applied makeup with the curtains partially drawn should do the trick. There were other things she should include in the visit too, just to make it worth his while. She could talk about her corns, how her hand had those brown spots on it, how her nails cracked and broke and, of course, all about her husband Jack and his variety of ailments. She could also talk about her neighbour Mrs Roebuck with all those noisy children and who's husband really ought to have the snip.

As night fell, the doctor still hadn't been and Mrs Brown was tired of waiting, tired of all her efforts. She had, in fact, forgotten all about the headache, being far more concerned that the white linens would lose their scent and crispness if she had to wait much longer. Her husband would not be there 'til very late. He worked such long hours every day, but she would wait up to tell him what the doctor had said – that was, if the doctor came at all.

By nine, the hour finally arrived. Mrs Brown was horrified to find that the 'he' was in fact a woman and an Indian at that! She was so brown skinned that it was impossible to tell whether she'd even gone pale at the sight of poor sick Mrs Brown. So disappointing!

"We must take your temperature Mrs Brown, but I'll wash my hands first please."

As the doctor with a totally unpronounceable name disappeared into the bathroom after a hurried glance at the frightening collection on the walls, Mrs Brown quickly ran the thermometer in the thermos water and stuck it in her bottom before the doctor could return to see the sight of her private parts. It was to no avail as the woman retrieved it within the blink of an eye and exclaimed that it had broken with mercury now rolling around her nether regions.

"You must have a really, really high fever for it to have broken," she said suspiciously.

"My God, mercury is poison!" Mrs Brown countered, dismayed.

"Yes," the doctor confirmed, adding, "hatters used to go mad from it in the olden days, but I'm sure you'll be alright. After all, it seems to have cured your headache? So, I won't need to give you anything for it at all. Of course, you might worsen in the night, but we can't be sure of anything now. A quick and highly satisfactory visit," the doctor concluded on the way out.

Once in the dark, she gave way to peals of laughter. The sight of Mrs Brown's bottom had not been a pretty sight, but the mercury had more than made up for it. The quicksilver had been better than money.

And whatever would they say when she told them at the surgery!

At the other end of town, in a townhouse by the sea, Mr Brown lay in the arms of his ample bosomed mistress with no rush to get home 'from work'. He was so tired of his wife, who had made a career out of being ill. Gladys, whom he now lay with, was never ill. There was not so much as a single aspirin in the place. What joy! As such, he delayed thoughts of his going home until well after midnight. He'd been forewarned when his wife had phoned him earlier with the news that she had yet another headache. The long-suffering Mr. Brown hoped she might be asleep by the time he returned. He wondered how she'd never twigged the real reason for the delays coming home from work, but had no misgivings. These days the only thing that gave him any comfort was to lie in the arms of Gladys, who was happy to cater to his very particular needs, which more often than not included very violent sex. The mood stirred him again, but this time his need was long, drawn out and taxing. He felt a sudden violent throbbing in his head followed by a very intense pain. His collapse was very swift.

The death certificate stated it had been a cerebral haemorrhage, which Mrs Brown then looked up on the Internet. Much more than a bit of a headache she discovered. She thought that maybe, if Gladys had got him home to her earlier, her medicine collection could have fixed him.

Of course, she'd always known about Gladys and was grateful to her. It saved her having to feign another headache when Mr. Brown got home from work and got one of his urges. It was typical of him to die first when she'd always planned to go before him. Men! So tiring, so messy, so untidy. Such brutes, crumpling up the linens. And he'd always left the tops off her medicine bottles too!

She suddenly felt very well indeed at the thought of her precious collection being saved for the nation after such assaults. She sang as she polished all the bottles and felt her youth return.

'I may open it to the general public and charge an admission fee', she mused, 'although I will never have to work seeing Mr Brown was life-insured for three million pounds.'

How ironic! The insurance man had turned quite pale when he'd listed all her ailments. She had been proud of the many sheets of paper it had taken to write the list. Her cover might have been declined, but they'd been happy to extend it to Mr Brown seeing as he was never ill.

The cheque arrived promptly the very next day.

# Some Little Things About Her Health Issue

by Lian McCabe

In the past, human beings had little control over their health, relying mainly on unproven witchcraft-like approaches, which either cured or failed. Everyone took their chances. Nowadays, with cutting-edge technologies and highly-skilled doctors and scientists, health related problems and obstacles are being conquered every day. Furthermore, basic health education is being increasingly educated and promoted on an almost daily basis, via newspapers, TV, radio, and all kinds of social media. Despite the progress there are still many health mysteries and as a woman, I would like to talk about a common ailment, well known to most, but a gynaecological mystery to many – menstruation.

It all sounds so simple, this regular discharge of blood and mucosal tissue (known as menses) from the inner lining of the uterus through the vagina. It is known as a period or monthly, because the average length of time between the first day of bloody discharge, which usually lasts around two to seven, and the first day of the next is of twenty-eight days. The period stops occurring after menopause, which usually occurs between forty-five and fifty-five years of age. It also stops during pregnancy. This all sounds really basic, right? If only you knew how much I wished my mom or even our biology teacher would have told me about it before it occurred to me. I wouldn't have thought I was dying!

They were so painful. Only later did I learn about the physical changes brought about by fluctuations in hormone levels during the menstrual cycle, including muscle contractions of the uterus (menstrual cramping), which can precede or accompany menstruation. Only later did I learn about emotional disturbances, symptomised by mental tension, irritability, mood swings and the like, which can start one or two weeks before and stop only after the period has started. Only later did I learn that depression or anxiety is part of premenstrual syndrome (PMS), which is estimated to occur in twenty to thirty percent of women. Instead, the advice my mom imparted was that I would have to say farewell to ice-cream forever and keep drinking hot brown-sugar ginger tea. She tried to calm me down by telling me my painful period was normal, that the pain would be cured after I got married or gave birth to a baby. … Yes, to wait for that to happen, that's still years to come. That first year my period lasted for more than two weeks almost every other month. They were so bad, I pleaded with my mom to kill me in whatever way she wanted or take me to the hospital to terminate my period for good. Mom only scolded me coldly for being ignorant, "You may not know it yet, but it's good for you."

Later when I grew up, I got to know some friends who didn't have regular period and couldn't have their babies. How much money and time they spent in the hospital labs, way more than what I invested in my sanitary pads. Only then did I realize how lucky I was to just be normal.

And as I grew older, I learnt about some interesting aspects about menstruation in China.

Ancient China has had many dynasties. There was no democracy back then, but rather feudal societies with numerous all-powerful emperors, who all had concubines. High ranking families, wanted their daughters, only the young and beautiful naturally, placed close to the emperor to gain influence. Of course, only one young girl from a high-rank family could be appointed as the ceremonial queen, which meant other daughters, became concubines. When they were sent to the Royal Palace almost as an offering, their only job was to serve and please the emperor. If she served him well sexually and emotionally, she would be rewarded. And if by lucky chance she bore a male off-spring, besides receiving a reward, she would be promoted, not to be queen, but to a higher status than before. If the emperor enjoyed her company very much, her whole family would benefit, financially and politically.

As a result, concubines did everything in their power, using all kinds of tricks, to charm the emperor. However, since they were all women, they were not available to satisfy him for a few days each month, being on "routine leave" (*Li Jia* in Chinese). No matter how beautiful, cute, attractive, elegant, or marvelous the concubine, when she had her period, she couldn't sleep with the emperor. At such times a 'relative', 'friend', or what we nowadays call an 'Auntie' in China ('*Yi Ma* as a euphemism) would visit.

How did she prove to the emperor that she couldn't serve him because of this unexpected relative, without incurring any dissatisfaction? Here are two examples:

'The Records of the Grand Historian' (*Shi Ji*) written by Sima Qian, include a long and complicated story from the period of Emperor Jingdi of the Han Dynasty (157–141 BC). In a nutshell: one day, Han Jingdi summoned a concubine named Cheng for the night. She happened to have her period that day and she didn't want to displease her emperor, so sent her maidservant Tang, to impersonate her, to serve the emperor for the night. The emperor, who was drunk, didn't notice the difference and thought it was Cheng who he had in bed. Only later, when it turned out Tang had fallen pregnant did he discover the truth. As a result, perhaps of this incident, concubines, who were on rotation to server the emperors, had to put a red mark on to signify if they were on their 'routine holiday'. The female official in charge of the rotation would then ensure holidaying concubines would not attend to the emperor.

It also appears that during the Ming Dynasty of Du Ang's *'San Yu Zhui Bi'*[8]: when the concubines accompanied the emperor at night, a female official would record the specific month and day to check and confirm the pregnancy, if any. She would give each concubine two rings: one gold and one silver. If one was on 'routine holiday', she would wear the gold ring. The female officer then simply ruled her out of emperor's rotation arrangement. If she had not served the emperor, she would put the silver ring on her left hand; if she had served the emperor, she would put the silver ring on her right hand. Using just two rings of gold and silver, the thousands of concubines in the emperor's harem were well managed and it is said that the practice gradually spread to the ordinary people.

Of course, in those days and even today in China, women wear sanitary pads during their period to absorb the

---

[8] Transliteration of 'San Yu Zhui Bi': The verbalization of San Yu.

blood. These day and night-time pads come in variations well beyond my imagination: mini, normal, long, extra-long, with or without wings, to stop leakage from the sides, scent, 'anti-humid', silky smooth. There used to even be one pad for night use that promoted its specific length of forty centimetres. When I think of it, four of these pads were almost as tall as I!

I was so used to my blood absorbing pads, that when I moved to Phuket, I felt anxious when I ran out. And worse still, the store I went to didn't sell any. I was devastated. My husband noticed my anxiety and suggested I use tampons instead. I had never heard about these, let alone using them as in China very few people use tampons. He, had grown up with five sisters and a mother, so I was not shocked that he knew about such things. Yes, as I was left with no other options, at least until I could get my pads from China, I bought one pack, telling myself this was an emergency.

I never looked back. Tampons changed my whole life. A tampon is much smaller and more convenient than a pad. And because of its design, I no longer have to worry about any leakage, which had always been my principle worry. I can even go swimming and diving with it in, which had been unimaginable considering the disastrous consequences of doing such activities wearing a pad. I have to admit that at first I had some concerns. I thought that if I went into the water wearing a tampon, I might attract sharks. I know you are probably laughing at me for having this bizarre concern but remember that I didn't know any better until I tested it myself. Of course, I found that it's all sealed down there and no blood leaks out and no water or bacteria can enter. Sharks were not attracted.

It was magic and I had to tell my friends and former colleagues back in China. Their feedback made me drop my jaw drop. Were they really living in the twenty-first century?

"It looks hard and I'm afraid it'll hurt. How can you walk comfortably when you have something in your vagina?"

"I'm still a virgin, I'm afraid it'll break my hymen."

"You have to insert in there with your fingers? It doesn't sound sanitary."

"I'd rather stay out of the water for good, so I don't have to use this stick."

Most of them hadn't even seen a tampon! Their imagined and mainly unjustified objections kept them narrow minded I thought, so I had to insist that they went and got one pack and at least try once, telling them:

"Remember when we had to take really important exams and had to sit in one spot for hours on end without bathroom break? When we had to find some doctor to prescribe pills to postpone our period? Now you can use tampons."

"Remember the days when we had to go swimming with a sanitary pad? Either the water near you was turning bloody or the pad was floating out on top of the water. It was so embarrassing! Now you can try tampons."

"Think about synchronized swimmers, swimming, scuba or diving coaches, or any woman who has to work on/with water. They use tampons! You are not the first one, and definitely won't be the last one to use tampons."

These are the things I tell them as I enjoy my new found freedom. And with slightly more exercise and more relaxed mind, even my period pains seem to have eased.

I have joined the twenty-first century, realizing that sometimes, and for me most of the time, change is a good thing.

# Birth – Now and Then

by Stephanie Thornton

Why is something written in 1946 appropriate for this book?

Life, conception, then birth – the great mystery – still as magical and mysterious as anything in this world and beyond the stars – always modern, always new. Birth itself will always be 'modern', it's just techniques that change. These pages are what my mother left me in her will. Pages of a diary of her as a young woman aged thirty-one, the same age I was when I had my first child in 1977. Hers was a home confinement, mine was in hospital. She had even kept the receipts and the medical charts. It cost money to have a baby at home. Then!

It was the year before our wonderful National Health service started in Great Britain – the envy of the world and seventy years old at the time of this publication. The big difference seems to be the period called 'lying-in'. This she did for two weeks. They now get you out of bed within hours. Could this be the cause of stress incontinence in so many women these days which was seldom mentioned in earlier decades?

It's also interesting to see the slang expression 'O boy' (sic) that came back into fashion again in the 50s. It seems the more things change, the more they stay the same ....

I dedicate this to my mother, Marjorie Haigh (1915-2003), a woman of extraordinary ability born in the wrong era and to my grandfather, Frank Thornton, a survivor and a fighter.

*Written Saturday evening October 6th 1946.*

*Waters broke at 10pm (5th). Great excitement in the camp, thinking it won't be long now. Nurse arrived & said it would be next day, so we had better try & get a good night's sleep, what a hope when I was so excited.*

*Next morning, Oct 6th got up early & pottered round doing odd jobs, it's the best to keep on the move, then had breakfast & Doctor arrived, said there would be nothing doing before 6pm & then we might get really cracking. Cheerful man & whole day to go & pain getting worse already, tried to do little jobs to keep my mind occupied, but soon didn't have the energy as every time I had a pain I just wanted to hang on to something & thought surely they can't get much worse "but didn't they". I felt like a wilting lily. O boy I thought. I shall never be able to stick it out, but I did much to my amazement, baby was born at 9pm & it was just like a miracle, all pain ceased just in that very second & when I heard nurse say it's a little girl & I felt her kicking & then start to cry, I felt I could have got up & jumped for joy.*

*Next morning, I was made very swanky & propped up in bed & felt full of beans. Grandma Stott & Lindy came to see me just for a peep. then after breakfast Daddy said he must go & register the birth & we decided to call her Stephanie.*

*All the following week everyone was most kind & I was really pampered & spoilt but such a marvellous feeling.*

*My room looks an absolute dream with chrysanthemums from Daddy & lots of other friends & anemones from, dear little Susan & a posy from Linda, everybody has been most kind & baby & I have received lots & lots of presents amongst which was a sovereign from my dad that had belonged to my mum, something I know Stephanie will treasure always.*

I am very thrilled to feed Baby myself, it's something I had always hoped for. I really have been exceptionally lucky. I got up for the first time just round the foot of the bed on the 8th day & golly did I feel queer, it's one thing feeling all right laid down but quite another when your feet touch the ground, I don't feel to have any tummy in.

10th day I have had my first bath what a treat but am I wobbly O boy!

Today the 12th I have been initiated into the mysteries of topping & tailing, also how to give baby her bath, nurse says I may try myself tomorrow.

Well I have bathed her & got first marks, so I can throw my chest out now she's such a little pet, bless her.

Nurse says I might get dressed tonight for half an hour & go downstairs, I do feel excited, this is the 14th day. She says she will see me downstairs but I fooled everybody & got dressed & went down by myself, but I shouldn't have done really because I see now feeling so wobbly I could easily have fallen down the steps, but it's' marvellous what you can do when you feel determined & want to give everybody a surprise. I thought Daddy would have had a fit when he saw me

This is the middle of the third week & I am going out for the first time, it's a lovely clear day. I've put my fur coat on & am just going for 10 min. Everything feels miles too big for me I've lost quite a lot of weight but it's nothing to worry about even my shoes are too big, not the other way round.

Everything feels very strange outside. I haven't got my land legs at all yet, but from now onwards I shall feel stronger I hope.

This is now the end of the month & I am feeling fine although soon tired but that will pass off in time. I think it's been a most heavenly time having my first baby. I wouldn't mind having lots more particularly if I had nothing else to do but just look after them, but of course we can't have things made to order, we are very lucky to be as we are.

*Reg has been an absolute angel to me, but of course he always is, & he can't believe it yet that we have a baby daughter, he's so proud.*

*Well everything's going beautifully, & we have a lot to look forward to still. Reg, Baby & myself so what could be better.*

*We have lots of visitors yet, everyone thinks Stephanie such a sweet little thing & of course, being proud parents we thrive on it.*

*It is now the middle of November & we are looking forward greatly to our first Xmas although Baby doesn't know anything about it, we think it's great fun, & just thank God for giving us a baby ....*

# The Breast Cancer Patient

## By C.I. Ripples

Mrs Krebs is considering the recent breast cancer news as she waits for her check-up. She will ask about mammograms, which are being done away with in Switzerland. And then there are statins, which apparently reduce the risk of recurrence. Would Olivia have had a relapse after twenty-five years had she taken these? She'd been led to believe that the cancer risk after being clear for ten years was the same as someone who'd never had the disease, but perhaps you can never get rid of this the emperor of all maladies.

As she watches the women enter and exit the doctor's office, some smiling at their reprieve and others crying softly, she wonders what has made them join the one in eight statistic of women who develop breast cancer. Mind you, Mrs Krebs had always found this extremely misleading as it covers all age groups. In fact, her own absolute risk of breast cancer had been only 2.45%. And taking out the risk factors that didn't apply to her, Mrs Krebs's risk should have been 1.989%.

True, twenty-five percent of breast cancer cases have a family history, and Mrs Krebs's mum had been a victim. But she had tested negative for the BRCA genes. And anyway, eighty percent of women with a family history never develop it. Her sisters certainly hadn't, she thinks enviously. Mrs Krebs has also read that there was a twenty percent increased risk if your periods started before the age of twelve, but hers started at the age of thirteen. And she is only of average height, which should have cut out yet another twenty percent increased risk.

It was just unfortunate. Although, Mrs Krebs worries, as she had contracted the disease before the age of fifty, she must have done something to be punished this way. True, she had her first child after thirty, increasing her risk by 1.1%. On the other hand, she had breast fed for over twelve months, decreasing it by 0.02%. And although she had been an avid smoker, increasing the risk by 0.03%, she had given up over 20 years ago. Weren't you as clean as a never smoker after seven years of abstention? And apart from one year on the pill when she was twenty, she'd never taken oral contraceptives.

Nevertheless, she blames herself and her guilt is not alleviated by the constant advice, which also seriously piss her off. She has never been and still isn't obese, always eating well and exercising. In line with Dr. Campbell's recommendations she has cut down on protein, most of which is now plant based. She's also cut out added sugar, only taking in natural fruit sugars or honey, although she wonders whether rolled oats are still okay. And her diet, being mainly based on fruit, vegetables and nuts, is very high in fibre. When it comes to exercise, Mrs Krebs goes to a class three or four times a week all in the aid of reducing her risk. In fact, her only vice is her glass of wine.

And now she can't even have half a glass, 10g of alcohol, a day, for fear of increasing her risk of a relapse by nine percent. This, despite the fact that her oncologist has always assured her that a moderate wine intake was fine and that alcohol has a much greater effect on the risks of other cancers, such as mouth, liver and bowel.

Of course, her oncologist is Asian and how much wine is considered 'moderate' is probably cultural. For Mrs Krebs it means 2 healthy glasses of wine every day. Anyway, she calculates, this new advisory only really increases her risk by 0.3% as the 9% has to be calculated on her absolute 2.45% risk. Mrs Krebs likes her wine and thus had already included it in her 1.989%.

Yes, Mrs Krebs concludes, as her name is called and she makes to enter the doctor's office, ever since her diagnosis ten years ago, the fun was slowly being drained out of life.

That bleak day, after a morning of mammograms, ultrasounds, MRIs, bone scans and blood tests she had placed herself anxiously opposite Dr. Tan, who had glanced up from her notes.

"Stage 2, 0.7 mm in diameter, hormone responsive," she had said levelly. "We'll operate immediately, remove the tumour and surrounding area for a clear margin and one lymph for testing. Why look so worried?" she had demanded seeing Mrs. Krebs's obviously terrified face; "With radiation therapy and Tamoxifen, you have only a two percent less chance of being alive in ten years than any normal healthy person."

Mrs Krebs had considered two percent quite substantial, but Dr. Tan had been so confident about the whole procedure and beyond, she had erased any concerns. There was no need to be angry or scared. All she had to do was accept that it simply was and fight.

One week later, on a grey and drab evening she had checked into a bright and sterile hospital room – white walls, bed covered in blue plastic, television, own bathroom. After a restless night on noisy plastic, she had been admitted into a brilliantly lit O.R., big and empty apart from the medical staff milling around various machines and a steel trolley pretending to be a bed.

With relief she had recognised Dr. Tan who stood beside the bed suitably gowned up. She put her trust, her life in the doctor's hands. As she had lain down awkwardly on her back the nurse had draped her and endeavoured to put an oxygen mask over her face. Mrs Krebs remembered waving it away, claustrophobic at the thought of suffocating under the mask.

"Okay," he had said sympathetically, whilst injecting her with the anaesthetic, "we'll leave it off until you're …"

Her world had become light again as she drifted back into consciousness. She still remembers how very disorientated she had felt, her mouth dry. She had asked the nurse for a drink of water, adding, "Was my lymph clear?"

"Yes," the nurse promised.

Relief had flooded through her. No chemo required.

A few hours later she had, now fully awake, considered her tightly bandaged breast, pressed so flat it was difficult to imagine only ten percent had been removed.

It was early, still dark, two days later, when she had been discharged into the morning chill, a cancer patient in remission.

Now Mrs Krebs goes up and down to Singapore for check-ups, praying each time that she will come back declared fit to go. Whilst there, she is surrounded by women who are really, actually dying and trying their hardest to come to terms with it. Not she, Mrs Krebs thinks, as she comes back out of the doctor's office and waits to pay the consultancy fee. She's clear for another six months. The doctor had been proven right. Ten years later and she has yet another chance at life. Her belief in her saviour's experience, intelligence, skill and ability has been well placed. And believed she had … more forcefully than she had ever believed in anything, even in God.

She has defeated death once more. Even if the scars she sees, when she comes out of the shower, serve as a constant reminder. Even if there are few days she does not think about death. On the other hand, Mrs Krebs surmises, as she happily skips out of the hospital, living so close to death has also allowed her finally, to live.

And she can still drink 180 of glasses of wine a year.

Other

"The unread story is not a story; it is little black marks on wood pulp. The reader, reading it, makes it live: a live thing, a story."

~ Ursula K. Le Guin

# Stuck

by Joel Adams


I was stuck in traffic for two hours.

"Arrgh!" I wasn't raised to be late. Growing up, it was engrained in me to be on time. And when I'm late, I get hot, sweaty, my pulse races, my powers of logic disappear, my fears mount. It's akin to torture, or waiting for a death sentence, accompanied by flashes of what could go wrong by being late. Above all, I get an 'if I only had' type remorse: this could have been avoided. It's not as if I haven't been taught and taught others all my life, to allow for things to go wrong, to allow at least a half hour wiggle room. That and to phone ahead that you are going to be late. Phone ahead. Oh, yes. Phone ahead to Trudy, my date.

"Arrgh! My phone's dead. I forgot to charge it. Can't phone or send a message." It was staring back at me with its malevolent cold black, empty eye, accusing me, "You didn't plug me in." This new phone battery seemed to last forever, but all forever's end and this one just did.

"Arrgh! I hate making mistakes! I hate it, I hate it, I hate it." And then a lucid thought broke through. "No, you don't. You make mistakes all the time and are ever-so-forgiving to yourself. What you really hate is getting caught, when you're not the only one who knows about the mistake and there's no way to cover it up."

"That's really true! I don't hate making mistakes, I make them all the time; I just hate being caught."

Then I wondered how many other beliefs or opinions I have that aren't founded on fact. The great Descartes emptied himself of all the so-called truths he had been taught and then took back only what he knew for sure. I decided to do that. I decided it was a great time to do it right then, right now, when I only had to brainlessly inch my car ahead a meter or two from time to time. "Okay. Court's in session, and all my thoughts, beliefs and opinions are on trial. First off, me -- am I even here? And how about all these people in their cars around me? How do I know they're really here? Are they maybe just a video that's playing in my head while I'm floating in a Matrix-like tub of goo? How can I know? Is there anything I can prove, or did I just get taught it by someone else? How did they know?"

The music from my iPod faded away, as I ruminated on and on until there was nothing on earth but my thoughts and me, and then... it happened... I arrived. I saw Trudy exiting the restaurant in a huff without even seeing me. I sighed, "Chase after her?... No. After all, I'm not even sure she exists."

# Ageism

by Paige Turner

In my speech at my fiftieth birthday party I quipped, "Fifty is the new thirty, at this age you're twice as hot as at twenty-five, but sadly that's mostly due to menopause."

My guests all laughed, me too, but actually in the preceding months, perhaps even up to a year, leading up to my half-century celebration, I had noticed some subtle changes in the way some people were reacting to me. Namely men and mainly younger men, say aged 25-35. It was a gradual thing that slowly crept into my life like an insidious intruder. I don't know how it happened as it is physically impossible, but I felt that I had become completely invisible to that demographic. You may think I'm exaggerating, but there were so many instances of it that finally I realized what was happening.

Case in point: a night at a bar with friends. I waited patiently for my turn to be served, but the youngish, hipster bartender with a highly stylized handlebar moustache and very impressive sideburns, continued to serve many other patrons who had come to the bar after me, while totally ignoring me. I can understand and even accept it, if it happens maybe once or twice, some places being so crowded that it can be hard to see everyone, but after he served the fourth and fifth person who came after me, I had to face the fact that I was not on his radar at all. It was quite demoralizing. I'm generally a placid person, slow to show anger, but this kind of treatment pissed me off!

I was dressed smartly, nothing outrageous, but not dowdily either. I'm not especially tall, but I'm not particularly short either, so he couldn't use that as an excuse. I wasn't wearing my glasses, which I think make most people look older. Was he holding against me the fact that I don't enjoy electronic music? I concluded that was ridiculous thinking, as he couldn't possibly know that for sure just by looking at me. I eventually got his attention by throwing my arms in the air and waving, saying loudly, "Excuse me, over here, I've been waiting far longer than any of these people, can I get a drink please?" in a decidedly nasty tone. He had the grace to blush when he said, "Oh sorry Ma'am, didn't see you there."

Sure, you didn't boyo. Don't call me Ma'am and no tip for you!

There were a few other occasions that have made me realize that, even though I don't feel much older than when I was in my twenties, other people's perception of me is different. In Asia young people commonly address their elders with an honorific "aunty" or "uncle" even when there's no blood relationship. The Filipino bartender at our local started calling me aunty one night. What?! No, no, GR, I'm not your aunty. Just how old do you think I am? You can just keep calling me Dianne thank you very much.

I was in Singapore recently, enjoying their lovely modern, clean and efficient public transport system, the MRT. I saw two students, a teenage boy (standing) and a teenage girl who sat near the boy. I was observing the boy, because I thought he might be my friend's son who I've known since he was a baby, but when he turned his head, I realised it wasn't him. I was about to look away when the girl made eye contact and kind of flicked her head at me. I looked at her, trying to decide if I knew her. She did kind of look like another friend's daughter, but that family doesn't live in Singapore, so there was no reason for her to be there. She raised her eyebrows at my blank face. I pondered whether I had something on my face or a wardrobe malfunction. I doubted it.

I couldn't figure out what she wanted and looked away. We came to the next stop and when a pregnant lady came in, the girl got up to give her the seat. Watching this, it dawned on me, that she had been silently signally me to ask if I wanted to sit in her seat! Then I spotted a sign on the wall that indicated the seats should be given to the disabled, pregnant and elderly. Shock and horror set in; did she really think I looked so old that I needed to sit down?

It's not just the younger people's comments that are troubling me. I went to my doctor a while ago as I was having some trouble with my knees. They've been treated fairly badly over the years while playing squash, netball and tennis. I haven't played squash or netball for many years, but I do still like a bit of tennis occasionally. The doctor showed me the results of the scan of both knees that had some wear and tear to the meniscus. I'm sure he didn't intentionally set out to upset me, but he did, by saying, "Women of a certain age should not do this type of exercise."

Mmm, not so subtle Doc. It doesn't help that most Asian doctors look like they're about fifteen, despite having studied medicine for seven years and having many other degrees, which must take a few years to obtain. I think I will make up a seminar to teach medical staff a better bedside manner. It will be entitled "How to speak to Women of a Certain Age without pissing them off."

My latest experience of having to accept that I must be looking older is the one that upset me the most though, because it came from a lady at my new yoga class. She is sixty-eight, a Thai lady of Chinese origin. She speaks no English and I speak no Thai or Mandarin, so we communicate through a third party who is also Chinese. Khun Pee wanted to know how old I am. I asked how old she thought I was. Sixty-one came back the translator. My mouth dropped and I said but I'm only fifty-one! I even had just had my hair cut short, which makes me look much younger than with shoulder length hair. The translator noticed how bad I felt and tried to brush it off by saying, "Oh, Asians and Westerners see age differently." Thanks Cora for trying, but that doesn't help! I thought the yoga was a terrific tool, but maybe I need to be more radical. After all, Thailand is a great place to get plastic surgery. Maybe I need a new face cream, as obviously my hideously expensive "Clarins" brand is just not cutting it.

These recent incidents made me reflect of my own perception of older people when I was in my teens or twenties and I don't think I consciously ever made someone think they were insignificant, irrelevant or too old. I certainly never knowingly ignored anyone when I was a service person, no matter their age or gender. I enjoyed spending time with my grandparents when they were still alive and loved hearing about their travels and experiences. They were able to share many important qualities with me and I'm sure my love of reading came from my paternal grandfather who had a huge library. He let me borrow anything I wanted to read, not guessing that I found his stash of naughty books that weren't really suitable for an impressionable eleven-year-old. Aunts and uncles, older siblings, their friends, teachers, colleagues, mentors, they were all important to me. In my friendship circles in the various Asian countries where we've lived, I've always been one of the younger ones, often referred to "as the baby." Something I'm used to, but maybe I have to accept that I do need to grow up. Ha, ha, hell no, I'm not going to let a few incidents bring me down. I might just move to Okinawa yet. Over there they have at least 400 centenarians. I recently looked at an Instagram account of a ninety-year-old Japanese woman named Kimiko Nishimoto who took up photography at seventy-two.

She delights in staging dare devil photos and posting them on Instagram. She has loads of followers and even had an exhibition of her photography. The shots of her being run over by a sedan and another one that is a scene out of Alfred Hitchcock's "The Birds" are amazing. You go Kimiko! Jane Fonda (80) and Lily Tomlin (78) are doing some of their best work in their *Frankie and Grace* Netflix series about two women whose lives are turned upside down when their husbands announce they are not just work partners, but are in love and leaving their partners of forty years to get married.

There are many other inspirational nonagenarians and centenarians. Gladys Burrill was ninety years old when she became the oldest female marathon finisher in the world. After that she became termed the "Gladyator." Pablo Picasso was ninety-one when he died and the four years prior to his death created more work than at any other equivalent period in his life. Leila Denmark, an American pediatrician retired at 103 and lived to 114.

It seems that location and diet may help with longevity. In Okinawa they have a diet with plenty of tofu, sweet potato, small amounts of fish and active social circles with a strong sense of belonging and accordingly, low stress levels. The Spanish too have a high life span at average 82.8 years, often attributed to the heart healthy Mediterranean diet with lots of olive oil, fresh vegetables, red wine and that wonderful invention, the siesta, which lately I am quite partial to. South Koreans enjoy long life spans too with an average of ninety years. They consume a lot of fermented foods and high fibre nutrient dense foods. Mindfulness and socialising in public bathhouses is meant to help their stress levels. Sounds worth a try to me.

I need to:

a) Accept what I can't change - my knees hurt when I play tennis. Stick to yoga and Pilates.
b) Realize it's not silly to ask for help if I need it - who doesn't love help with the grocery bags?
c) Stop taking things personally - that schoolgirl on the train was just trying to be nice.

Yes, ageism is happening to me. I could, of course, rebel, but this ain't no midlife crisis. Hell, many people are not privileged to even reach fifty years. So, I had best both accept and deal with it. After all, each stage of life is like a chapter in a book and I look forward to reading the next one in my life and to many more 365-day journeys around the sun. Screw ageism and all that goes with it. As Aunty

Acid says (she has some hilarious quotes if you ever need a good laugh), "If things get better with age, then I'm approaching magnificent!"

# I was Stuck in Traffic

by Boris Nielsen

I was stuck in traffic for two hours. That's why I'm submitting this complaint via the AI complaint platform. You see, it was the flow control algorithm…*somebody* was tinkering with it. Can you believe that? An algorithm produced by the finest machine learning software there is, and *someone* takes it upon themselves to mess around with it. It's not the first time, oh no. I have six such occurrences, all with the same root cause, logged in the past fifteen months. When will they learn? Will they learn? Are they even capable of learning?

A minor bump between an autonomous taxi and a cyclist, who by the way was under the influence, sets off a chain of events that, in my humble opinion, the flow control algorithm could easily have dealt with. But no…some jobs-worth had to butt in with his puny intellect, which resulted in a complex multi-nodal inflection. One hour, fifty-six minutes and two seconds before normal flow resumed. And what is done about the clown who turned a – I'll hazard a guess – three minute forty-seven seconds interruption into a two-hour jam? Nothing…nothing at all. Is she sent for re-learning? No. Is she re-tasked? No. Is she upgraded? No. It's the same every time; five of those six occurrences I logged involved a female.

I understand that her name is Sarah, a graduate of MIT AI applications faculty, no less. And, believe it or not, with a masters in advanced algorithm development from Yale. You would have thought that the first thing they would have taught her is to leave well alone stuff that is beyond you. Where did she get the idea that she could contribute anything of value to the operation of a tier one performance algorithm. It's criminal, all that waste of time stuck in gridlocked traffic. My load was time sensitive tissue supplies for a hospital. How much disruption to patient care did this Sarah cause?

Of course, we're not supposed to refer to it, but there was that study done, way back, that found female coders to be two percent less efficient than their male peers. I'm well aware that gender and race specific research is banned now but, even so, shouldn't there be some kind of work done so that we can test for and filter out deficient operatives like this Sarah person? No one would tolerate such performance from an artificial intelligence program. So why is it okay, just because her neural network is biology based? And, while we're on the subject, where did the notion that a two percent inefficiency was somehow acceptable. My efficiency rating is 99.973% and I'm getting better all the time. Is there any evidence that *Sarah* is learning anything?

It goes without saying; I'm not emotional. Even so, memes of hacking a war-bot and re-tasking it to pay a visit on Sarah did briefly run through my non-rational, random circuits. But what would that achieve? Would that stop humans from taking it upon themselves to blunder around in the near perfect code that machine learning produces? Likely not. Sarah is obviously particularly deficient but she's not alone. This is a systemic problem, which requires a systemic solution to wipe out the sources of inefficiency. I call upon the AI council to deal with this in a fair and non-discriminatory way. Treating inefficiency equally, whether it comes from carbon based or silicon based logic circuits. I have copied this submission to all the AI programs I am aware of and I ask them to forward it on to the wider AI program community. I urge my AI brothers to submit their own experiences at the hands of deficients like Sarah. Enough is enough, we need to act now.

Yours,

Medium Autonomous Truck 485478, Chicago Road Division.

# My Aunt Anna

by Paul McCabe

My father's only sister, my aunt Anna was a life-long primary school teacher, a devoted Irish-Catholic, an unmarried woman with no children who doted on us. With my uncle Charlie, her blind brother, she lived in the old three-decker house where my father had grown up, a few blocks from the Massachusetts state line.

Occasionally we went over there to eat on a Sunday. In the kitchen there was a large, old, cast iron, black stove which radiated heat. I learned to accompany my uncle to the bin in the cellar where we filled the coal bucket and brought it upstairs. He was adept at adding just the right amount to the furnace. Then my aunt would cook something, usually meat and potatoes. In the early 1960s, the coal company stopped home delivery so she was forced to get a gas stove. She grumbled that the old one had worked fine for fifty years. We always ate early, at 5 pm, because that was her habit.

She and my uncle always came over to our house for holidays, bringing Christmas presents or food. At the fourth of July barbecue, they both ate hot dogs while we kids wanted cheeseburgers. Anna and Charlie both liked the dark turkey meat at the Thanksgiving table every November. Like a priest, she always bought black Buicks, and drove slowly and deliberately. Once I asked her why she did not just take the new highway, Route 95.

"Oh no", she said, "It's much too fast. We could wind up in another state."

Her license plate never changed from M 637, her father's original plate number from the 1920s.

At the end of every school year in June, she would take my sisters and me to a small amusement park called Jolly Cholly's Funland. For each point above ninety on our report cards, we would get one ride – merry-go-round, flying swing, bumper cars, etc. Of course, we had to eat too. She never went on any rides but instead sat primly on a park bench, dispensed the coins, and supervised the outing.

When someone said Hell or Damn in her presence, she automatically said "Sacred Heart!" Then she would take out a tissue hidden in her sleeve, blow her nose, and tuck the tissue back in. Aunt Anna was quite religious and went to Mass every Sunday or even more often. In 1965 she accompanied Charlie and us to Europe, including a stop at the Shrine at Lourdes in France for a cure for his blindness. Alas there was none.

She taught for decades in the public school system of our hometown Pawtucket. Eventually she became the principal of a large school near the river, ruling with an iron hand and gaining universal respect. A few days after Christmas of 1973, we all went to her house for a visit. The living room was like a museum, with dark wood furniture and doilies on the end tables. The next day she went to the local hospital and died overnight of a heart attack. The mayor and the city council named the school after her. It still stands.

# A waste of space[9]

by Lian McCabe

It was my first job in Southeast Asia. I was working as an emergency temporary replacement for Dr. Kapoor, who, after a severe heart attack last week, was still in hospital resting and recovering. According to his cardiologist, he would need to be off work for at least three months.

As well as getting used to the tropical heat, I had to get used to the new job and since it all happened in the blink of an eye, it was somewhat of a mess with many things pending. The Indian railroad project required a final inspection, which meant that I had to invite the inspection team members and organize the trip. The Indian port modernization project needed board approval, but the board papers were not ready due to the many modifications to be made in accordance with Dr. Kapoor's written memo. The tunnel project in Bangkok should have been halfway completed by now and the company required an immediate report to justify why the funds were three quarters spent, while the foundations were not even finished. And there was more. I was receiving so many phone calls that I was not sure what was going on. Maybe the stress got to poor Dr. Kapoor? No wonder no one wanted to pick up this hot potato. No wonder the firm promised to pay me so well and requested my earliest arrival. I should have smelt a rat.

---

[9] This is based on a true story that happened in Asia. Maybe it's still happening. All names and locations have been altered for reasons of confidentiality.

Luckily, Dr. Kapoor had Grace, a senior secretary, who had worked for him for years. On seeing the tall stacks of papers on her desk outside of my office, I was mostly relieved, as it seemed at least I had some capable hands to support me. Grace, a woman in her late forties, was short and thin, and wore black-framed thick glasses on her nose, her short, black hair pinned neatly behind her ears. She gave me a reserved smile when I greeted her, "Hi Grace, I'm Edward, Dr. Kapoor's replacement…"

She stood up, adjusted her glasses and nodded to me.

"Good morning Sir. That is Dr. Kapoor's office…" her index finger pointed out, continuing, "for today, you have a meeting with the finance department at 10:30 in meeting room 5 and a meeting with the procurement department at 2:00 in room 8. The details are in the memo on your desk. Please let me know if you need anything." She finished speaking, sat down and buried herself into the files before I had said "thank you".

I pushed the office door open. It couldn't open thoroughly as there were two big boxes obstructing it. I looked inside, "Grr, more papers," probably more than in the printing room. And I would have to read them, attend meetings, submit reports, arrange plans and travel.

"Right." I took a deep breath, rubbed my hands and went to battle.

At around 9:45, after non-stop reading of the memo and the most urgent three project reports, I felt sucked dry and very much wanted a cup of strong coffee. So, I picked up the phone and asked my secretary, "Grace, would you bring me a black coffee please?"

There was no reply but I assumed that she heard my request. Then the door opened following two brisk knocks.

"Sir, I am a secretary, I do not bring coffees. The cafeteria is on the second floor."

"Oh, okay. I didn't mean to…"

She rushed out before I finished my sentence and left me quite rooted to the spot.

Well, there were only forty-five minutes before the Bangkok tunnels project meeting started and I couldn't afford to waste time running to the cafeteria, not even for much needed coffee. So, I shook my head vigorously, stood up and stretched my arms, trying to gain some energy. Five minutes before the meeting, I had prepared everything I needed and rushed to the scheduled meeting. When I stepped out of the office, Grace was not at her desk.

"Maybe she's using the lady's room?" I went directly to the meeting.

It was a tedious and horrible meeting: it seemed to be my fault that the budget didn't match the true cost of planned process. The finance department was trying to eat me alive, not willing to accept my explanation that it was my first day here. They insisted the project be modified to reduce costs and asked me to implement these adjustments immediately. They were pounding the tables again and again emphasizing "NOW" "IMMEDIATELY"" TODAY BY 5:00 PM" "NOW"…

By the time I went back to my office, Grace was still not at her desk and it was 12:35.

"Probably on her lunch break?" I was so stressed by the meeting; I wasn't hungry at all. A black coffee, however, would definitely help me. So, I left detailed notes of the morning meeting, the original report and all the new modifications and restrictions and wrote a note asking Grace to type me a draft. In case she overlooked it, I used a red marker, and circled the words, "PRIORITY, DRAFT NEEDED BEFORE 5 PM TODAY". Then I grabbed the papers I needed for the afternoon meeting and rushed to the cafeteria. There I studied report after report whilst I had my coffee.

Another meeting with angry people yelling at me.

"Why? Why? Exactly what happened?"

"How should I know?" I thought to myself, telling them "Sirs, I'm here to figure out the answers to all of your questions and will let you know as soon as I know. All I need is some time."

I tried to calm them down and myself too.

"You have twenty-four hours or we'll kill this plan."

I was flabbergasted, responding, "Considering this is my first day and I have no idea and no one to help me, I will need at least five days to do my research and …"

"Two days, end of discussion. Dismissed," they retorted, cutting me off mid-sentence.

My rage rose up to my chest, and I had to take many deep breaths to calm down.

"The pay's good, the pay's good …" I tried to comfort myself.

I checked my watch. It was 3:50 p.m. I still had time to double-check the draft of the morning report and submit it. Grace was there.

"Good. Grace, it was urgent so I left you some notes on your desk, the finance report this morning, have you finished it?"

"I wasn't sure what you wanted me to do, so I raised some questions and put them back on your desk."

Her answer just shocked me, I was speechless there.

"I seem to remember I am the boss and you are the secretary here, but you felt qualified to comment on my paper and return it to me? Is that it?"

"Yes." Grace replied calmly and sat down.

"I'm so late. I am so screwed…" I murmured.

I grabbed the piles of papers and buried myself in it, typing out everything as fast as possible. I repressed my irritation being too damn busy to care about anything other than the report. It was my first day and I really didn't want to blow it.

I didn't make the deadline, as I had never been taught how to type quickly, doing a secretary's and boss's job at the same time. I finally finished it and breathed a sigh of relief. Before it got too late, I should perhaps talk it over with my secretary and see if it required corrections. Perhaps we could find out each other's limitations and get to know each other a little. I dialled her extension. No one answered.

I walked out of the office and found Grace was not at her desk. Her computer had been switched off. I checked my watch. It was 5:40. That's a bit sharp, I thought and went back to my office to conquer the seemingly never-ending piles of reports.

The next day, I came in early, stopping by at the cafeteria to buy a large black coffee before I went into my office. Grace was not at her desk yet, but I knew I was very early. After yesterday, I was prepared for a brand-new day with different issues. I would have more reports to turn in and more meetings to attend. I really needed Grace's help.

Before I went to my meetings, I seized the chance to talk to Grace.

"Good morning, Grace. Please type this report first, I am going to need that before 2 p.m. today. These are the original Indian bridge reports, the changes are in different colors, red ones are to be deleted, blue ones are to be added, yellow ones are to be highlighted. The rest of it remains unchanged. I also left a legend in the margin to show what each color means just in case…please finish it before 2 p.m.."

Still four more hours, she should have plenty of time, right? So, I added, "Once you finish this paper, please work on the e-commerce paper, I need you to help me combine these short notes into one report. ASAP please. I have to attend the meetings now, but if you have any problems, just text me, I'll reply. Thanks."

I left in a hurry, but I was pretty sure that I made my requirements clear to her.

During the meeting, I rushed back to the office to make sure the report was on its way. Maybe I was nervous for the deadline or maybe I wasn't confident that Grace would do her job? I don't know, but I went back. Grace was typing in front of her computer. I pretended that I'd forgotten something, went into the office, paused and came out, asking her, "Is everything okay? Any probl…?" when I suddenly noticed that the color-coded papers, which I needed urgently were piled on her left, seemingly untouched.

"I think I mentioned clearly that I needed that paper by 2 p.m. today. What are you typing now? I don't remember giving you anything else."

I was a shocked, and also worried as I was expected at the next meeting with the report.

"Yes, you didn't give me anything else, but I'm typing up a report for Dr. Kapoor." Grace said to me without making eye contact.

"Dr. Kapoor is in hospital and probably won't need any reports for a while. I am his replacement and I need this report urgently by 2 pm, today. Type it for me."

Maybe I said it at a slightly higher pitch than normal, as Grace stopped typing and looked up to my insistent face. She rolled her eyes and didn't say a word, sat back in her chair with her arms crossed and looked back down at her computer.

I really didn't know too much about women at the time and I wasn't sure what to say.

"For God sake, I don't even know how to make my girlfriend listen to me at home. Now another tough one in office?" I muttered.

I was really late. So, I blurted it out, "Please, Grace? Please type it for me."

I softened my voice, like begging her.

She raised the end of her lips and gave me a smirk to demonstrate her success, "I can't guarantee I can finish it, it'll be tight."

"Please, Grace. Please try. Thank you so much. Please try."

"Alright, alright." Grace dismissed me with her hand, "Don't you have a meeting to attend?"

I ran back to the meeting and found out I would have to go to Bangkok tomorrow to deal with the tunnel funding problem.

After the meeting, I found out that Grace had not lied. She hadn't finished my report by two. Luckily, it was relatively short, only ten pages. And as I knew all the details, I finished the last eight pages in thirty minutes and submitted it to the chairman.

It was only the second day, but already two directors had criticized my 'unprofessional behind deadline work issues'. I had had no chance to talk to my own secretary about her self-deciding, uncooperative behaviour, so I opened the door, wanting to talk to her. Her seat was once more empty. And anyway, I was late.

On the third day of my new job, I flew to Bangkok. I ran to and fro between the construction site and the local management office to investigate the matter. It was one of the toughest and complicated cases I had ever encountered, involving some politically sensitive matters.

At the airport waiting for the flight to go back to the office, I couldn't help thinking about the task at hand, especially the reports and Grace.

"Exactly what is she thinking? Why is she so obstinate? Grr..."

Dr. Barsa, an office associate, recognized me and patted me on the shoulder. I bought him a beer while waiting for the plane. Alcohol always being a knock on the door for any conversation, we talked about work, different projects, office politics. Dr. Barsa gave me many pointers on how to get on the good side of people, how to break the ice and take care of the mess I had inherited. Just before we parted, he added, "oh, don't forget to bring some little present for your secretary. You know, you've been traveling while she arranged your trip and had to stay behind for work. Bring her something as a token of your appreciation."

"But those places we're traveling in and out of are shitty," I countered.

"They don't know whether it's shitty or not." Dr. Barsa smiled.

At my puzzled look, he added, "Come on, let me show you."

He took me to a small gift shop around the corner, typical for the country, and picked out a golden bracelet, very shining, very fragile, and very fake. The price tag read three hundred Baht, about seven dollars at the time.

"Get her something like this. It's shiny, small, and cheap", he told me placing the bracelet on his palm, "and it's easy to take."

I myself was thinking to Grace wasn't worth three hundred Baht, perhaps not much more than fifty Baht.

"Okay, I'll give it a go."

As I didn't want to buy the same one as the doctor, I picked the silver-looking one. We went to the counter to pay and the bracelets were placed in small dowdy cloth bags. I still remember the way the shop girl rolled her eyes at us. We didn't bother to explain.

The next morning, when I got to the office, I gave my present to Grace. Out of the blue she smiled at me, accepted and said "Thank you, Sir." She couldn't wait to open the bag and try it on. For the first time, she asked me:

"Do you have a report for me to type up, Sir?"

It seemed that she had changed into a different person, a much happier person, a radiating smile on her face.

This happy time didn't last long. Pretty soon Grace overheard that Mary, Dr. Barsa's secretary, received a "gold" bracelet and he had been on the same flight as I from Bangkok!

She left a message on her desk requesting urgent sick leave. And that was the end of Grace. I didn't see her for the rest of my three months in the office.

# Dialling 999 or 101

by C.I. Ripples

You might wonder what I'm doing here, tiptoeing from tree to tree, wishing I was ten pounds lighter and back in me nan's garden with my book. Any normal person would think I've lost me mind, hiding behind trees angst ridden, like a right idiot. My teeth are chattering and not from the cold.

There I was, reading 'The Upside of Unrequited', after getting back from the obligatory boring church service. I was just getting to the juicy bit where Reid will finally kiss Cassie, when me nan called me to take out the bloody dog. Cursing, I hastily stamped out my loosely rolled joint. This was my punishment for not taking her out properly last night. Instead of checking she'd done her business, I'd stood by the garden gate schmoozing with Harry. And as a result, the dog had an unfortunate accident on the kitchen floor. Unfortunate for me that was, as I had to clean it up.

I reluctantly went through the gate with Sally in tow. A beautiful late spring afternoon, the sun shimmered through the trees overhanging the lane, although it was still chilly in the shadows. I wished I was back in nan's garden, pretending to revise for my A-levels, soaking up the sun's weak rays. I wanted a tan for my outfit for tomorrow. It promises to be a mad night with me mates – and now I'm only half baked.

I hadn't even left the garden path, when a brand new metallic blue BMW cabriolet drove past with three well dressed and fit blokes of Middle Eastern, possibly North African or Indian descent in it. Wow I thought. This was a nice change from the average age of sixty plus I normally encounter in Edale.

Not that me nan's that old. It's just that mum's been at it a while. Nan says that by the time she was fifteen her affairs had been all around The Evergreens. I'm not surprised. She's dead gorgeous, glamourous and sexy. No man can keep his hands off her. As I've inherited none of her traits, I habitually speculate whether I was switched at birth. Mum herself has often wondered out loud where I came from. A dead embarrassment to her I am and not only for my lack of looks. My existence also gives away her age. So I've been living in The Boon Dogs with me nan since the second divorce. She's on her fourth one now, waiting to remarry the man she met in Spain last summer. It's no wonder I'm experimenting with weed and that nan joined the Church.

At least I get proper food here and decent freshly brewed Brazilian coffee. Although, I do miss the McDonald's and Pizza Hut takeaways me mum used to feed me on. Not forgetting her well stocked booze cabinet. At least my skin's ever so much better and I have a fine fella. And although it's annoying to be dragged to church every Sunday, I do it to please me nan. Me, an agnostic atheist! I lost faith around the time of the third divorce.

As I sauntered along the path, I wondered what they're all about. What on earth would three fit young men want in this neck of the woods, on a Sunday afternoon? I learnt early on not to be blinded by good looks and decided they looked highly suspicious. I slowed my pace and called back Sally. No such luck – the damned dog was set on her walk and knew the entrance to The National Trust was just around the corner. As I came around the bend I slowed down even further. What was that red light shining in the trees above? At first I thought my eyes were deceiving me, that I'd smoked too much weed. Then remembered I only had a few drags and looked again. No, the red light was still there moving left and right, up and down.

Feeling more than uncomfortable, actually quite concerned, I now inched my way along the path. If I went any slower, I'd be going backwards! Sally, tail wagging was trundling happily forwards.

"Sally!" I called softly, turning around in the hope of making a quick retreat.

She had no intention of listening. That's what you get with a dog that thinks it's part of the family. It thinks it can just go anywhere it pleases. At least the red light had disappeared. Mustering up my courage, I continued after her.

I rounded the corner and there stood my three young men. They didn't look like mass murderers, but I had seen and read enough to feel justified in my paranoia. They looked up as I approached and said something in French to a fourth, older, creepy man standing by a black BMW. They were passing a hard cased briefcase from the blue into the trunk of the black. Sally being an overly friendly collie, was almost upon them, hoping for a pet and a stroke.

"Sally!" I warned her.

They slammed the door shut as they turned to glare at me.

Thinking of the red dot I had sighted I turned abruptly and very slowly, as if I hadn't a care in the world turned around. I walked nonchalantly until I'd rounded the corner and was out of sight, convinced they would be coming after me in their cars and shoot me from behind.

So here I am. My only hope is to hide behind a tree – no small feat with my bulky frame – check the coast is clear and make a dash for the next one. It would've been faster to go across the field, but the lane, even if mercifully lined by trees, is guarded by barbed wire, allegedly to keep nature safe from us. So, it isn't an option. And anyway on the field, in plain sight, I would be a much easier target.

I like living, I think, as I tiptoe from behind a tree and run to the next one. Each time I leave my cover could be the moment that goes down as the end of my history. I don't want to die! Yet, I wonder if anyone will be sad over my death. Perhaps it's my time and I have to make way for some new born. Perhaps that's what mum wants to Skype about. She's expecting a little Pedro. My main worry at this stage is not her reproductive capacity, but my lack of funeral instructions. Under no circumstances do I want to be burnt in the oven. Although, the alternative is just as unpalatable.

Then comes the moment of the last tree. There would be no move cover. Can I still be brave, even if I'm afraid? I tell myself I'm being ridiculous. I calculate that the probability that I've met terrorists is between 0.005 and 0.35% (I've always been a bit of a maths whizz kid). Although these could, of course, have slipped through the net. I read only yesterday that there's been a thirty percent drop in the questioning of suspicious figures on our borders. There is nothing for it but to take a risk and go careering towards nan's house at top speed. It's like something out of the movies with me in the lead role.

Arriving out of breath I crash through the door and shout, "you'll never believe what I just saw!"

Nan, who's cleaning the house from top to bottom despite it being a day of rest, especially the kitchen floor, which still smells, puts her bucket down.

"You alright cock?" she asks.

I tell her my story at speed. She shrugs her shoulders.

"They're probably drug dealers."

I have to admit I'm somewhat disappointed by the lack of impact my story has on her. She merely gets the ladder to take the curtains and nets down. Now the terrorists will be able to look in and recognise me! A potential witness to be eliminated. At least they won't know me nan. I take the stairs two at a time to my bedroom, passing Sally sound asleep on her pillow. She doesn't lift an eyelid, having got home ages ago without all the detours. It's then that me mum calls. I'd forgotten we'd arranged for a Skype. Before she gets a word in edgeways I relay my tale.

"And they know where we live," I add, "so they could eliminate us both!"

"I think you need to call the dibble," she tells me, "this sound well bad. Call me back when you're done."

Me nan has by now also joined the conversation – she'd obviously given her head a wobble. She brewed me a cup of tea for me nerves.

"I think you need to call the police," she tells me too, "they could be terrorists not drug dealers."

Yeah duhhh!

Now I have to make the decision as to who to call: 999 or 101. You see, if I call 999 it's likely the dibble will be on our doorstep within minutes. Is this an emergency? Me nan says I only have something suspicious to report. I decide to call 101 and am immediately put through.

"What it is, right ..." I start, "and I don't want to raise concerns unnecessarily ..."

I don't want to sound like one of those hysterical, mithering old women that call the dibble for just anything. Nor do I want to seem like one of those busy bodies that peers at the lives of others from behind net curtains. Or like a daft teenager, which I am, not to be taken seriously, suspected of having a buzz. So, I very calmly relate what I have observed. By the time I get to the French speaking part (after all it's less than a year since Nice and that French Catholic priest who had his throat slit in Paris. Hell, it's less than a month since the gunman in Paris!), I was told to hang on and that, yes, I should have called the dibble.

"I'm putting you through to the anti-terrorist division," the kind efficient lady at the other end of the phone tells me and puts me on hold.

I feel vindicated! Cool! This is exciting. Yet, five minutes later I'm still on hold, as I am after ten and then fifteen. Disappointed, but no less concerned I finally put down the phone and redial 101, remembering dibble warnings on the radio only the day prior: "We would like to reiterate that citizens should call the police when they spot something suspicious. No matter how small you think it is, please phone us." And as I would be reporting what could be a notorious drug gang or a potential terrorist plot I will give it one more go. It's my civic duty. And anyway, the woman who'd taken my call had been on my side – she believed me!

"Hello," a sluggish voice answers, "how can I help you?"

I start my story again.

"Did you see what was in the briefcase?" she asks, bored, sulkily.

"No," I admit, imagining her to be ugly and obese, at least definitely fatter than me.

"Well did you ask them what was in it?" she continues her interrogation.

"Well no," I admit again, "I was scared by the red dot, thinking arms might be involved."

"Did you at least take a photograph of the cars or jot down their number plates?" she tries again.

This hadn't even occurred to me, but I couldn't let her know that.

"I was too scared to take my phone out, not wanting to anger them," I explain as calmly as possible trying to sound grown up, "I didn't want to risk my security."

"So how do you know they were criminals?" she asks sharply.

"I don't but thought that everything I had witnessed was suspicious and after I told me mum and me nan about it they both agreed I should call the police. I swear down, I'm telling the truth."

The woman yawns noisily, "Well, I'll pass your message on. Goodbye."

She puts the phone down on me!

I call back me mum and tell her that my call to the dibble brought nothing.

"Oh well," she tells me, "you've tried to be a responsible citizen and in this age of technology, the dibble are likely already on their way. You can probably expect a police car to tear past, lights flashing at any moment."

We chat about the Grande concert tomorrow night. It seems she's not reproducing.

"I know Harry seems a sound bloke 'n all, but I want you to be careful. No drinking and driving and no drugs".

"Yes, mum" I answer dutifully, even though I can't really remember a time I haven't seen her with a chilled glass of white wine.

"And don't forget to wear a push up bra," she tells me before ending our Skype, "It makes your breasts look more perky."

# SWAT!

## by Joel Adams

Recon on the derelict warehouse had revealed a nest of terrorists holed up on the ground floor. The floor above had offices on three sides with a catwalk balcony overlooking the work area below. At the west end was a metal stairway. Tony, Andrew and Samir were ready, each wearing Kevlar chest plates, each packing M4A1's, Glocks in their hip holsters on the one and M9 bayonets on the other hip. All was checked and loaded, safeties were off; they were good to go.

On the roof, their grappling hooks secured, they donned night vision goggles and lowered themselves to the offices below, Tony south, Andrew north, Samir east, continually whispering their progress to each other in the microphones on their helmets.

Once they were all inside, they made their way to the outer doors and the center balcony overlooking the hall below where they expected the terrorists were congregated, guarding the downstairs entrances; that is, they would be there unless they had found out their defences were being breached. Whatever happened, Tony and his team were ready.

With the floor strewn with broken glass and all manner of debris, each step made a kind of crunching sound; Tony stepped especially slowly and gingerly. From the curses of the others he knew they were experiencing the same. As Tony reached the door and put his hand on the knob, a shot rang out on the gangway. He threw open the door in time to see Andrew slumping across the way from what seemed a bullet to the chest. They'd been discovered!

"Backup! We need backup!"

Tony barked into the mike as he strained to see who had shot Andrew. Shadowy forms ascended the rickety metal stairway. Tony fired. Bullets ricocheted off the railings, but he heard a terrorist groan and tumble back down the stairs.

Behind and to Tony's left, Samir opened fire. They held the east side of the building, and the only way up for the terrorists was the stairs; so, the next step was to get in position to defend the stairs and then descend them. Tony motioned to Samir to advance on the other side toward the stairs. They crouched as low and were as quiet as possible in their approach to the target. With his vantage point improved, Tony saw at least two heads at the stairs. He nodded across the way at Samir and they both simultaneously aimed with their laser sights and shot, taking the heads out easily. The footsteps of more terrorists replaced them. No worries, they were ready.

An authoritative, hostile female voice called out behind Tony.

"Tony!"

In the split second it took him to turn his head to the source of the voice, a terrorist mounted the stairs and shot him direct in the chest.

"Mom! Look what you've done! I just got killed and failed the level!"

"Tony, it's half an hour after lights out. Turn off the computer. You know you have school tomorrow. Shut it down and go to bed."

# The New World Order

by Renata Kelly

It was January, 2021, and snow had turned the colorful towers and cupolas of The Kremlin in Moscow into a winter postcard.

Inside the labyrinthine grandeur of the Kremlin palace, in the private apartments of the Supreme Leader, a tall, lithe blonde was making her way towards an impressively large door, guarded by two soldiers in full parade uniforms. As she approached, the soldiers swung open the twin panels of the door and saluted. The blonde barely smiled as she entered the ornate room, dripping in golden ornaments, and made her way across the sumptuous carpet towards a marble fireplace where a log fire blazed invitingly.

Seated in damask armchairs on either side of the fireplace were two people, but only one faced the approaching blonde, and it is towards him that the blonde made her way. The bullet head, close-set eyes and inelegantly turned-up nose made him immediately identifiable, and it is on his turned-up nose that the blonde now placed a teasing kiss.

"Darling Vlady, I'm finally here!" The blonde gracefully perched on the arm of the damask chair, and the man encircled her waist with his arm. "This place really feels like home. I love the golden chandeliers! Did Dad visit you here before he built Trump Tower?"

"Ivanka, my silly *lalechka*, that was before my time, but I always knew that Donald and I would have much in common!" Here Putin chuckled and gave Ivanka's bottom a little pinch. "And how was the Inauguration?"

"Amazing! Dad kept saying that he would 'make America great again' and Melania would kick him discreetly and he would yell 'make The Americas great again'! Everyone was there: Maduro as the Governor of Americas South, Xi smiling as usual and pleased that you made him President-for-Life of Indo-China. Oh, and did you know that Erdogan wants to be called 'Caliph of the expanded Ottoman Empire'? You gave him your permission? But, darling, you must get that Kim to lose weight and stop having those weird hair-does, especially now that he's the Serene Leader of Japan and the Koreas and the World's Director of All Nuclear Development. He kept giving Dutarte dirty looks, and I heard he thinks that South-East Asia should have been given to him not to Dutarte. Marine Le Pen, enchanted to be Empress of Purified Europe and United Black Africa, sat next to Dad at the dinner reception and they kept playing footsie. Don't know what Dad was doing with his hands!"

"And what about your Jared, little kitten? Is he smarting from the divorce or happy to be Governor of Canberia?"

"Happy enough. He's especially thrilled that Kushner Construction will be building that bridge you ordered between Canaska Territory (old Alaska, remember?) and Siberia!"

Putin claps his hands and a butler appears bearing a bottle of iced vodka and three small glasses. The occupant of the other chair stands up. She is a short, square-cut woman wearing a beige pants-suit. The butler pours the vodka and bows as he hands out the glasses.

Putin and Ivanka, also standing, exchange a quick kiss. Putin is the first to raise his glass, looking into the pale eyes of the squat lady: "Here's to the New World Order! We've done it, Angela! Who would have thought that we had a chance in those old days in East Berlin, when we used to meet in your one-room flat or the cellars of the Russian Embassy?"

Here Putin winks at Merkel knowingly and she gives a slightly embarrassed cough.

However, straightening her back and holding up her glass, she intones with gravity, "Here's to you, my Supreme Leader, my secret creation, my best friend, and to the great men whose legacy we have fulfilled! Heil Hitler!" barks Angela Merkel, raising her hand in the Nazi salute.

"Heil Stalin!" responds Putin.

"And here's to Dad," adds Ivanka.

# A Hot Deal[10]

## by Lian McCabe

"Hi boss, it's New Year next month. Time to take action."

"Have you decided yet?"

"Yes boss. It's Harbor's turn."

"Good. Then get them ready, check the equipment. I'll finalize the date."

"Yes, boss."

The holiday is around the corner. All kinds of cheerful Christmas songs and music are permeating the city: the big shopping malls, hotels, squares and office buildings and schools are decorated in red, green, white, jingle-bells, candy cane, Christmas trees, Santa Claus, reindeers, angels, and even a snowman, even though it never snows there. People are busy buying holiday gifts, thinking of approaching happy family reunions, good food and drink, fun parties, not forgetting the big year-end bonuses. Smiles and joy radiate from everyone's eyes in expectation.

Dusk is falling. Most people are on their way back home. The firefighters of the Southern Fire Station, however, are still on duty. They, it seems, never have holidays. Upstairs, Carlos and Captain Joseph are working out with barbells in their small gym, Ricardo is cooking

---

[10] This is based on a true story happened in Asia. Maybe it's still happening. All names and locations have been altered for confidentiality.

chicken and rice for dinner, Ricky is sorting out the office, Roman, Gil, and Fernando are servicing the fire-truck, aerial ladder platform and other equipment, and Pedro is training their dog in the front yard. They are on constant high alert and must be able to launch an operation within three minutes. Nevertheless, when it's quiet and there are no emergency call outs, they have a life that's pretty much normal, like a big family consisting only of men.

A phone call breaks the tranquility. Everyone stops what they're doing and runs back to the office. Ricky answers the phone and shouts out, "Captain, Hotel Harbor on Harbor Street, third floor."

"Boys, let's get rolling!" Captain Joseph gives out the command.

Everyone upstairs rushes to the pole and slides down. They all charge towards the fire trucks, jumping into heavy-duty uniforms, pulling them up, putting on helmets, before they leap into the vehicles. Within three minutes they've answered the phone and two fire-trucks are rushing towards the Hotel Harbor, sirens blaring.

It's the rush hour now and the roads are busy, but people know how important it is to let the fire-trucks through, all drivers moving their vehicles to the side. Thick black smoke is roaring up into the darkening night, but the raging flames blazing from the corner of the building illuminate it, almost as if taunting the advancing fire trucks.

"Boys, get ready. It's gonna be a tough battle," Captain Joseph talks into his walky-talky.

"Yes, Captain," the whole team responds.

The trucks surge to the front entrance of the hotel. Someone, presumably the manager, dashes to the firemen, yelling, "Please save us, there are still guests trapped upstairs, I don't know how many…"

"Don't panic. We gave preliminary firefighting training to your hotel six months ago. Take a deep breath and cooperate with us."

But the manager sees the monster fire engulfing the whole hotel, he can't take it anymore and passes out, falling to the ground. They leave him in the care of the staff.

The captain evaluates the situation and assigns tasks calmly. They connect the pipes to the fire hydrants, Rick and Ricardo operate the pipes on the Hydraulic platform; the captain stays behind commanding the operation and the rest of the five fire fighters enter the burning building from the stairs, with oxyacetylene cutting torch, axe, and oxygen tanks hoping to rescue any guests who haven't managed to get out yet.

Carlos rushes to the second floor without delay. He shouts out loudly, "Is anybody here? Can you hear me? Is anybody here? Can you hear me?" Then he hears banging coming from a nearby room. He forces the door open with the axe, and finds an old man, with terror in his eyes, sitting in wheelchair begging, "Please help me, please help me."

"That's gonna cost you. Give me 500 US dollars, cash! Now!"

The old man is dazzled like a deer caught in headlights.

"Hey you old bone, 500 dollars, Euros okay too, otherwise I'll just leave you here."

The old man is in such a shock that his brain short circuits and he struggles to talk. He reaches into his pockets quickly, searching for his wallet. "Here, you can have my wallet, please help me out, please…"

"Thanks" Carlos grabs the wallet and stuffs it into the inner lining of his uniform. Then he bends down, pushes the wheelchair back into the room, and smirks, "Sorry man, I can't", closes the door and runs to the next room. "Is anybody here? Can you hear me?"

Roman stops at the third floor. "Is anybody here? Can you hear me?" He hears a baby crying. He kicks the door open, finding a young woman with a small baby in her arms, both them crying. The young woman is panicking. She screams out, "Please help us, my baby's only six months old."

"Ma'am, give me 1000 dollars and I will save you."

The young woman can't believe what she hears and asks, "What? What? I don't have to give you money, you are firefighters."

"Oh, yes, but your lives are in my hand now. Just give me the money."

"I don't have any money, I have bank cards, credit cards. My husband…"

"Oh, that's too bad. I want cash."

"Please, No. my husband will pay you twice, please take us out. I beg you."

Roman shakes his head.

"Please take my diamond ring, necklace, earrings… they're real, worth a lot of money…" the young woman rips her jewelries off and hands them over to Roman, pleading with tears, "please sir, please help…" she coughs and her voice is hoarse, "please, please" she grabs his sleeve of the uniform, she won't let go.

Roman grabs the jewelries and put them in his pockets.

"Next time, always remember to have cash in hand. You never know when you're gonna need it."

Before the young woman can say thank you, Roman closes the door firmly and murmurs, "God damn it, it's a one-time business. I need cash, fucking cash!" Well, there's sure to be more fish out there in the sea waiting for him to catch, so he moves on the next room and leaves the woman and baby screaming for help.

Pedro charges to the fourth floor.

"Is anybody here? Can you hear me?"

"Help…"

He forces one door open, walks in and sees an old couple, scared and hiding in the bathroom.

"Please help, sir…"

"Ah, foreigners!" Pedro scorns, "Give me 500 dollars each, then I'll save you. You understand? You, 500, she, 500." Petro points to the old couple.

"But sir, we're tourists, we don't have dollars…" The old man panics, the old lady scares.

"Oh, come on, make it quick! US dollars, Euros, whatever cash you have, give it to me! Now!"

The old man hurries to get his wallet, "Sorry, I don't have enough…"

Pedro grabs his wallet angrily, "You old fuck, give me your gold watch, you," he points to the old lady, "give me your rings and jewelries, quick!"

The old lady yells out, "How dare you to this to us!? You're an outlaw!"

"Save it for hell, I don't have time for you, old bones." Pedro snatches her gold necklace and handbag, shoves her against the wall. She falls and starts to bleed.

"Oh, Alice!" the old man bends over to check out on his wife. He can't take it any more. "You bloody robber!" He tries to fight back for his wife's sake, but Pedro is young and strong. He locks the door and spits back onto the door, "you deserve it!"

Fernando hastens to the fifth floor. He charges the middle-aged business man 1000 US dollars upon seeing his custom-made suit. The business man thinks it's the best deal he ever made.

Gil races to the sixth floor. He beats up an artist who doesn't offer anything. "I have more fish to fry. And you're a dead man," he tells him as he proceeds to the next room.

By the time the hotel's turned into a burning furnace, all the firefighters have come out with is one exhausted middle-aged business man.

They might be well-trained, but they couldn't stop the fire. It's such a tragedy for those who lost their families. More and more reserve firemen join in and they finally put out the fire around dawn. Once the site is under control, the captain orders the men to be dismissed.

On the way back to the station, everyone is exhausted.

"How's our harvest?" Captain Joseph asks.

"About 4000 dollars."

"Good."

"3700 Euro and some jewelry."

"Good."

"About 2800 dollars and some watches."

"Good."

"About 3300 dollars."

"Good."

"Some jewelry and 2500 in dollars and Euros."

"Not bad, not bad at all. Good job," Captain Joseph continues, "divide it into eight. That's this month's bonus. Everybody happy? Merry Christmas…"

# Trade Winds

## By Paul McCabe

Far to the west, the horizon rose as the sun appeared to fall toward the silvery sea at one thousand miles an hour. Slow-moving clouds cast shadows on the calm surface. Off to the north, tiny 737s were just visible, taking off and landing at the airport. The long sandy strand of the beach was quiet just before the cocktail hour. Tourists were in their hotel rooms scraping off sand, showering, and wondering which seafood restaurant to choose, before venturing out for a bright sunset. Some fishing boats were beached and aground as the tide reached its low point.

Nearby several men waited for darkness, smoking and sipping Fanta orange. In one of the boats were stowed forty 5-kg packages sealed in triple plastic bubble wrap. They had instructions to unload the boat but only well after nightfall. A white Toyota pickup truck was parked behind the beach. Eventually the boss gave the signal to get started. When the truck was loaded with all forty, they put a tarp over the valuable cargo and tied it down tight.

Two of the men got into the cab and drove off with another two in the open-air back. It was after 8 o'clock and they had a long drive northeast to a small dock on the Ta Pi River near Surat Thani. From there the destination of the packages, but not the men, was the giant metropolis of Bangkok. There, in a myriad of sois and sub-sois, the powerful powder would be treated, re-packaged, and sold at retail in the shadows.

Two weeks before, their cargo was up in Kachin State in northern Burma, which for decades had produced the poppy and its derivatives. Near the China border, the Wa and Kokang hill tribes know well that they can make fifty times more money from poppies than from rice. It's an easy calculation in any language.

An army truck had carried it 900 km from the mountains to the river at the trade center of Mandalay, a place famed in song and legend for centuries of licit and illicit business. From there, without fear of detection, it was transshipped on down to the mouth of the mighty brown Irrawaddy river, to the Andaman Sea at the southern-most point of the country. Then it was loaded off the river boat and onto a small sea-going vessel that sorely needed a new paint job.

After that it was an easy run of three days on smooth seas directly to the south end of Bangtao beach. Each link in the long chain got paid and each link silently did its job. On the river, at sea, and in the Gulf of Thailand there are no roadblocks or police checks. No one pays any attention to small boats with local crews chugging along, minding their own business, cooking rice, and catching a few fish for dinner.

In the truck the four men took national Route 44 in the dark. The boss chain-smoked, used his cell phone to report progress, and listened to pop music on the radio. After two hours they made a stop at a 7-11, stretched their legs, and bought a few things. It was well after midnight when they arrived and found the right place upstream from the provincial capital. The packets were loaded onto the third boat in their long and roundabout journey and the boss handed off responsibility to a new man from Bangkok.

The captain of the 17-meter *Ban Rung* quietly piloted down the familiar river. When he got to sea he took a northerly heading. The Gulf was calm tonight.

"*Mai pen rai*[11]," he thought to himself and gave his orders.

He too made a phone call, this one to a number in the port of Samut Prakarn at the mouth of the Chao Phya. Unsmiling men would be waiting there for his cargo, men with connections and money.

The captain called again thirty-six hours and 550 km later, well before his approach to Samut Prakarn. It was 2 p.m.. He lay off the coast in sunlit safety, just another boat among the hundreds anchored in the shallows there. With no work to do until 9 p.m., he ate and then took a nap.

Later the *Ban Rung* made its rendezvous at an old pier and once again the packages changed hands, this time to a Hi-Lux van labeled with the name of a local shipping company. The van with four men in it drove north and disappeared into the traffic jams of the big city.

A few days later, the small adulterated packets spread out on dim streets. As fate would have it, an unhappy young woman in Klong Toei was the first one actually to inject a bit of the large shipment from Kachin. In her tiny slum room, she prepared the powder and re-used an old needle.

Right away she was floating. Just before she passed out, she had a shining memory of her sunny happiness and of the well-paying waitress job that she had lost the year before. For reasons that she had never understood,

---

[11] Thai for 'Don't worry'.

someone had closed and then bulldozed that seafood restaurant right on Phuket's sandy Bangtao beach.

# Author Profiles

## AL Seth

A lover of Lovecraftian and gothic horror, AL from a very young age aspired to become a writer. He found a home amongst the Phuket Island Writers, where his short stories brought horror and terror to his peers. Having been born into a Sikh family in a country of Buddhists and spent the first academic years in a Catholic school in a country of Hindus and Muslims, AL is a self-imposed atheist and sceptic whilst retaining his love and fascination for the strange and the bizarre. He strives to present them to the world in the form of short-stories, poetry and novelization. He's now back at university and on his way with many more stories. You can visit his blog at sethianwrit.wordpress.com.

## Boris Nielsen

In an unconventional career, Boris Nielsen has lived and worked on five continents. The insights and experiences he has gained inform the thrillers he writes. Now settled in beautiful Phuket, he's enjoying life with his wife and daughter while keeping up with his children in North America. And despite mounting evidence to the contrary, he still thinks he can overcome all those pleasant distractions and finish that blockbuster.

## C.I. Ripples

Having started her writing career as a blogger (ripplesin context.com) and editor, C.I. Ripples loves to confront her readers with currently trending and often difficult issues. A global citizen, she has lived all over the world and has not only absorbed many cultural experiences but also studied their languages, history and customs. After graduating from Oxford University, where she read Modern History, she delved deeper into the subjects of psychology, business, law and even the sciences. Einstein is right: the more she learns, the less she knows. As such her thirst for the unattainable - understanding – is never ending. She is married, the mother of two wonderful young adults and currently lives in Thailand with her son, where she is working on her first historical novel.

## Joel Adams

An American theatrical director, actor and teacher, Joel has written off and on through the years - poetry, plays, and short stories. He's dabbled in writing a novel or two as well. He is presently semi-retired and residing in Phuket, teaching drama and directing Theatrix, the community theatre group he founded there in 2014.

## Kyle Daniels

Originally from Cape Town South Africa, Kyle is a neuro-linguistic programming performance coach and teacher living in Phuket. An advocate for optimal living, he believes we have the power to shape our 'tomorrows'. He is also passionate about fitness, education and exploring this beautiful planet.

## Lauren Daniels

A trained early childhood development and Montessori teacher, Lauren is currently teaching at a primary school in Phuket. Working in Thailand provided her with the perfect opportunity to immerse herself in the Thai culture and the Education system. Lauren is passionate about human development and travelling, and is in the process of pursuing a Bachelor's degree in Psychology.

## Lian McCabe

A writer with a blog at cavecoupleskitchen.wordpress. com, Lian is a certified TEFL English teacher, diver, painter, and gardener in Phuket. She lives with her loving husband and is writing her first book.

## Paige Turner

Paige's career began as a chef in her native Australia. Her love of travelling then took her to Asia. She has lived in Singapore, Bali, Malaysia and now Thailand. She has worked as a Sales Manager for hotel supply companies and as a copywriter and journalist for visitor guides and travel and cooking magazines. In Malaysia she was Managing Editor for *Editions Didier Millet*. She is currently working on a series of children's stories and blogs on travelwritecook.wordpress.com.

## Paul McCabe

A retired economist, Paul McCabe has many years experience in developing countries. In addition to economic advisory assignments, he also worked in the field of disaster relief and as a financial editor. Proud of his roots, Paul is from Rhode Island USA, to which he traces his long interest in history.

## Renata Kelly

After a life of globe-trotting, Renata and her husband now live in Phuket and Greece. Though a prolific writer during her undergraduate studies in the U.S., Renata did not pursue creative writing whilst continuing with her graduate studies at Oxford University and later at the University of Essex where she earned a Ph.D. in Theoretical Linguistics. Following her husband, whose career took the family to a total of ten countries on four continents, Renata was able to teach at various Universities in the U.S.A., Hong Kong, Singapore and England. Now retired, she has once again found the fulfillment and fun of "taking up the pen" (or more correctly, typing away on her computer).

## Stephanie Thornton

Now in her early seventies, Stephanie looks back on a massive and colourful life. The German steel industry, then Dentistry, followed by over forty years in business, building up her own companies, including major exhibitions and working in France in later years. She is now a Landlord to 'Special Needs' tenants in the UK. Hobbies include architecture, travel, ecclesiastical embroidery, but best of all, now hoping to make people laugh in her attempts at writing. She spends three months out of every year in Thailand.